DEATH COMES TO PEMBERLEY

P. D. James was born in Oxford in 1920 and educated at Cambridge High School for Girls. From 1949 to 1968 she worked in the National Health Service and subsequently in the Home Office, first in the Police Department and later in the Criminal Policy Department. All that experience has been used in her novels. She is a Fellow of the Royal Society of Literature and of the Royal Society of Arts and has served as a governor of the BBC, a member of the Arts Council, where she was Chairman of the Literary Advisory Panel, on the Board of the British Council, and as a magistrate in Middlesex and London. She is an Honorary Bencher of the Honourable Society of the Inner Temple. She has won awards for crime writing in Britain, America, Italy and Scandinavia, including the Mystery Writers of America Grandmaster Award and the National Arts Club Medal of Honor for Literature (US). She has received honorary degrees from seven British universities, was awarded an OBE in 1983, and was created a life peer in 1991. In 1997 she was elected President of the Society of Authors.

She lives in London and Oxford and has two daughters, five grandchildren and eight great-grandchildren.

Death Comes to Pemberley

P. D. JAMES

faber and faber

First published in 2011
by Faber and Faber Ltd
Bloomsbury House
74–77 Great Russell Street
London WC1B 3DA

This paperback edition first published in 2012

Typeset by Faber and Faber Ltd
Printed and bound by CPI Group (UK) Ltd, Croydon CRO 4YY

A CIP record for this book
is available from the British Library

ISBN 978–0–571–28360–6

2 4 6 8 10 9 7 5 3

To Joyce McLennan

Friend and personal assistant who has typed my
novels for thirty-five years

With affection and gratitude

Contents

Author's Note

I owe an apology to the shade of Jane Austen for involving her beloved Elizabeth in the trauma of a murder investigation, especially as in the final chapter of *Mansfield Park* Miss Austen made her views plain: 'Let other pens dwell on guilt and misery. I quit such odious subjects as soon as I can, impatient to restore everybody not greatly in fault themselves to tolerable comfort, and to have done with all the rest.' No doubt she would have replied to my apology by saying that, had she wished to dwell on such odious subjects, she would have written this story herself, and done it better.

P. D. James, 2011

Prologue

The Bennets of Longbourn

It was generally agreed by the female residents of Meryton that Mr and Mrs Bennet of Longbourn had been fortunate in the disposal in marriage of four of their five daughters. Meryton, a small market town in Hertfordshire, is not on the route of any tours of pleasure, having neither beauty of setting nor a distinguished history, while its only great house, Netherfield Park, although impressive, is not mentioned in books about the county's notable architecture. The town has an assembly room where dances are regularly held but no theatre, and the chief entertainment takes place in private houses where the boredom of dinner parties and whist tables, always with the same company, is relieved by gossip.

A family of five unmarried daughters is sure of attracting the sympathetic concern of all their neighbours, particularly where other diversions are few, and the situation of the Bennets was especially unfortunate. In the absence of a male heir, Mr Bennet's estate was entailed on his cousin, the Reverend William Collins, who, as Mrs Bennet was fond of loudly lamenting, could turn her and her daughters out of the house before her husband was cold in his grave. Admittedly, Mr Collins had attempted to make such redress as lay in his power. At some inconvenience to himself, but with the approval of his formidable patroness Lady Catherine de Bourgh, he had left his parish at Hunsford in

Kent to visit the Bennets with the charitable intention of selecting a bride from the five daughters. This intention was received by Mrs Bennet with enthusiastic approval but she warned him that Miss Bennet, the eldest, was likely to be shortly engaged. His choice of Elizabeth, the second in seniority and beauty, had met with a resolute rejection and he had been obliged to seek a more sympathetic response to his pleading from Elizabeth's friend Miss Charlotte Lucas. Miss Lucas had accepted his proposal with gratifying alacrity and the future which Mrs Bennet and her daughters could expect was settled, not altogether to the general regret of their neighbours. On Mr Bennet's death, Mr Collins would install them in one of the larger cottages on the estate where they would receive spiritual comfort from his administrations and bodily sustenance from the leftovers from Mrs Collins's kitchen augmented by the occasional gift of game or a side of bacon.

But from these benefits the Bennet family had a fortunate escape. By the end of 1799 Mrs Bennet could congratulate herself on being the mother of four married daughters. Admittedly the marriage of Lydia, the youngest, aged only sixteen, was not propitious. She had eloped with Lieutenant George Wickham, an officer in the militia which had been stationed at Meryton, an escapade which was confidently expected to end, as all such adventures deserve, in her desertion by Wickham, banishment from her home, rejection from society and the final degradation which decency forbade the ladies to mention. The marriage had, however, taken place, the first news being brought by a neighbour, William Goulding, when he rode past the Longbourn coach and the newly married Mrs Wickham placed her hand on the open window so that he could see the ring. Mrs Bennet's sister, Mrs Philips, was assiduous in circulating her version of the elopement, that the couple had been on their way to Gretna Green but had made a short stop in London to enable Wickham to inform a godmother of his forthcoming nuptials, and, on the arrival of Mr Bennet in search of his daughter, the couple had accepted the family's suggestion that the intended marriage could more conveniently take place in London. No one believed this fabrication, but it was acknowledged that Mrs Philips's ingenuity in devising it deserved at least a show of credulity. George Wickham, of course, could never be accepted in Meryton again to rob the female servants of their virtue and the shopkeepers of their profit, but it was agreed that, should his wife come among them, Mrs Wickham should be afforded the tolerant forbearance previously accorded to Miss Lydia Bennet.

There was much speculation about how the belated marriage had been achieved. Mr Bennet's estate was hardly worth two thousand pounds a year, and it was commonly felt that Mr Wickham would have held out for at least five hundred and all his Meryton and other bills being paid before consenting to the marriage. Mrs Bennet's brother, Mr Gardiner, must have come up with the money. He was known to be a warm man, but he had a family and no doubt would expect repayment from Mr Bennet. There was considerable anxiety in Lucas Lodge that their son-in-law's inheritance might be much diminished by this necessity, but when no trees were felled, no land sold, no servants put off and the butcher showed no disinclination to provide Mrs Bennet with her customary weekly order, it was assumed that Mr Collins and dear Charlotte had nothing to fear and that, as soon

3

as Mr Bennet was decently buried, Mr Collins could take possession of the Longbourn estate with every confidence that it had
remained intact.

But the engagement which followed shortly after Lydia's
marriage, that of Miss Bennet and Mr Bingley of Netherfield
Park, was received with approbation. It was hardly unexpected;
Mr Bingley's admiration for Jane had been apparent from their
first meeting at an assembly ball. Miss Bennet's beauty, gentleness and the naive optimism about human nature which
inclined her never to speak ill of anyone made her a general
favourite. But within days of the engagement of her eldest to
Mr Bingley being announced, an even greater triumph for Mrs
Bennet was noised abroad and was at first received with in-
credulity. Miss Elizabeth Bennet, the second daughter, was to
marry Mr Darcy, the owner of Pemberley, one of the greatest
houses in Derbyshire and, it was rumoured, with an income of
ten thousand pounds a year.

It was common knowledge in Meryton that Miss Lizzy hated
Mr Darcy, an emotion in general held by those ladies and gentlemen who had attended the first assembly ball at which Mr Darcy
had been present with Mr Bingley and his two sisters, and at
which he had given adequate evidence of his pride and arrogant
disdain of the company, making it clear, despite the prompting
of his friend Mr Bingley, that no woman present was worthy to
be his partner. Indeed, when Sir William Lucas had introduced
Elizabeth to him, Mr Darcy had declined to dance with her, later
telling Mr Bingley that she was not pretty enough to tempt him.
It was taken for granted that no woman could be happy as Mrs
Darcy for, as Maria Lucas pointed out, 'Who would want to have

that disagreeable face opposite you at the breakfast table for the rest of your life?'

But there was no cause to blame Miss Elizabeth Bennet for taking a more prudent and optimistic view. One cannot have everything in life and any young lady in Meryton would have endured more than a disagreeable face at the breakfast table to marry ten thousand a year and to be mistress of Pemberley. The ladies of Meryton, as in duty bound, were happy to sympathise with the afflicted and to congratulate the fortunate but there should be moderation in all things, and Miss Elizabeth's triumph was on much too grand a scale. Although they conceded that she was pretty enough and had fine eyes, she had nothing else to recommend her to a man with ten thousand a year and it was not long before a coterie of the most influential gossips concocted an explanation: Miss Lizzy had been determined to capture Mr Darcy from the moment of their first meeting. And when the extent of her strategy had become apparent it was agreed that she had played her cards skilfully from the very beginning. Although Mr Darcy had declined to dance with her at the assembly ball, his eyes had been frequently on her and her friend Charlotte who, after years of husband-seeking, was extremely adroit at identifying any sign of a possible attachment, and had warned Elizabeth against allowing her obvious partiality for the attractive and popular Lieutenant George Wickham to cause her to offend a man of ten times his consequence.

And then there was the incident of Miss Bennet's dinner engagement at Netherfield when, due to her mother's insistence on her riding rather than taking the family coach, Jane had caught a very convenient cold and, as Mrs Bennet had planned, was forced to stay for several nights at Netherfield. Elizabeth, of course, had set out on foot to visit her, and Miss Bingley's good manners had impelled her to offer hospitality to the unwelcome visitor until Miss Bennet recovered. Nearly a week spent in the company of Mr Darcy must have enhanced Elizabeth's hopes of success and she would have made the best of this enforced intimacy.

Subsequently, at the urging of the youngest Bennet girls, Mr Bingley had himself held a ball at Netherfield, and on this occasion Mr Darcy had indeed danced with Elizabeth. The chaperones, ranged in their chairs against the wall, had raised their lorgnettes and, like the rest of the company, studied the pair carefully as they made their way down the line. Certainly there had been little conversation between them but the very fact that Mr Darcy had actually asked Miss Elizabeth to dance and had not been refused was a matter for interest and speculation.

The next stage in Elizabeth's campaign was her visit, with Sir William Lucas and his daughter Maria, to Mr and Mrs Collins at Hunsford Parsonage. Normally this was surely an invitation which Miss Lizzy should have refused. What possible pleasure could any rational woman take in six weeks of Mr Collins's company? It was generally known that, before his acceptance by Miss Lucas, Miss Lizzy had been his first choice of bride. Delicacy, apart from any other consideration, should have kept her away from Hunsford. But she had, of course, been aware that Lady Catherine de Bourgh was Mr Collins's neighbour and patroness, and that her nephew, Mr Darcy, would almost certainly be at Rosings while the visitors were at the parsonage. Charlotte, who kept her mother informed of every detail of her married life, including the health of her cows, poultry and husband, had written subsequently to say that Mr Darcy and his cousin, Colonel Fitzwilliam, who was also visiting Rosings, had called at the parsonage frequently during Elizabeth's stay and that Mr Darcy on one occasion had visited without his cousin when Elizabeth had been on her own. Mrs Collins was certain that this distinction must confirm that he was falling in love and wrote that, in her opinion, her friend would have taken either gentleman with alacrity had an offer been made; Miss Lizzy had however returned home with nothing settled.

But at last all had come right when Mrs Gardiner and her husband, who was Mrs Bennet's brother, had invited Elizabeth to accompany them on a summer tour of pleasure. It was to have been as far as the Lakes, but Mr Gardiner's business responsibilities had apparently dictated a more limited scheme and they would go no further north than Derbyshire. It was Kitty, the fourth Bennet daughter, who had conveyed this news, but no one in Meryton believed the excuse. A wealthy family who could afford to travel from London to Derbyshire could clearly extend the tour to the Lakes had they wished. It was obvious that Mrs Gardiner, a partner in her favourite niece's matrimonial scheme, had chosen Derbyshire because Mr Darcy would be at Pemberley, and indeed the Gardiners and Elizabeth, who had no doubt enquired at the inn when the master of Pemberley would be at home, were actually visiting the house when Mr Darcy returned. Naturally, as a matter of courtesy, the Gardiners were introduced and the party invited to dine at Pemberley, and if Miss Elizabeth had entertained any doubts about the wisdom of her scheme to secure Mr Darcy, the first sight of Pemberley had confirmed her determination to fall in love with him at the first convenient moment. Subsequently he and his friend Mr Bingley had returned to Netherfield Park and had lost no time in calling at Longbourn where the happiness of Miss Bennet and Miss Elizabeth was finally and triumphantly secured. The engagement, despite its brilliance, gave less pleasure than had Jane's. Elizabeth had never been popular, indeed the more perceptive of the Meryton ladies occasionally suspected that Miss Lizzy was privately laughing at them. They also accused her of being sardonic, and although there was uncertainty about the meaning of the word, they knew that it was not a desirable quality in a woman, being one which gentlemen particularly disliked. Neighbours whose jealousy of such a triumph exceeded any satisfaction in the prospect of the union were able to console themselves by averring that Mr Darcy's pride and arrogance and his wife's caustic wit would ensure that they lived together in the utmost misery for which even Pemberley and ten thousand a year could offer no consolation.

Allowing for such formalities without which grand nuptials could hardly be valid, the taking of likenesses, the busyness of lawyers, the buying of new carriages and wedding clothes, the marriage of Miss Bennet to Mr Bingley and Miss Elizabeth to Mr Darcy took place on the same day at Longbourn church with surprisingly little delay. It would have been the happiest day of Mrs Bennet's life had she not been seized with palpitations during the service, brought on by fear that Mr Darcy's formidable aunt, Lady Catherine de Bourgh, might appear in the church door to forbid the marriage, and it was not until after the final blessing that she could feel secure in her triumph.

It is doubtful whether Mrs Bennet missed the company of her

second daughter, but her husband certainly did. Elizabeth had always been his favourite child. She had inherited his intelligence, something of his sharp wit, and his pleasure in the foibles and inconsistencies of their neighbours, and Longbourn House was a lonelier and less rational place without her company. Mr Bennet was a clever and reading man whose library was both a refuge and the source of his happiest hours. He and Darcy rapidly came to the conclusion that they liked each other and thereafter, as is common with friends, accepted their different quirks of character as evidence of the other's superior intellect. Mr Bennet's visits to Pemberley, frequently made when he was least expected, were chiefly spent in the library, one of the finest in private hands, from which it was difficult to extract him, even for meals. He visited the Bingleys at Highmarten less frequently since, apart from Jane's excessive preoccupation with the comfort and well-being of her husband and children, which occasionally Mr Bennet found irksome, there were few new books and periodicals to tempt him. Mr Bingley's money had originally come from trade. He had inherited no family library and had only thought of setting one up after his purchase of Highmarten House. In this project both Darcy and Mr Bennet were very ready to assist. There are few activities so agreeable as spending a friend's money to your own satisfaction and his benefit, and if the buyers were periodically tempted to extravagance, they comforted themselves with the thought that Bingley could afford it. Although the library shelves, designed to Darcy's specification and approved by Mr Bennet, were as yet by no means full, Bingley was able to take pride in the elegant arrangement of the volumes and the gleaming leather of the bindings, and occasionally even opened a book and was seen reading it when the season or the weather was unpropitious for hunting, fishing or shooting.

Mrs Bennet had only accompanied her husband to Pemberley on two occasions. She had been received by Mr Darcy with kindness and forbearance but was too much in awe of her son by marriage to wish to repeat the experience. Indeed, Elizabeth suspected that her mother had greater pleasure in regaling her neighbours with the wonders of Pemberley, the size and beauty of the gardens, the grandeur of the house, the number of servants and the splendour of the dining table than she had in experiencing them. Neither Mr Bennet nor his wife were frequent visitors of their grandchildren. Five daughters born in quick succession had left them with a lively memory of broken nights, screaming babies, a head nurse who complained constantly, and recalcitrant nursery maids. A preliminary inspection shortly after the birth of each grandchild confirmed the parents' assertion that the child was remarkably handsome and already exhibiting a formidable intelligence, after which they were content to receive regular progress reports.

Mrs Bennet, greatly to her two elder daughters' discomfort, had loudly proclaimed at the Netherfield ball that she expected Jane's marriage to Mr Bingley to throw her younger daughters in the way of other wealthy men, and to general surprise it was Mary who dutifully fulfilled this very natural maternal prophecy. No one expected Mary to marry. She was a compulsive reader but without discrimination or understanding, an assiduous practiser at the pianoforte but devoid of talent, and a frequent deliverer of platitudes which had neither wisdom nor wit. Certainly she never displayed any interest in the male sex. An assembly ball was a penance to be endured only because it offered an opportunity for her to take centre stage at the pianoforte and, by the judicious use of the sustaining pedal, to stun the audience into submission. But within two years of Jane's marriage, Mary was the wife of the Reverend Theodore Hopkins, the rector of the parish adjacent to Highmarten.

The Highmarten vicar had been indisposed and Mr Hopkins had for three Sundays taken the services. He was a thin, melancholy bachelor, aged thirty-five, given to preaching sermons of inordinate length and complicated theology, and had therefore naturally acquired the reputation of being a very clever man, and although he could hardly be described as rich, he enjoyed a more than adequate private income in addition to his stipend. Mary, a guest at Highmarten on one of the Sundays on which he preached, was introduced to him by Jane at the church door after the service and immediately impressed him by her compliments on his discourse, her endorsement of the interpretation he had taken of the text, and such frequent references to the relevance of Fordyce's sermons that Jane, anxious for her husband and herself to get away to their Sunday luncheon of cold meats and salad, invited him to dinner on the following day. Further invitations followed and within three months Mary became Mrs Theodore Hopkins with as little public interest in the marriage as there had been display at the ceremony.

One advantage to the parish was that the food at the vicarage notably improved. Mrs Bennet had brought up her daughters to appreciate the importance of a good table in promoting domestic harmony and attracting male guests. Congregations hoped that the vicar's wish to return promptly to conjugal felicity might shorten the services, but although his girth increased, the length of his sermons remained the same. The two settled down in perfect accord, except initially for Mary's demand that she should have a book room of her own in which she could read in peace. This was acquired by converting the one good spare bedroom for her sole use, with the advantage of promoting domestic amity while making it impossible for them to invite their relations to stay.

By the autumn of 1803, in which year Mrs Bingley and Mrs Darcy were celebrating six years of happy marriage, Mrs Bennet had only one daughter, Kitty, for whom no husband had been found. Neither Mrs Bennet nor Kitty was much concerned at the matrimonial failure. Kitty enjoyed the prestige and indulgence of being the only daughter at home, and with her regular visits to Jane, where she was a great favourite with the children, was enjoying a life that had never before been so satisfactory. The visits of Wickham and Lydia were hardly an advertisement for matrimony. They would arrive in boisterous good humour to be welcomed effusively by Mrs Bennet, who always rejoiced to see her favourite daughter. But this initial goodwill soon degenerated into quarrels, recriminations and peevish complaints on the part of the visitors about their poverty and the stinginess of Elizabeth's and Jane's financial support, so that Mrs Bennet was as glad to see them leave as she was to welcome them back on their next visit. But she needed a daughter at home and Kitty, much improved in amiability and usefulness since Lydia's departure, did very well. By 1803, therefore, Mrs Bennet could be regarded as a happy woman so far as her nature allowed and had even been known to sit through a four-course dinner in the presence of Sir William and Lady Lucas without once referring to the iniquity of the entail.

Book One

The Day before the Ball

1

At eleven in the morning of Friday 14th October 1803 Elizabeth Darcy sat at the table in her sitting room on the first floor of Pemberley House. The room was not large but the proportions were particularly pleasing and the two windows gave a view of the river. This was the room Elizabeth had chosen for her own use, to be fitted out entirely as she wished, furniture, curtains, carpets and pictures selected from the riches of Pemberley and disposed as she desired. Darcy himself had supervised the work and the pleasure in her husband's face when Elizabeth had taken possession, and the care taken by everyone to comply with her wishes, had made her realise, more even than had the more ostentatious glories of the house, the privileges that adhered to Mrs Darcy of Pemberley.

The room which gave her almost as much delight as the sitting room was Pemberley's splendid library. It was the work of generations and now her husband had the interest and joy of adding to its riches. The library at Longbourn was Mr Bennet's domain and even Elizabeth, his favourite child, entered it only by invitation. The library at Pemberley was as freely open to her as it was to Darcy, and with his tactful and loving encouragement she had read more widely and with greater enjoyment and comprehension in the last six years than in all the past fifteen, augmenting an education which, she now understood, had never been other than rudimentary. Dinner parties at Pemberley could not be more different from those she had sat through at Meryton when the same group of people spread the same gossip and exchanged the same views, enlivened only when Sir William Lucas recalled at length yet another fascinating detail of his investiture at the Court of St James. Now it was always with regret that she would catch the eyes of the ladies and leave the gentlemen to their masculine affairs. It had been a revelation to Elizabeth that there were men who valued intelligence in a woman.

It was the day before Lady Anne's ball. For the last hour she and the housekeeper, Mrs Reynolds, had been checking that the preparations so far were in order and that everything was going ahead smoothly, and now Elizabeth was alone. The first ball had taken place when Darcy was a year old. It was held to celebrate the birthday of his mother and, except for the period of mourning when her husband died, the ball had taken place every year until Lady Anne's own death. Held on the first Saturday after the October full moon, it usually fell due within days of Darcy's and Elizabeth's wedding anniversary, but this they always planned to spend quietly with the Bingleys, who had married on the same day, feeling that the occasion was too intimate and precious to be celebrated with public revelry and, at Elizabeth's wish, the autumn ball was still named for Lady Anne. It was regarded by the county as the most important social event of the year. Mr Darcy had voiced his concern that it might not be a propitious year in which to hold the ball, with the expected war with France already declared and the growing fear in the south of the country where invasion by Bonaparte was daily expected. The harvest too had been poor, with all that meant to country life. A number of gentlemen, raising worried eyes from their account books, were inclined to agree that there should be no ball this year, but were met with such outrage from their wives and the certainty of at least two months of domestic discomfort that they finally agreed that nothing was more conducive to good morale than a little harmless entertainment, and that Paris would rejoice exceedingly and take new heart were that benighted city to learn that the Pemberley ball had been cancelled.

The entertainment and seasonal diversions of country living are neither as numerous nor enticing as to make the social obligations of a great house a matter of indifference to those neighbours qualified to benefit from them, and Mr Darcy's marriage, once the wonder of his choice had worn off, at least promised that he would be more frequently at home than formerly and encouraged the hope that this new wife would recognise her responsibilities. On Elizabeth and Darcy's return from their wedding journey, which had taken them as far as Italy, there were the customary formal visits to be sat through and the usual congratulations and small talk to be endured with as much grace as they could manage. Darcy, aware from childhood that Pemberley could always bestow more benefits than it could receive, endured these meetings with creditable equanimity and Elizabeth found in them a secret source of entertainment as her neighbours strove to satisfy curiosity while maintaining their reputation for good breeding. The visitors had a double pleasure: to enjoy their prescribed half-hour in the grace and comfort of Mrs Darcy's drawing room before later engaging with their neighbours in reaching a verdict on the dress, agreeableness and suitability of the bride and the couple's chance of domestic felicity. Within a month a consensus had been reached: the gentlemen were impressed by Elizabeth's beauty and wit, and their wives by her elegance, amiability and the quality of the refreshments. It was agreed that Pemberley, despite the unfortunate antecedents of its new mistress, now had every promise of taking its rightful place in the social life of the county as it had done in the days of Lady Anne Darcy.

Elizabeth was too much of a realist not to know that these antecedents had not been forgotten and that no new families could move into the district without being regaled with the wonder of Mr Darcy's choice of bride. He was known as a proud man for whom family tradition and reputation were of the first importance and whose own father had increased the family's social standing by marrying the daughter of an earl. It had seemed that no woman was good enough to become Mrs Fitzwilliam Darcy, yet he had chosen the second daughter of a gentleman whose estate, encumbered with an entail which would cut out his children, was little bigger than the Pemberley pleasure gardens, a young woman whose personal fortune was rumoured to be only five hundred pounds, with two sisters unmarried and a mother of such loud-mouthed vulgarity that she was unfit for respectable society. Worse still, one of the younger girls had married George Wickham, the disgraced son of old Mr Darcy's steward, under circumstances which decency dictated could only be spoken of in whispers, and had thus saddled Mr Darcy and his family with a man he so despised that the name Wickham was never mentioned at Pemberley and the couple were excluded entirely from the house. Admittedly Elizabeth was herself respectable and it was finally accepted even by the doubters that she was pretty enough and had fine eyes, but the marriage was still a wonder and one that was particularly resented by a number of young ladies who, on their mothers' advice, had refused several reasonable offers to keep themselves available for the glittering prize and were even now nearing the dangerous age of thirty with no prospect in sight. In all this Elizabeth was able to comfort herself by recalling the response she had given to Lady Catherine de Bourgh when that outraged sister of Lady Anne had pointed out the disadvantages which would accrue to Elizabeth if she were presumptuous enough to become Mrs Darcy. 'These are heavy misfortunes, but the wife of Mr Darcy must have such extraordinary sources of happiness necessarily attached to her situation that she could, upon the whole, have no cause to repine.'

The first ball at which Elizabeth had stood as hostess with her husband at the top of the staircase to greet the ascending guests had in prospect been somewhat of an ordeal, but she had survived the occasion triumphantly. She was fond of dancing and could now say that the ball gave her as much pleasure as it did her guests. Lady Anne had meticulously set out in her elegant handwriting her plans for the occasion, and her notebook, with its fine leather cover stamped with the Darcy crest, was still in use and that morning had been laid open before Elizabeth and Mrs Reynolds. The guest list was still fundamentally the same but the names of Darcy's and Elizabeth's friends had been added, including her aunt and uncle, the Gardiners, while Bingley and Jane came as a matter of course and this year, as last, would be bringing their house guest, Henry Alveston, a young lawyer who, handsome, clever and lively, was as welcome at Pemberley as he was at Highmarten.

Elizabeth had no worries about the success of the ball. All the preparations, she knew, had been made. Logs in sufficient quantity had been cut to ensure that the fires would be kept up, particularly in the ballroom. The pastry cook would wait until the morning to prepare the delicate tarts and savouries which were so enjoyed by the ladies, while birds and animals had been slaughtered and hung to provide the more substantial meal which the men would expect. Wine had already been brought up from the cellars and almonds had been grated to provide the popular white soup in sufficient quantities. The negus, which would greatly improve its flavour and potency and contribute considerably to the gaiety of the occasion, would be added at the last moment. The flowers and plants had been chosen from the hothouses ready to be placed in buckets in the conservatory for Elizabeth and Georgiana, Darcy's sister, to supervise their arrangement tomorrow afternoon; and Thomas Bidwell, from his cottage in the woodland, would even now be seated in the pantry polishing the dozens of candlesticks which would be required for the ballroom, the conservatory and the small sitting room reserved for the female guests. Bidwell had been head coachman to the late Mr Darcy, as his father had been to the Darcys before him. Now rheumatism in both his knees and his back made it impossible for him to work with the horses, but his hands were still strong and he spent every evening of the week before the ball polishing the silver, helping to dust the extra chairs required for the chaperones and making himself indispensible.

Tomorrow the carriages of the landowners and the hired chaises of the humbler guests would bowl up the drive to disgorge the chattering passengers, their muslin gowns and glittering head-dresses cloaked against the autumn chill, eager again for the remembered pleasures of Lady Anne's ball.

In all the preparations Mrs Reynolds had been Elizabeth's reliable helpmeet. Elizabeth and she had first met when, with her aunt and uncle, she had visited Pemberley and had been received and shown round by the housekeeper, who had known Mr Darcy since he was a boy and had been so profuse in his praise, both as a master and as a man, that Elizabeth had for the first time wondered whether her prejudice against him had done him an injustice. She had never spoken of the past to Mrs Reynolds, but she and the housekeeper had become friends and Mrs Reynolds, with tactful support, had been invaluable to Elizabeth, who had recognised even before her first arrival at Pemberley as a bride that being mistress of such a house, responsible for the well-being of so many employees, would be very different from her mother's task of running Longbourn. But her kindness and interest in the lives of her servants made them confident that this new mistress had their welfare at heart and all was easier than she had expected, in fact less onerous than managing Longbourn since the servants at Pemberley, the majority of long service, had been trained by Mrs Reynolds and Stoughton, the butler, in the tradition that the family were never to be inconvenienced and were entitled to expect immaculate service.

Elizabeth missed little of her previous life, but it was to the servants at Longbourn that her thoughts most frequently turned:

Hill the housekeeper, who had been privy to all their secrets, including Lydia's notorious elopement, Wright the cook, who was uncomplaining about Mrs Bennet's somewhat unreasonable demands, and the two maids who combined their duties with acting as ladies' maids to Jane and herself, arranging their hair before the assembly balls. They had become part of the family in a way the servants at Pemberley could never be, but she knew that it was Pemberley, the house and the Darcys, which bound family, staff and tenants together in a common loyalty. Many of them were the children and grandchildren of previous servants, and the house and its history were in their blood. And she knew, too, that it was the birth of the two fine and healthy boys upstairs in the nursery – Fitzwilliam, who was nearly five and Charles, who was just two – which had been her final triumph, an assurance that the family and its heritage would endure to provide work for them and for their children and grandchildren and that there would continue to be Darcys at Pemberley.

Nearly six years earlier Mrs Reynolds, conferring over the guest list, menu and flowers for Elizabeth's first dinner party, had said, 'It was a happy day for us all, madam, when Mr Darcy brought home his bride. It was the dearest wish of my mistress that she would live to see her son married. Alas, it was not to be. I knew how anxious she was, both for his own sake and for Pemberley, that he should be happily settled.'

Elizabeth's curiosity had overcome discretion. She had occupied herself by moving papers on her desk without looking up, saying lightly, 'But not perhaps with this wife. Was it not settled by Lady Anne Darcy and her sister that a match should be made between Mr Darcy and Miss de Bourgh?'

'I am not saying, madam, that Lady Catherine might not have had such a plan in mind. She brought Miss de Bourgh to Pemberley often enough when Mr Darcy was known to be here. But it would never have been. Miss de Bourgh, poor lady, was always sickly and Lady Anne placed great store on good health in a bride. We did hear that Lady Catherine was hoping Miss de Bourgh's other cousin, Colonel Fitzwilliam, would make an offer, but nothing came of it.'

Recalling her mind to the present, Elizabeth slipped Lady Anne's notebook into a drawer and then, reluctant to leave the peace and solitude which she could not now hope to enjoy until the ball was safely over, walked over to one of the two windows which gave a view of the long curving drive to the house and the river, fringed by the famous Pemberley wood. This had been planted under the direction of a notable landscape gardener some generations earlier. Each tree at the edge, perfect in form and hung with the warm golden flags of autumn, stood a little apart from the others as if to emphasise its singular beauty, and the planting then became denser as the eyes were cunningly drawn towards the rich loam-smelling solitude of the interior. There was a second and larger wood to the north-west in which the trees and bushes had been allowed to grow naturally and which had been a playground and secret refuge from the nursery for Darcy as a boy. His great-grandfather who, on inheriting the estate, became a recluse, had built a cottage there in which he had shot himself, and the wood – referred to as the woodland to distinguish it from the arboretum – had induced a superstitious fear in the servants and tenants of Pemberley and was seldom visited. A narrow lane ran through it to a second entrance to Pemberley, but this was used mainly by tradesmen and the guests to the ball would sweep up the main drive, their vehicles and horses accommodated in the stables and their coachmen entertained in the kitchens while the ball was in progress.

Lingering at the window and putting aside the concerns of the day, Elizabeth let her eyes rest on the familiar and calming but ever-changing beauty. The sun was shining from a sky of translucent blue in which only a few frail clouds dissolved like wisps of smoke. Elizabeth knew from the short walk which she and her husband usually took at the beginning of the day that the autumn sunshine was deceptive, and a chilling breeze, for which she was ill prepared, had driven them quickly home. Now she saw that the wind had strengthened. The surface of the river was creased with small waves which spent themselves among the grasses and shrubs bordering the stream, their broken shadows trembling on the agitated water.

She saw that two people were braving the morning chill; Georgiana and Colonel Fitzwilliam had been walking beside the river and now were turning towards the greensward and the stone steps leading to the house. Colonel Fitzwilliam was in uniform, his red tunic a vivid splash of colour against the soft blue of Georgiana's pelisse. They were walking a little distanced but, she thought, companionably, occasionally pausing as Georgiana clutched at her hat which was in danger of being swept away by the wind. As they approached, Elizabeth drew back from the window, anxious that they should not feel that they were being spied upon, and returned to her desk. There were letters to be written, invitations to be replied to, and decisions to be made on whether any of the cottagers were in poverty or grief and would welcome a visit conveying her sympathy or practical help.

She had hardly taken up her pen when there was a gentle knock on the door and the reappearance of Mrs Reynolds. 'I'm sorry to disturb you madam, but Colonel Fitzwilliam has just come in from a walk and has asked whether you can spare him some minutes, if it is not too inconvenient.'

Elizabeth said, 'I'm free now, if he would like to come up.'

Elizabeth thought she knew what he might have to communicate and it would be an anxiety which she would have been glad to be spared. Darcy had few close relations and from boyhood his cousin, Colonel Fitzwilliam, had been a frequent visitor to Pemberley. During his early military career he had appeared less often but during the last eighteen months his visits had become shorter but more frequent and Elizabeth had noticed that there had been a difference, subtle but unmistakable, in his behaviour to Georgiana – he smiled more often when she was present and showed a greater readiness than previously to sit by her when he could and engage her in conversation. Since his visit last year for Lady Anne's ball there had been a material change in his life. His elder brother, who had been heir to the earldom, had died abroad and he had now inherited the title of Viscount Hartlep and was the acknowledged heir. He preferred not to use his present title, particularly when among friends, deciding to wait until he succeeded before assuming his new name and the many responsibilities it would bring, and he was still generally known as Colonel Fitzwilliam.

He would, of course, be looking to marry, especially now when England was at war with France and he might be killed in action without leaving an heir. Although Elizabeth had never concerned herself with the family tree, she knew that there was no close male relative and that if the colonel died without leaving a male child the earldom would lapse. She wondered, and not for the first time, whether he was seeking a wife at Pemberley and, if so, how Darcy would react. It must surely be agreeable to him that his sister should one day become a countess and her husband a member of the House of Lords and a legislator of his country. All that was a reason for justifiable family pride, but would Georgiana share it? She was now a mature woman and no longer subject to guardianship, but Elizabeth knew that it would grieve Georgiana greatly if she contemplated marriage with a man of whom her brother could not approve; and there was the complication of Henry Alveston. Elizabeth had seen enough to make her sure that he was in love, or on the verge of love, but what of Georgiana? Of one thing Elizabeth was certain, Georgiana Darcy would never marry without love, or without that strong attraction, affection and respect which a woman could assure herself would deepen into love. Would not that have been enough for Elizabeth herself if Colonel Fitzwilliam had proposed while he was visiting his aunt, Lady Catherine de Bourgh, at Rosings? The thought that she might unwittingly have lost Darcy and her present happiness to grasp at an offer from his cousin was even more humiliating than the memory of her partiality for the infamous George Wickham and she thrust it resolutely aside.

The colonel had arrived at Pemberley the previous evening in time for dinner, but apart from greeting him they had been little together. Now, as he quietly knocked and entered and at her invitation took the proffered chair opposite her beside the fire, it seemed to her that she saw him clearly for the first time. He was five years Darcy's senior, but when they had first met in the drawing room at Rosings his cheerful good humour and attractive liveliness had emphasised his cousin's taciturnity and he had seemed the younger. But all that was over. He now had a maturity and a seriousness which made him seem older than she knew him to be. Some of this must, she thought, have been due to his army service and the great responsibilities he bore as a commander of men, while the change in his status had brought with it not only a greater gravity but, she thought, a more visible family pride and indeed a trace of arrogance, which were less attractive.

He did not immediately speak and there was a silence during which she made up her mind that, as he had asked for a meeting, it was for him to speak first. He seemed to be concerned how best to proceed but did not appear either embarrassed or ill at ease. Finally, leaning towards her, he spoke. 'I am confident, my dear cousin, that with your keen eye and your interest in the lives and concerns of other people you will not be entirely ignorant of what I am about to say. As you know, I have been privileged since the death of my aunt Lady Anne Darcy to be joined with Darcy as guardian of his sister and I think I can say that I have carried out my duties with a deep sense of my responsibilities and a fraternal affection for my ward which has never wavered. It has now deepened into the love which a man should feel for the woman he hopes to marry and it is my dearest wish that Georgiana should consent to be my wife. I have made no formal application to Darcy but he is not without perception and I am not without hope that my proposal will have his approval and consent.'

Elizabeth thought it wiser not to point out that, since Georgiana had reached her majority, no consent was now necessary. She said, 'And Georgiana?'

'Until I have Darcy's approval I cannot feel justified in speaking. At present I acknowledge that Georgiana has said nothing to give me grounds for active hope. Her attitude to me as always is one of friendship, trust and, I believe, affection. I hope that trust and affection may grow into love if I am patient. It is my belief that, for a woman, love more often comes after marriage than before it and, indeed, it seems to me both natural and right that it should. I have, after all, known her since her birth. I acknowledge that the age difference might present a problem, but I am only five years older than Darcy and I cannot see it as an impediment.'

Elizabeth felt she was on dangerous ground. She said, 'Age may be no impediment, but an existing partiality may well be.'

'You are thinking of Henry Alveston? I know that Georgiana likes him but I see nothing to suggest a deeper attachment. He is an agreeable, clever and excellent young man. I hear nothing but good of him. And he may well have hopes. Naturally he must look to marry money.'

Elizabeth turned away. He added quickly, 'I intend no imputation of avarice or insincerity, but with his responsibilities, his admirable resolve to revive the family fortune and his energetic efforts to restore the estate and one of the most beautiful houses in England, he cannot afford to marry a poor woman. It would condemn them both to unhappiness, even penury.'

Elizabeth was silent. She was thinking again of that first meeting at Rosings, of their talking together after dinner, the music and the laughter and his frequent visits to the parsonage, his attentions to her which had been too obvious to escape notice. On the evening of the dinner party Lady Catherine had certainly seen enough to worry her. Nothing escaped her sharp inquisitive eye. Elizabeth remembered how she had called out, 'What is it you are talking of? I must have a share in the conversation.' Elizabeth knew that she had begun to wonder whether this man was one with whom she could be happy, but the hope, if it had been strong enough to be called a hope, had died when a little later they had met, perhaps by accident, perhaps by design on his part, when she had been walking alone in the grounds of Rosings and he had turned to accompany her back to the vicarage. He had been deploring his poverty and she had teased him by asking what disadvantages this poverty brought to the younger son of an earl. He had replied that the younger sons 'cannot marry where they like'. At the time she had wondered whether the remark had held a warning and the suspicion had caused her some embarrassment which she had attempted to hide by turning the conversation into a pleasantry. But the memory of the incident had been far from pleasant. She had not needed Colonel Fitzwilliam's warning to remind her of what a girl with four unmarried sisters and no fortune could expect in marriage. Was he saying that it was safe for a fortunate young man to enjoy the company of such a woman, even to flirt with discretion, but prudence dictated that she must not be led to hope for more? The warning might have been necessary but it had not been well done. If he had never entertained the thought of her it would have been kinder had he been less openly assiduous in his attentions.

Colonel Fitzwilliam was aware of her silence. He said, 'I may hope for your approval?'

She turned to him and said firmly, 'Colonel, I can have no part in this. It must be for Georgiana to decide where her happiness may best lie. I can only say that if she does agree to marry you I would fully share my husband's pleasure in such a union. But this is not a matter I could influence. It must be for Georgiana.'

'I thought she may have spoken to you?'

'She has not confided in me and it would not be proper for me to raise this matter with her until, or if, she chooses to do so.'

This seemed for a moment to satisfy him, but then, as if under a compulsion, he returned to the man he suspected could be his rival. 'Alveston is a handsome and agreeable young man and he speaks well. Time and greater maturity will no doubt moderate a certain overconfidence and a tendency to show less respect for his elders than is proper at his age and which is regrettable in one so able. I doubt not that he is a welcome guest at Highmarten but I find it surprising that he is able to visit Mr and Mrs Bingley so frequently. Successful lawyers are usually not so prodigal with their time.'

Elizabeth made no reply and he perhaps thought that the criticism, both actual and implied, had been injudicious. He added, 'But then he is usually in Derbyshire on Saturday or Sunday or when the courts are not sitting. I assume he studies whenever he is at leisure.'

Elizabeth said, 'My sister says that she has never had a guest who spent so much time at work in the library.'

Again there was a pause and then, to her surprise and discomfort, he said, 'I take it that George Wickham is still not received at Pemberley?'

'No, never. Neither Mr Darcy nor I have seen him or been in touch since he was at Longbourn after his marriage to Lydia.'

There was another and longer silence after which Colonel Fitzwilliam said, 'It was unfortunate that Wickham was made so much of when a boy. He was brought up with Darcy as if they were brothers. In childhood it was probably beneficial to both; indeed, given the late Mr Darcy's affection for his steward, after the latter's death it was a natural beneficence to take some responsibility for his child. But for a boy of Wickham's temperament – mercenary, ambitious, inclined to envy – it was dangerous for him to enjoy a privilege which, once boyhood was over, he could not share. They went to different colleges at university and he did not, of course, take part in Darcy's tour of Europe. Changes in his status and expectations were perhaps made too drastically and too suddenly. I have reason to believe that Lady Anne Darcy saw the danger.'

Elizabeth said, 'Wickham could not have expected to share the grand tour.'

'I have no knowledge of what he did expect except that it was always greater than his deserts.'

Elizabeth said, 'The early favours shown may have been to an extent imprudent and it is always easy to question the judgement of others in matters of which we may be imperfectly informed.'

The colonel shifted uneasily in his chair. He said, 'But there could be no excuse for Wickham's betrayal of trust in his attempted seduction of Miss Darcy. This was an infamy which no difference in birth or upbringing could excuse. As a fellow guardian of Miss Darcy I was, of course, informed of the disgraceful affair by Darcy, but it is a matter which I have put out of my mind. I never speak of it to Darcy and I apologise for speaking of it now. Wickham has distinguished himself in the Irish campaign and is now something of a national hero, but that cannot wipe out the past although it may provide him with opportunities for a more respectable and successful life in the future. I should not have mentioned his name in your presence.'

Elizabeth made no reply and, after a brief pause, he got to his feet, bowed and was gone. She was aware that the conversation had given satisfaction to neither. Colonel Fitzwilliam had not received the wholehearted approval and assurance of her support for which he had hoped and Elizabeth feared that if he failed to win Georgiana the humiliation and embarrassment would wreck a friendship which had lasted since boyhood and which she knew her husband held dear. She had no doubt that Darcy would approve of Colonel Fitzwilliam as a husband for Georgiana. What he hoped above all for his sister was safety, and she would be safe; even the difference in age would probably be seen as an advantage. In time Georgiana would be a countess and money would never be a worry to the fortunate man who married her. She wished that the question could be settled one way or another. Perhaps events would come to a head tomorrow at the ball – a ball with its opportunities for sitting out together, for whispered confidences as the dancers went down, was well known for bringing events, happy or unhappy, to a conclusion. She only hoped that all concerned should be satisfied, then smiled at the presumption that this could ever be possible.

Elizabeth was gratified by the change in Georgiana since Darcy and she had married. At first Georgiana had been surprised, almost shocked, to hear her brother being teased by his wife, and how often he teased in return and they laughed together. There had been little laughter at Pemberley before Elizabeth's arrival, and under Elizabeth's tactful and gentle encouragement Georgiana had lost some of her Darcy shyness. She was now confident in taking her place when they entertained, more ready to venture her opinions at the dinner table. As Elizabeth grew in understanding of her sister, she suspected that under the shyness and reserve Georgiana had another Darcy characteristic: a strong will of her own. But how far did Darcy recognise this? Within part of his mind was not Georgiana still the vulnerable fifteen year old, a child needing his safe watchful love if she were to escape disaster? It was not that he distrusted his sister's honour or her virtue – such a thought for him would be close to blasphemy – but how far did he trust her judgement? And for Georgiana, Darcy, since their father's death, had been head of the family, the wise and dependable older brother with something of the authority of a father, a brother greatly loved and never feared, since love cannot live with fear, but held in awe. Georgiana would not marry without love, but neither would she marry without his approval. And what if it came to a choice between Colonel Fitzwilliam, his cousin and childhood friend, heir to an earldom, a gallant soldier who had known Georgiana all her life, and this handsome and agreeable young lawyer who admittedly was making his name but of whom they knew very little? He would inherit a barony, and an ancient one, and Georgiana would have a house which, when Alveston had

31

made his money and restored it, would be one of the most beautiful in England. But Darcy had his share of family pride and there could be no doubt which candidate offered the greater security and the more glittering future.

The colonel's visit had destroyed her peace, leaving her worried and a little distressed. He was right in saying he should not have mentioned Wickham's name. Darcy himself had had no contact with him since they met at the church when Lydia was married, a marriage which could never have taken place without his lavish expenditure of money. She was confident that this secret had never been divulged to Colonel Fitzwilliam, but he had, of course, known of the marriage and he must have suspected the truth. Was he, she wondered, attempting to reassure himself that Wickham had no part in their life at Pemberley and that Darcy had bought Wickham's silence to ensure that the world would never be able to say that Miss Darcy of Pemberley had a sullied reputation? The colonel's visit had made her restless and she began pacing to and fro, trying to calm fears which she hoped were irrational and to regain some of her former composure.

Luncheon with only four of them at the table was brief. Darcy had an appointment with his steward and had returned to his study to wait for him. Elizabeth had arranged to meet Georgiana in the conservatory where they would inspect the blooms and green boughs the head gardener had brought from the hothouses. Lady Anne had liked many colours and complicated arrangements but Elizabeth preferred to use only two colours with the green and to arrange them in a variety of vases, large and small, so that every room contained sweet-smelling flowers.

Tomorrow the colours would be pink and white, and Elizabeth and Georgiana worked and consulted among the pungent scent of long-stemmed roses and geraniums. The hot, humid atmosphere of the conservatory was oppressive and she had a sudden wish to breathe fresh air and feel the wind on her cheeks. Was it perhaps the unease occasioned by Georgiana's presence and the colonel's confidence which lay like a burden on the day?

Suddenly Mrs Reynolds was with them. She said, 'Dear madam, Mr and Mrs Bingley's coach is coming up the drive. If you hurry you will be at the door to receive them.'

Elizabeth gave a cry of delight and, with Georgiana following, ran to the front door. Stoughton was already there to open it just as the carriage drew slowly to a stop. Elizabeth ran out into the cool breath of the rising wind. Her beloved Jane had arrived and for a moment all her unease was subsumed in the happiness of their meeting.

2

The Bingleys were not long at Netherfield after their marriage. Bingley was the most tolerant and good-natured of men but Jane realised that being in such close proximity to her mother would not contribute to her husband's comfort or her peace of mind. She had a naturally affectionate nature and her loyalty and love for her family were strong, but Bingley's happiness came first. Both had been anxious to settle close to Pemberley and when their lease at Netherfield ended, they stayed for a short time in London with Mrs Hurst, Bingley's sister, and then moved with some relief to Pemberley, a convenient centre from which to search for a permanent home. In this Darcy took an active part. Darcy and Bingley had been to the same school but the difference in age, although of only a couple of years, meant that they saw little of each other in boyhood. It was at Oxford that they became friends. Darcy – proud, reserved and already ill at ease in company – found relief in Bingley's generous good nature, easy sociability and cheerful assumption that life would always be good to him, and Bingley had such faith in Darcy's superior wisdom and intelligence that he was reluctant to take any action on matters of importance without his friend's approbation.

Darcy had advised Bingley to buy rather than build, and as Jane was already carrying their first child, it seemed desirable to find a home urgently, and one into which they could move with the minimum of inconvenience. It was Darcy, active on his friend's behalf, who found Highmarten, and both Jane and her husband were delighted with it at first sight. It was a handsome modern house built on rising ground with a wide attractive view from all its windows, commodious enough for family life and with well laid-out gardens and a manor large enough for Bingley to hold shooting parties without inviting unfavourable comparison with Pemberley. Dr McFee, who for years had looked after the Darcy family and the Pemberley household, had visited and pronounced the situation healthy and the water pure, and the formalities were quickly settled. Little was required except the purchase of furniture and redecoration, and Jane, with Elizabeth's help, had much pleasure in moving from room to room, deciding on the colour of wallpaper, paint and curtains. Within two months of finding the property, the Bingleys were installed and the two sisters' happiness in their marriages was complete.

The two families saw each other frequently and there were few weeks in which a carriage did not travel between Highmarten and Pemberley. Jane would very rarely be parted from her children for more than a night – the four-year-old twins, Elizabeth and Maria, and young Charles Edward, now nearly two – but knew that they could be safely left in the experienced and competent hands of Mrs Metcalf, the nurse who had cared for her husband when a baby, and she was happy to spend two nights at Pemberley for the ball without the problems inevitable in transferring three children and their nurse for so short a visit. She had, as always, come without her maid, but Elizabeth's capable young maid, Belton, was happy to look after both sisters. The Bingleys' coach and coachman were consigned to the care of Wilkinson, Darcy's coachman, and after the customary bustle of greeting, Elizabeth and Jane, arm in arm, climbed the stairs to the room always assigned to Jane on her visits, with Bingley's dressing room next door. Belton had already taken charge of Jane's trunk and was hanging up her evening dress and the gown she would wear for the ball and would be with them in an hour to help them change and to dress their hair. The sisters, who had shared a bedroom at Longbourn, had been particularly close companions since childhood and there was no matter on which Elizabeth could not speak to Jane, knowing that she would be totally reliable in keeping a confidence and that any advice she gave would come from her goodness and loving heart.

As soon as they had spoken to Belton they went as usual to the nursery to give Charles the expected hug and sweetmeat, to play with Fitzwilliam and listen to his reading – he was soon

35

to leave the nursery for the schoolroom and a tutor – and to settle down for a brief but comfortable chat with Mrs Donovan. She and Mrs Metcalf had fifty years' experience between them and the two benevolent despots had early established a close alliance, defensive and offensive, and ruled supreme in their nurseries, beloved by their charges and trusted by the parents, although Elizabeth suspected that Mrs Donovan thought the only function of a mother was to produce a new baby for the nursery as soon as the youngest had outgrown his first caps. Jane gave news about the progress of Charles Edward and the twins and their regime at Highmarten was discussed and approved by Mrs Donovan, not surprisingly since it was the same as hers. There was then only an hour before it was time to dress for dinner so they made their way to Elizabeth's room for the comfortable exchange of small items of news on which the happiness of domestic life so largely depended.

It would have been a relief to Elizabeth to have confided to Jane about a more important concern, the colonel's intended proposal to Georgiana. But although he had not enjoined secrecy, he must surely have expected that she would first talk to her husband, and Elizabeth felt that Jane's delicate sense of honour would be offended, as would be her own, if her sister were given the news before Elizabeth had had a chance to speak to Darcy. But she was anxious to talk about Henry Alveston and was glad when Jane herself introduced his name by saying, 'It is good of you to again include Mr Alveston in your invitation. I know how much it means to him to come to Pemberley.'

Elizabeth said, 'He is a delightful guest and we are both glad to see him. He is well mannered, intelligent, lively and good looking, and is therefore a paradigm of a young man. Remind me how he became intimate with you. Did not Mr Bingley meet him at your lawyer's office in London?'

'Yes, eighteen months ago, when Charles was visiting Mr Peck to discuss some investments. Mr Alveston had been called to the office with a view to his representing one of Mr Peck's clients in court and, as both visitors arrived early, they met in the waiting room and later Mr Peck introduced them. Charles was greatly taken with the young man and they had dinner together afterwards when Mr Alveston confided his plan to restore the family fortune and the estate in Surrey, which his family has held since 1600 and to which, as an only son, he feels a strong obligation and attachment. They met again at Charles's club and it was then that Charles, struck by the young man's look of exhaustion, issued an invitation in both our names for him to spend a few days at Highmarten; Mr Alveston has since become a regular and welcome visitor whenever he can get away from court. We understand that Mr Alveston's father, Lord Alveston, is eighty and in poor health and for some years has been unable to provide the energy and leadership which the estate requires, but the barony is one of the oldest in the country and the family is well respected. Charles learned from Mr Peck, and indeed from others, how much Mr Alveston is admired in the Middle Temple, and both of us have become fond of him. He is a hero to young Charles Edward and a great favourite with the twins who always receive his visits with frisks of delight.'

To be good with her children was a sure path to Jane's heart and Elizabeth could well understand the attraction of Highmarten for Alveston. The life of an overworked bachelor in London could offer little comfort and Alveston obviously found in

Mrs Bingley's beauty, her kindness and gentle voice, and in the cheerful domesticity of her home, a welcome contrast to the raucous competition and social demands of the capital. Alveston, like Darcy, had early assumed the burden of expectations and responsibility. His resolve to restore the family fortune was admirable, and the Old Bailey, its challenges and successes, was probably a prototype of a more personal struggle.

There was a silence, then Jane said, 'I hope that neither you, my dear sister, nor Mr Darcy is made uneasy by his presence here. I must confess that, watching his and Georgiana's obvious pleasure in each other's company, I thought it possible that Mr Alveston might be falling in love, and if that would distress Mr Darcy or Georgiana we shall, of course, ensure that the visits cease. But he is an estimable young man and if I am right in my suspicion and Georgiana returns his partiality, I have every confidence that they could be happy together, but Mr Darcy may have other plans for his sister and, if so, it may be both wise and kind that Mr Alveston should no longer come to Pemberley. I have noticed during recent visits that there is a change in Colonel Fitzwilliam's attitude to his cousin, a greater willingness to talk with her and to be at her side. It would be a brilliant match and she would adorn it, but I do wonder how happy she would be in that vast northern castle. I saw a picture of it last week in a book in our library. It looks like a granite fortress with the North Sea almost breaking against its walls. And it is so far from Pemberley. Surely Georgiana would be unhappy to be so distant from her brother and the house she loves so well.'

Elizabeth said, 'I suspect that with both Mr Darcy and Georgiana, Pemberley comes first. I remember when I visited with my aunt and uncle, and Mr Darcy asked me what I thought of the house, my obvious delight in it pleased him. If I had been less than genuinely enthusiastic I don't think he would have married me.'

Jane laughed. 'Oh, I think he would, my dear. But perhaps we should not discuss this matter further. Gossip about the feelings of others when we cannot fully understand them, and they may not understand them themselves, can be an unconscious cause of distress. Perhaps I was wrong to mention the colonel's name. I know, my dear Elizabeth, how much you love Georgiana and, living with you as her sister, she has grown into a more assured as well as a beautiful young woman. If she has indeed two suitors the choice must of course be hers, but I cannot imagine she would consent to marry against her brother's wishes.'

Elizabeth said, 'The matter may come to a head after the ball, but I own that it is an anxiety to me. I have grown to love Georgiana dearly. But let us put it aside for now. We have the family dinner to look forward to. I must not spoil it for either of us or our guests by worries which may be groundless.'

They said no more, but Elizabeth knew that for Jane there could be no problem. She believed firmly that two attractive young people who obviously enjoyed each other's company might very naturally fall in love and that love should result in a happy marriage. And here there could be no difficulty about money: Georgiana was rich and Mr Alveston rising in his profession. But money weighed little with Jane; provided there was sufficient for a family to live in comfort, what matter which partner it was who brought money to the union? And the fact, which to others would be paramount, that the colonel now was a viscount and that his wife would in time become a countess while

Mr Alveston would be only a baron, would weigh nothing with Jane. Elizabeth resolved that she would attempt not to dwell on possible difficulties but that, after the ball, she must soon find an early opportunity to talk to her husband. Both had been so busy that she had hardly set eyes on him since morning. She would not be justified in speculating to him about Mr Alveston's feelings unless Mr Alveston or Georgiana raised the matter, but he should be told as soon as possible of the colonel's intention to speak of his hope that Georgiana would consent to be his wife. She wondered why the thought of such an alliance, brilliant as it was, gave her an unease which she could not reason away, and tried to put this uncomfortable feeling aside. Belton had arrived and it was time for Jane and herself to get ready for dinner.

3

On the eve of the ball, dinner was served at the customary and fashionable hour of six thirty but when the numbers were few it was usual for it to be held in a small room adjacent to the formal dining room, where up to eight could sit in comfort at the round table. In past years the larger room had been necessary because the Gardiners, and occasionally Bingley's sisters, had been guests at Pemberley for the ball, but Mr Gardiner never found it easy to leave his business, nor his wife to be parted from her children. What they both liked best was a summer visit when Mr Gardiner could enjoy the fishing and his wife enjoyed nothing better than to explore the grounds with Elizabeth in a single-horse phaeton. The friendship between the two women was long-standing and close and Elizabeth had always valued her aunt's advice. There were matters on which she would have been glad of it now.

Although the dinner was informal, the party naturally moved together to enter the dining room in pairs. The colonel at once offered his arm to Elizabeth, Darcy moved to Jane's side and Bingley, with a little show of gallantry, offered his arm to Georgiana. Seeing Alveston walking alone behind the last pair, Elizabeth wished she had arranged things better, but it was always difficult to find a suitable unescorted lady at short notice and convention had not before mattered at these pre-ball dinners. The empty chair was between Georgiana and Jane, and when Alveston took it, Elizabeth detected his transitory smile of pleasure.

As they seated themselves the colonel said, 'So Mrs Hopkins is not with us again this year. Isn't this the second time she has missed the ball? Does your sister not enjoy dancing, or has the Reverend Theodore theological objections to a ball?'

Elizabeth said, 'Mary has never been fond of dancing and has asked to be excused, but her husband has certainly no objection to her taking part. He told me on the last occasion when they dined here that in his view no ball at Pemberley attended by friends and acquaintances of the family could have a deleterious effect on either morals or manners.'

Bingley whispered to Georgiana, 'Which shows that he has never imbibed Pemberley white soup.'

The remark was overheard and provoked smiles and some laughter. But this light-heartedness was not to last. There was an absence of the usual eager talk across the table, and a languor from which even Bingley's good-humoured volubility seemed unable to rouse them. Elizabeth tried not to glance too frequently at the colonel, but when she did she was aware how often his eyes were fixed on the couple opposite. It seemed to Elizabeth that Georgiana, in her simple dress of white muslin with a chaplet of pearls in her dark hair, had never appeared more lovely, but there was in the colonel's gaze a look more speculative than admiring. Certainly the young couple behaved impeccably, Alveston showing Georgiana no more attention than was natural, and Georgiana turning to address her remarks equally between Alveston and Bingley, like a young girl dutifully following social convention at her first dinner party. There was one moment, which she hoped the colonel had not detected. Alveston was mixing Georgiana's water and wine and, for a few seconds, their hands touched and Elizabeth saw the faint flush grow and fade on Georgiana's cheeks.

Seeing Alveston in his formal evening clothes, Elizabeth was struck again by his extraordinary good looks. He was surely not unaware that he could not enter a room without every woman present turning her eyes towards him. His strong mid-brown hair was tied back simply at the nape of his neck. His eyes were a darker brown under straight brows, his face had an openness and strength which saved him from any imputation of being too handsome, and he moved with a confident and easy grace. As she knew, he was usually a lively and entertaining guest, but tonight even he seemed afflicted by the general air of unease. Perhaps, she thought, everyone was tired. Bingley and Jane had come only eighteen miles but had been delayed by the high wind, and for Darcy and herself the day before the ball was always unusually busy.

The atmosphere was not helped by the tempest outside. From time to time the wind howled in the chimney, the fire hissed and spluttered like a living thing and occasionally a burning log would break free, bursting into spectacular flames and casting a momentary red flush over the faces of the diners so that they looked as if they were in a fever. The servants came and went on silent feet, but it was a relief to Elizabeth when the meal at last came to an end and she was able to catch Jane's eye and move with her and Georgiana across the hall into the music room.

4

While the dinner was being served in the small dining room, Thomas Bidwell was in the butler's pantry cleaning the silver. This had been his job for the last four years since the pain in his back and knees had made driving impossible, and it was one in which he took pride, particularly on the night before Lady Anne's ball. Of the seven large candelabra which would be ranged the length of the supper table, five had already been cleaned and the last two would be finished tonight. The job was tedious, time-consuming and surprisingly tiring, and his back, arms and hands would all ache by the time he had finished. But it wasn't a job for the maids or for the lads. Stoughton, the butler, was ultimately responsible, but he was busy choosing the wines and overseeing the preparation of the ballroom, and regarded it as his responsibility to inspect the silver once cleaned, not to clean even the most valuable pieces himself. For the week preceding the ball it was expected that Bidwell would spend most days, and often far into the night, seated aproned at the pantry table with the Darcy family silver ranged before him – knives, forks, spoons, the candelabra, silver plates on which the food would be served, the dishes for the fruit. Even as he polished he could picture the candelabra with their tall candles throwing light on bejewelled hair, heated faces and the trembling blossoms in the flower vases.

He never worried about leaving his family alone in the woodland cottage, nor were they ever frightened there. It had lain desolate and neglected for years until Darcy's father had restored it and made it suitable for use by one of the staff. But although it was larger than a servant could expect and offered peace and privacy, few were prepared to live there. It had been built by Mr Darcy's great-grandfather, a recluse who lived his life mostly alone, accompanied only by his dog, Soldier. In that cottage he had even cooked his own simple meals, read and sat contemplating the strong trunks and tangled bushes of the wood which were his bulwark against the world. Then, when George Darcy was sixty, Soldier became ill, helpless and in pain. It was Bidwell's grandfather, then a boy helping with the horses, who had gone to the cottage with fresh milk and found his master dead. Darcy had shot both Soldier and himself.

Bidwell's parents had lived in the cottage before him. They had been unworried by its history, and so was he. The reputation that the woodland was haunted arose from a more recent tragedy which occurred soon after the present Mr Darcy's grandfather succeeded to the estate. A young man, an only son who worked as an under-gardener at Pemberley, had been found guilty of poaching deer on the estate of a local magistrate, Sir

Selwyn Hardcastle. Poaching was not usually a capital offence and most magistrates dealt with it sympathetically when times were hard and there was much hunger, but stealing from a deer park was punishable by death and Sir Selwyn's father had been adamant that the full penalty should be exacted. Mr Darcy had made a strong plea for leniency in which Sir Selwyn refused to join. Within a week of the boy's execution his mother had hanged herself. Mr Darcy had done what he could, but it was believed that the dead woman had held him chiefly responsible. She had cursed the Darcy family, and the superstition took hold that her ghost, wailing in grief, could be glimpsed wandering among the trees by those unwise enough to visit the woodland after dark, and that this avenging apparition always presaged a death on the estate.

Bidwell had no patience with this foolishness but the previous week the news had reached him that two of the housemaids, Betsy and Joan, had been whispering in the servants' hall that they had seen the ghost when venturing into the woodland as a dare. He had warned them against speaking such nonsense which, had it reached the ears of Mrs Reynolds, might have had serious consequences for the girls. Although his daughter, Louisa, no longer worked at Pemberley, being needed at home to help nurse her sick brother, he wondered if somehow the story had reached her ears. Certainly she and her mother had become more meticulous than ever about locking the cottage door at night and, when returning late from Pemberley, he had been instructed to give a signal by knocking three times loudly and four times more quietly before inserting his key.

The cottage was reputed to be unlucky but only in recent years had ill luck touched the Bidwells. He still remembered, as keenly as if it were yesterday, the desolation of that moment when, for the last time, he had taken off the impressive livery of Mr Darcy of Pemberley's head coachman and said goodbye to his beloved horses. And now for the past year his only son, his hopes for the future, had been slowly and painfully dying.

If that were not enough, his elder daughter, the child from whom he and his wife had never expected trouble, was causing anxiety. Things had always gone well with Sarah. She had married the son of the innkeeper at the King's Arms in Lambton, an ambitious young man who had moved to Birmingham and established a chandlery with a bequest from his grandfather. The business was flourishing, but Sarah had become depressed and overworked. There was a fourth baby due in just over four years of marriage and the strain of motherhood and helping in the shop had brought a despairing letter asking for help from her sister Louisa. His wife had handed him Sarah's letter without comment but he knew that she shared his concern that their sensible, cheerful, buxom Sarah had come to such a pass. He had handed the letter back after reading it, merely saying, 'Louisa will be sadly missed by Will. They've always been close. And can you spare her?'

'I'll have to. Sarah wouldn't have written if she wasn't desperate. It's not like our Sarah.'

So Louisa had spent the five months before the birth in Birmingham helping to care for the other three children and had remained for a further three months while Sarah recovered. She had recently returned home, bringing the baby, Georgie, with her, both to relieve her sister and so that her mother and brother could see him before Will died. But Bidwell himself had never been happy about the arrangement. He had been almost as anxious as his wife to see their new grandson, but a cottage where a dying man was being nursed was hardly suitable for the care of a baby. Will was too ill to take much more than a cursory interest in the new arrival and the child's crying at night worried and disturbed him. And Bidwell could see that Louisa was not happy. She was restless and, despite the autumnal chill, she seemed to prefer walking in the woodland, the baby in her arms, than to be at home with her mother and Will. She had even, as if by design, been absent when the rector, the elderly and scholarly Reverend Percival Oliphant, made one of his frequent visits to Will, which was strange because she had always liked the rector, who had taken an interest in her from her childhood, lending her books and offering to include her in his Latin class with his small group of private pupils. Bidwell had refused the invitation – it would only give Louisa ideas above her station – but still, it had been made. Of course, a girl was often anxious and nervous as her wedding approached, but now that Louisa was at home why did not Joseph Billings visit the cottage regularly as he used to do? They hardly saw him. He wondered whether the care of the baby had brought home both to Louisa and to Joseph the responsibilities and risks of the married state and caused them to reconsider. He hoped not. Joseph was ambitious and serious, and some thought, at thirty-four, too old for Louisa, but the girl seemed fond of him. They would be settled in Highmarten within seventeen miles of himself and Martha and would be part of a comfortable household with an indulgent mistress, a generous master, their future secured, their lives

stretching ahead, predictable, safe, respectable. With all that before her, what use to a young woman were learning and Latin?

Perhaps all would right itself when Georgie was back with his
mother. Louisa would be travelling with him tomorrow and it
had been arranged that she and the baby were to go by chaise
to the King's Arms at Lambton, from where they would travel
post to Birmingham where Sarah's husband, Michael Simpkins,
would meet them to drive home in his trap and Louisa would
return to Pemberley by post the same day. Life would be easier
for his wife and Will when the baby had been taken home, but
when he returned to the cottage on Sunday after helping to put
the house to rights after the ball, it would be strange not to see
Georgie's chubby hands held out in welcome.

These troubled thoughts had not prevented him from con-
tinuing with his work but, almost imperceptibly, he had
slackened his pace and for the first time had let himself wonder
whether the silver cleaning had become too tiring for him to
undertake alone. But that would be a humiliating defeat. Resolutely pulling the last candelabrum towards him, he took up a
fresh polishing cloth and, easing his aching limbs in the chair,
bent again to his task.

5

In the music room the gentlemen did not keep them waiting
long and the atmosphere lightened as the company settled themselves comfortably on the sofa and chairs. The pianoforte was
opened by Darcy and the candles on the instrument were lit. As

soon as they had seated themselves, Darcy turned to Georgiana and, almost formally as if she were a guest, said that it would be a pleasure for them all if she would play and sing. She got up with a glance at Henry Alveston and he followed her to the instrument. Turning to the party she said, 'As we have a tenor with us, I thought it would be pleasant to have some duets.'

'Yes!' cried Bingley enthusiastically. 'A very good idea. Let us hear you both. Jane and I were trying last week to sing duets together, were we not, my love? But I won't suggest that we repeat the experiment tonight. I was a disaster, was I not, Jane?'

His wife laughed. 'No, you did very well. But I'm afraid I have neglected practising since Charles Edward was born. We will not inflict our musical efforts on our friends while we have in Miss Georgiana a more talented musician than you or I can ever hope to be.'

Elizabeth tried to give herself over to the music but her eyes and her thoughts were with the couple at the piano. After the first two songs a third was entreated and there was a pause as Georgiana picked up a new score and showed it to Alveston. He turned the pages and seemed to be pointing to passages which he thought might be difficult, or perhaps where he was uncertain how to pronounce the Italian. She looked up at him, and then played a few bars with her right hand and he smiled his acquiescence. Both of them seemed unaware of the waiting audience. It was a moment of intimacy which enclosed them in their private world, yet reached out to a moment when self was forgotten in their common love of music. Watching the candlelight on the two rapt faces, their smiles as the problem was solved and Georgiana settled herself to play, Elizabeth felt that this was no fleeting attraction based on physical proximity, not even in a shared love of music. Surely they were in love, or perhaps on the verge of love, that enchanting period of mutual discovery, expectation and hope.

It was an enchantment she had never known. It still surprised her that between Darcy's first insulting proposal and his second successful and penitent request for her love, they had only been together in private for less than half an hour: the time when she and the Gardiners were visiting Pemberley and he unexpectedly returned and they walked together in the gardens, and the following day when he rode over to the Lambton inn where she was staying to discover her in tears, holding Jane's letter with news of Lydia's elopement. He had quickly left within minutes and she had thought never to see him again. If this were fiction, could even the most brilliant novelist contrive to make credible so short a period in which pride had been subdued and prejudice overcome? And later, when Darcy and Bingley returned to Netherfield and Darcy was her accepted lover, the courtship, so far from being a period of joy, had been one of the most anxious and embarrassing of her life as she sought to divert his attention from her mother's loud and exuberant congratulations which had almost gone as far as thanking him for his great condescension in applying for her daughter's hand. Neither Jane nor Bingley had suffered in the same way. The good-natured and love-obsessed Bingley either did not notice or tolerated his future mother-in-law's vulgarity. And would she herself have married Darcy had he been a penniless curate or a struggling attorney? It was difficult to envisage Mr Fitzwilliam Darcy of Pemberley as either, but honesty compelled an answer. Elizabeth knew that she was not formed for the sad contrivances of poverty.

The wind was still rising and the two voices were accompanied by the moaning and howling in the chimney and the fitful blazing of the fire, so that the tumult outside seemed nature's descant to the beauty of the two blending voices and a fitting accompaniment to the turmoil in her own mind. She had never before been worried by a high wind and would relish the security and comfort of sitting indoors while it raged ineffectively through the Pemberley woodland. But now it seemed a malignant force, seeking every chimney, every cranny, to gain entrance. She was not imaginative and she tried to put the morbid imaginings from her, but there persisted an emotion which she had never known before. She thought, *Here we sit at the beginning of a new century, citizens of the most civilised country in Europe, surrounded by the splendour of its craftsmanship, its art and the books which enshrine its literature, while outside there is another world which wealth and education and privilege can keep from us, a world in which men are as violent and destructive as is the animal world. Perhaps even the most fortunate of us will not be able to ignore it and keep it at bay for ever.*

She tried to restore tranquillity in the blending of the two voices, but was glad when the music ended and it was time to pull on the bell-rope and order the tea.

The tea tray was brought in by Billings, one of the footmen. She knew that he was destined to leave Pemberley in the spring when, if all went well, he could hope to succeed the Bingleys' butler when the old man at last retired. It was a rise in importance and status, made the more welcome to him as he had become engaged to Thomas Bidwell's daughter Louisa the Easter before last and she would accompany him to Highmarten as chief parlourmaid. Elizabeth, in her first months at Pemberley, had been surprised at the family's involvement in the life of their servants. On Darcy's and her rare visits to London they stayed in their townhouse or with Bingley's sister, Mrs Hurst, and her husband, who lived in some grandeur. In that world the servants lived lives so apart from the family that it was apparent how rarely Mrs Hurst even knew the names of those who served her. But although Mr and Mrs Darcy were carefully protected from domestic problems, there were events – marriages, betrothals, changes of job, illness or retirement – which rose above the ceaseless life of activity which ensured the smooth running of the house, and it was important both to Darcy and Elizabeth that these rites of passage, part of that still largely secret life on which their comfort so much depended, should be recognised and celebrated.

Now Billings put down the tea tray in front of Elizabeth with a kind of deliberate grace, as if to demonstrate to Jane how worthy he was of the honour in store. It was, thought Elizabeth, to be a comfortable situation both for him and his new wife. As her father had prophesied, the Bingleys were generous employers, easy-going, undemanding and particular only in the care of each other and their children.

Hardly had Billings left when Colonel Fitzwilliam got up from his seat and walked over to Elizabeth. 'Will you forgive me, Mrs Darcy, if I now take my nightly exercise? I have it in mind to ride Talbot beside the river. I'm sorry to break up so happy a family meeting but I sleep ill without fresh air before bed.'

Elizabeth assured him that no excuses were necessary. He raised her hand briefly to his lips, a gesture that was unusual in him, and made for the door.

Henry Alveston was sitting with Georgiana on the sofa. Looking up, he said, 'Moonlight on the river is magical, Colonel, although perhaps best seen in company. But you and Talbot will have a rough ride of it. I do not envy you battling against this wind.'

The colonel turned at the door and looked at him. His voice was cold. 'Then we must be grateful that you are not required to accompany me.' With a farewell bow to the company he was gone.

There was a moment of silence in which the colonel's parting words and the singularity of his night ride were in every mind, but in which embarrassment inhibited comment. Only Henry Alveston seemed unconcerned although, glancing at his face, Elizabeth had no doubt that the implied criticism had not been lost on him.

It was Bingley who broke the silence. 'Some more music, if you please, Miss Georgiana, if you are not too tired. But please finish your tea first. We must not impose on your kindness. What about those Irish folksongs which you played when we dined here last summer? No need to sing, the music itself is enough, you must save your voice. I remember that we even had some dancing, did we not? But then the Gardiners were here, and Mr and Mrs Hurst, so we had five couples, and Mary was here to play for us.'

Georgiana returned to the pianoforte with Alveston standing turning the pages, and for a time the lively tunes had their effect. Then, when the music ended, they made desultory conversation, exchanging views which had been expressed many times before and family news, none of which was new. Half an hour later, Georgiana made the first move and said her goodnights, and when she had pulled the bell-rope to summon her maid, Alveston lit and handed her a candle and escorted her to the door. After she had left, it seemed to Elizabeth that the rest of the party were all tired but lacked the energy actually to get up and say their goodnights. It was Jane who next made a move and, looking at her husband, murmured that it was time for bed. Elizabeth, grateful, soon followed her example. A footman was summoned to bring in and light the night candles, those on the pianoforte were blown out, and they were making their way to the door when Darcy, who was standing by the window, gave a sudden exclamation.

'My God! What does that fool of a coachman think he's doing? He'll have the whole chaise over! This is madness. And who on earth are they? Elizabeth, is anyone else expected tonight?'

'No one.'

Elizabeth and the rest of the company crowded to the window and there in the distance saw a chaise, lurching and swaying down the woodland road towards the house, its two sidelights blazing like small flames. Imagination provided what was too distant to be seen – the manes of the horses tossed by the wind, their wild eyes and straining shoulders, the postilion heaving at the reins. It was too distant for the wheels to be heard and it seemed to Elizabeth that she was seeing a spectral coach of legend flying soundlessly through the moonlit night, the dreaded harbinger of death.

Darcy said, 'Bingley, stay here with the ladies and I'll see what this is about.'

But his words were lost in a renewed howling of the wind in the chimney and the company followed him out of the music room, down the main staircase and into the hall. Stoughton and Mrs Reynolds were already there. At a gesture from Darcy, Stoughton opened the door. The wind rushed in immediately, a cold, irresistible force seeming to take possession of the whole house, extinguishing in one blow all the candles except those in the high chandelier.

The coach was still coming at speed, rocking round the corner at the end of the woodland road to approach the house. Elizabeth thought that it would surely rattle past the door. But now she could hear the shouts of the coachman and see him struggling with the reins. The horses were pulled to a halt and stood there, restless and neighing. Immediately, and before he could dismount, the coach door was opened and in the shaft of light from Pemberley they saw a woman almost falling out and shrieking into the wind. With her hat hanging by its ribbons round her neck and her loose hair blowing about her face, she seemed like some wild creature of the night, or a mad woman escaped from captivity. For a moment Elizabeth stood rooted, incapable of action or thought. And then she recognised that this wild shrieking apparition was Lydia and ran forward to help. But Lydia pushed her aside and, still screaming, thrust herself into Jane's arms, nearly toppling her. Bingley stepped forward to assist his wife and together they half-carried Lydia to the door. She was still howling and struggling as if unaware of who was supporting her, but once inside, protected from the wind, they could hear her harsh broken words.

'Wickham's dead! Denny has shot him! Why don't you find

him? They're up there in the woodland. Why don't you do something? Oh God, I know he's dead!'

And then the sobs became moans and she slumped in Jane's and Bingley's arms as together they urged her gently towards the nearest chair.

Book Two

The Body in the Woodland

1

Instinctively Elizabeth had moved forward to help but Lydia thrust her aside with surprising strength, crying, 'Not you, not you.' Jane took over, kneeling beside the chair and holding both Lydia's hands in hers, gently murmuring reassurance and sympathy, while Bingley, distressed, stood impotently by. And now Lydia's tears changed to an unnatural whooping as if she were fighting for breath, a disturbing sound which seemed hardly human.

Stoughton had left the front door slightly ajar. The postilion, standing by the horses, seemed too shocked to move and Alveston and Stoughton dragged Lydia's trunk from the chaise and carried it into the hall. Stoughton turned to Darcy. 'What about the two other pieces of luggage, sir?'

'Leave them in the chaise. Mr Wickham and Captain Denny will presumably be travelling on when we find them so there is no point in leaving their baggage here. Get Wilkinson, will you Stoughton. Rouse him if he's in bed. Tell him to fetch Dr McFee. He had better take the chaise; I don't want the doctor riding through this wind. Tell him to give Dr McFee my compliments and explain that Mrs Wickham is here at Pemberley and requires his attention.'

Leaving the women to cope with Lydia, Darcy moved quickly to where the coachman was standing by the horses' heads. He had been gazing anxiously at the door but, at the approach of Darcy, drew himself up and stood stiffly to attention. His relief on seeing the master of the house was almost palpable. He had done his best in an emergency and now normal life had returned and he was doing his job: standing by his horses and awaiting instructions.

Darcy said, 'Who are you? Do I know you?'

'I'm George Pratt, sir, from the Green Man.'

'Of course. You are Mr Piggott's coachman. Tell me what happened in the woodland. Make it clear and concise, but I want to know the whole story, and quickly.'

Pratt was obviously anxious to tell it and immediately broke into rapid speech. 'Mr Wickham and his lady and Captain Denny came to the inn this afternoon but I wasn't there when they arrived. Come eight o'clock or thereabouts this evening Mr Piggott told me I was to drive Mr and Mrs Wickham and the captain to Pemberley when the lady was ready, using the back road through the woodland. I was to leave Mrs Wickham at the house to go to the ball, or so she was saying earlier to Mrs Piggott. After that my orders was to take the two gentlemen to the King's Arms at Lambton and then return with the chaise to the inn. I heard Mrs Wickham saying to Mrs Piggott that the gentlemen would be travelling on to London the next day and that Mr Wickham was hopeful of getting employment.'

'Where are Mr Wickham and Captain Denny?'

'I don't rightly know, sir. When we was about halfway into the woodland Captain Denny knocked to stop the chaise and got out. He shouted something like, "I'm finished with it and with you. I'll have no part in it," and ran off into the woodland. Then Mr Wickham went after him, shouting to him to come back and not be a fool, and Mrs Wickham started screaming for him not to leave her and made to follow, but after she got down from the coach, she thought better of it and got back in. She was hollering something dreadful and making the horses nervous so that I could hardly hold them, and then we heard the shots.'

'How many?'

'I couldn't rightly say, sir, things being all awry with the captain making off and Mr Wickham running after him and the lady yelling, but I heard one shot for certain, sir, and maybe one or two more.'

'How long after the gentlemen left did you hear the shots?'

'Could be fifteen minutes, sir, maybe longer. I know we was standing there an awful long time expecting the gentlemen to come back. But I heard shots all right. It was then Mrs Wickham started screaming that we'd all be murdered and ordered me to drive at speed to Pemberley. It seemed the best thing to do, sir, seeing as how the gentlemen were not there to give orders. I thought they was lost in the woodland but I couldn't go looking for them, sir, not with Mrs Wickham screaming murder and the horses in a right state.'

'No, of course not. Were the shots close?'

'Close enough, sir. I reckon someone was shooting maybe within a hundred yards.'

'Right. Well, I'll need you to take a party of us back to where the gentlemen went into the woodland and we'll go in search.'

It was apparent that this plan was so deeply unwelcome to Pratt that he ventured an objection. 'I was to go on to the King's

Arms in Lambton, sir, and then back to the Green Man. Those was my clear orders, sir. And the horses will be sore afeared of going back into the woodland.'

'Obviously there is no point in going on to Lambton without Mr Wickham and Captain Denny. From now on you take your orders from me. They will be clear enough. It is your job to control the horses. Wait here, and keep them quiet. I will settle matters later with Mr Piggott. You will not be in any trouble if you do what I say.'

Inside Pemberley, Elizabeth turned to Mrs Reynolds and spoke quietly. 'We need to get Mrs Wickham to bed. Is there one made up in the south guest room on the second floor?'

'Yes madam, and a fire has already been lit. This room and two others are always prepared for Lady Anne's ball in case we get another October night like the one in '97 when the snow was four inches deep and some guests who had made a long journey could not get home. Shall we take Mrs Wickham there?'

Elizabeth said, 'Yes that would be best, but in her present state she cannot be left alone. Someone will have to sleep in the same room.'

Mrs Reynolds said, 'There is a comfortable sofa as well as a single bed in the dressing room next door, madam. I can get the sofa moved in with blankets and pillows. And I expect Belton is still up and waiting for you. She must be aware that something is wrong and she is utterly discreet. I suggest that at present she and I take turns at sleeping on the sofa in Mrs Wickham's room.'

Elizabeth said, 'You and Belton should get your sleep tonight. Mrs Bingley and I should be able to manage.'

Returning to the hall, Darcy saw Lydia being half-carried up the stairs by Bingley and Jane, led by Mrs Reynolds. The whooping had sunk into quieter sobbing, but she wrenched herself free from Jane's supporting arms and, turning, fixed a furious gaze on Darcy. 'Why are you still here? Why don't you go and find him? I heard the shots, I tell you. Oh my God – he could be injured or dead! Wickham could be dying and you just stand there. For God's sake go!'

Darcy said calmly, 'We are getting ready now. I shall bring you news when we have any. There is no need to expect the worst. Mr Wickham and Captain Denny may be already heading this way on foot. Now try to rest.'

Murmuring reassurance to Lydia, Jane and Bingley had at last gained the top step and, following Mrs Reynolds, moved out of sight down the corridor. Elizabeth said, 'I am afraid Lydia will make herself ill. We need Dr McFee; he could give her something to calm her.'

'I have already ordered the chaise to collect him, and now we must go into the woodland to look for Wickham and Denny. Has Lydia been able to tell you what happened?'

'She managed to control her weeping long enough to blurt out the main facts and to demand that her trunk be brought in and unlocked. I could almost believe that she is still expecting to go to the ball.'

It seemed to Darcy that the great entrance hall of Pemberley, with its elegant furniture, the beautiful staircase curving up to the gallery, and the family portraits, had suddenly become as alien as if he were entering it for the first time. The natural order which from boyhood had sustained him had been overturned and for a moment he felt as powerless as if he were no longer master in his house, an absurdity which found relief in an irritation over details. It was not Stoughton's job, nor was it Alveston's, to carry luggage, and Wilkinson, by long tradition, was the only member of the household who, apart from Stoughton, took his orders directly from his master. But at least something was being done. Lydia's luggage had been carried in and the Pemberley chaise would go now to fetch Dr McFee. Instinctively he moved to his wife and gently took her hand. It was as cold as death but he felt her reassuring, answering pressure and was comforted.

Bingley had now come down the stairs and was joined by Alveston and Stoughton. Darcy briefly recounted what he had learned from Pratt, but it was apparent that Lydia, despite her distress, had indeed managed to gasp out the essentials of her story.

Darcy said, 'We need Pratt to point out where Denny and Wickham left the carriage, so we shall be taking Piggott's chaise. You had better stay here, Charles, with the ladies, and Stoughton can guard the door. If you will be part of this, Alveston, we should be able to manage between us.'

Alveston said, 'Please use me, sir, in any way in which I can be of help.'

Darcy turned to Stoughton. 'We may need a stretcher. Is there not one in the room next to the gunroom?'

'Yes sir, the one we used when Lord Instone broke his leg in the hunt.'

'Then fetch it, will you. And we shall need blankets, some brandy and water and lanterns.'

Alveston said, 'I can help with those,' and immediately the two of them were gone.

It seemed to Darcy that they had spent too long talking and making arrangements, but looking at his watch he saw that only fifteen minutes had passed since Lydia's dramatic arrival. It was then that he heard the sound of hoofs and, turning, saw a horseman galloping on the greensward at the edge of the river. Colonel Fitzwilliam had returned. Before he had time to dismount, Stoughton came round the corner of the house carrying a stretcher over his shoulder followed by Alveston and a manservant, their arms laden with two folded blankets, the bottles of brandy and water and three lanterns. Darcy went up to the colonel and rapidly gave him a concise account of the night's events and what they had in mind.

Fitzwilliam listened in silence, then said, 'You are mounting quite an impressive expedition to satisfy one hysterical woman. I daresay the fools have lost themselves in the woodland, or one of them has tripped over a tree root and sprained an ankle. They are probably even now limping to Pemberley or the King's Arms, but if the coachman also heard shots we had better go armed. I'll get my pistol and join you in the chaise. If the stretcher is needed you could do with an extra man and a horse would be an encumbrance if we have to go into the depths of the woodland, which seems likely. I will bring my pocket compass. Two grown men getting themselves lost like children is stupid enough, five would be ludicrous.'

He mounted his horse and quickly trotted towards the stables. The colonel had offered no explanation of his absence and Darcy, in the trauma of the evening's events, had given no thought to him. He reflected that wherever Fitzwilliam had been, his return was inopportune if he were to hold up the enterprise or demand information and explanations which no one could yet supply, but it was true that they could do with an extra man. Bingley would stay to look after the women, and he could, as always, rely on Stoughton and Mrs Reynolds to ensure that all doors and windows were secure and to cope with any inquisitive servants. But there was no undue delay. His cousin was back within a few minutes and he and Alveston lashed the stretcher to the chaise, the three men got in and Pratt mounted the leading horse.

It was then that Elizabeth appeared and ran up to the chaise. 'We're forgetting Bidwell. If there's any trouble in the woodland, he should be with his family. Perhaps he is already. Has he left to go home yet do you know, Stoughton?'

'No madam. He is still polishing the silver. He was not expecting to go home until Sunday. Some of the indoor staff are still working, madam.'

Before Elizabeth could reply, the colonel got quickly out of the chaise saying, 'I'll fetch him. I know where he will be – in the butler's pantry,' and he was gone.

Glancing at her husband's face, Elizabeth saw his frown and knew that he was sharing her surprise. Now that the colonel had arrived it was apparent that he was determined to take control of the enterprise in all its aspects, but she told herself that this was not perhaps surprising; he was, after all, accustomed to assuming command in moments of crisis.

He returned quickly, but without Bidwell, saying, 'He was so distressed at leaving his work half-finished that I did not press the matter. As usual on the night before the ball Stoughton has already arranged for him to stay overnight. He will be working all day tomorrow, and his wife will not expect to see him until Sunday. I told him that we would check that all is well at the cottage. I hope I have not exceeded my authority.'

Since the colonel had no authority over the Pemberley servants to be exceeded, there was nothing Elizabeth could say.

At last they moved off, watched from the door by a small group consisting of Elizabeth, Jane, Bingley and the two servants. No one spoke and when, minutes later, Darcy looked back, the great door of Pemberley had been closed and the house stood as if deserted, serene and beautiful in the moonlight.

2

No part of the Pemberley estate was neglected but, unlike the arboretum, the woodland to the north-west neither received nor required much attention. Occasionally a tree would be felled to provide winter fuel or timber for structural repairs to the cottages, and bushes inconveniently close to the path would be cut back or a dead tree chopped down and the trunk hauled away. A narrow lane rutted by the carts delivering provisions to the servants' entrance led from the gatehouse to the wide courtyard at the rear of Pemberley, beyond which were the stables. From the courtyard, a door to the back of the house led to a passage and the gunroom and steward's office.

The chaise, burdened with the three passengers, the stretcher and two bags belonging to Wickham and Captain Denny, was slow-moving and all three passengers sat in silence which, in Darcy, was close to an unaccountable lethargy. Suddenly the chaise shook to a stop. Rousing himself, Darcy looked out and felt the first sharp rain stinging his face. It seemed to him that a great fissured cliff face hung over them, bleak and impenetrable which, even as he looked, trembled as if about to fall. Then his mind took hold of reality, the fissures in the rock widened to become a gap between closely planted trees, and he heard Pratt urging the unwilling horses onto the woodland path.

Slowly they moved into loam-smelling darkness. They had been travelling under the eerie light of the full moon which seemed to be sailing before them like some ghostly companion, at one moment lost and then reappearing. After some yards, Fitzwilliam said to Darcy, 'We would be better on foot from now on. Pratt may not be precise in memory and we need to keep a close watch for the place where Wickham and Denny entered the woodland and where they may have come out. We can see and hear better outside the chaise.'

They got out of the chaise carrying their lanterns and, as Darcy had expected, the colonel took his place at the front. The ground was softened with fallen leaves so that their footfalls were muted and Darcy could hear little but the creak of the chaise, the harsh breathing of the horses and the rattle of the reins. In places the boughs overhead met to form a dense arched tunnel from which only occasionally he could glimpse the moon, and in this cloistered darkness all he could hear of the wind was a faint rustling of the thin upper twigs, as if they were still the habitation of the chirping birds of spring.

As always when he walked in the woodland, Darcy's thought turned to his great-grandfather. The charm of the woodland for that long-dead George Darcy must have lain partly in the wood's

66

diversity, its secret footpaths and unexpected vistas. Here in his remote tree-guarded refuge where the birds and small animals could come unimpeded to his home, he could believe that he and nature were one, breathing the same air, guided by the same spirit. As a boy playing in the woodland, Darcy had always sympathised with his great-grandfather and he had early realised that this seldom-mentioned Darcy, who had abdicated his responsibility to the estate and the house, was an embarrassment to his family. Before shooting his dog, Soldier, and himself, he had left a brief note asking to be buried with the animal, but this impious request had been ignored by the family and George Darcy lay with his forebears in the enclosed family section of the village churchyard, while Soldier had his own woodland grave with a granite headstone carved simply with his name and the date of his death. From childhood Darcy had been aware that his father had feared that there might be some inherited weakness in the family and had early indoctrinated in him the great obligations which would lie on his shoulders once he inherited, responsibilities for both the estate and those who served and depended on it, which no elder son could ever reject.

Colonel Fitzwilliam set a slow pace, swinging his lantern from side to side and occasionally calling a halt so that he could take a closer look at the occluding foliage, searching for any signs that someone had broken through. Darcy, aware that the thought was ungenerous, reflected that the colonel, exercising his prerogative to take charge, was probably enjoying himself. Trudging in front of Alveston, Darcy walked in a bitterness of spirit broken from time to time by surges of anger, like the rush of an incoming tide. Was he never to be free of George Wickham? These were the woods in which the two of them had played as boys. It was a time he could once recall as carefree and happy, but had that boyhood friendship really been genuine? Had the young Wickham even then been harbouring envy, resentment and dislike? Those rough boyish games and mock fights which sometimes left him bruised – had Wickham perhaps been deliberately over-boisterous? The petty, hurtful remarks now rose into his consciousness, beneath which they had lain untroubling for years. How long had Wickham been planning his revenge? The knowledge that his sister had only avoided social disgrace and ignominy because he was rich enough to buy her would-be seducer's silence was so bitter that he almost groaned aloud. He had tried to put his humiliation out of mind in the happiness of his marriage but now it returned, made stronger by the years of repression, an intolerable burden of shame and self-disgust made more bitter by the knowledge that it was only his money that had induced Wickham to marry Lydia Bennet. It had been a generosity born of his love for Elizabeth, but it had been his marriage to Elizabeth which had brought Wickham into his family and had given him the right to call Darcy brother and made him an uncle to Fitzwilliam and Charles. He might have been able to keep Wickham out of Pemberley but he could never banish him from his mind.

After five minutes they reached the path which led from the road to Woodland Cottage. Trodden regularly over the years, it was narrow but not hard to find. Before Darcy had time to speak, the colonel moved at once towards it, lantern in hand. Handing his firearm to Darcy, he said, 'You had better have this. I am not expecting any trouble and it will only frighten Mrs Bidwell and her daughter. I will check that they are all right and tell Mrs Bidwell to keep the door locked and on no account to let anyone in. I had better let Mrs Bidwell know that the two gentlemen may be lost in the woodland and that we are seeking them. There is no point in telling her anything else.'

Then he was gone and was immediately out of sight, the sound of his departure deadened by the density of the wood. Darcy and Alveston stood still in silence. The minutes seemed to lengthen and, looking at his watch, Darcy saw that the colonel had been gone for nearly twenty minutes before they heard the rustle of parted branches and he reappeared.

Taking back his gun from Darcy, he said curtly, 'All is well. Mrs Bidwell and her daughter both heard the sound of gunfire which they thought was close but not immediately outside the cottage. They locked the door at once and heard nothing more. The girl – Louisa is it not? – was on the verge of hysteria but her mother managed to quieten her. It is unfortunate that this is the night when Bidwell is not at home.' He turned to the coachman. 'Keep a sharp eye and stop when we get to the place where Captain Denny and Mr Wickham left the chaise.'

He again took his place at the head of the little procession and they walked slowly on. From time to time Darcy and Alveston raised their lanterns high, looking for any disturbance in the undergrowth, listening for any sound. Then, after about five minutes, the chaise rocked to a stop.

Pratt said, 'About here I reckon, sir. I remember this oak tree on the left and those red berries.'

Before Fitzwilliam could speak Darcy asked, 'In which direction did Captain Denny go?'

'To the left, sir. There's no path that I could see but he just charged into the wood as if the bushes wasn't there.'

'How long before Mr Wickham followed him?'

'No more than a second or two, I reckon. Like I said, sir, Mrs Wickham clutched at him and tried to stop him going, and kept hollering after him. But when he didn't come back and she heard the shots she told me to start moving and get to Pemberley as quick as possible. She was screaming, sir, the whole way, saying as how we was all going to be murdered.'

Darcy said, 'Wait here, and don't leave the chaise.' He turned to Alveston, 'We had better take the stretcher. We shall look fools if they've just got lost and are wandering unharmed, but those shots are worrying.'

Alveston untied and dragged down the stretcher from the chaise. He said to Darcy, 'And bigger fools if we get lost ourselves. But I expect you know these woodlands well, sir.'

Darcy said, 'Well enough, I hope, to find my way out of them.'

It was not going to be easy to manoeuvre the stretcher through the undergrowth but, after discussion of the problem, Alveston shouldered the rolled canvas and they set off.

Pratt had made no reply to Darcy's command that he should stay with the chaise but it was apparent that he was unhappy at being left alone and his fear communicated itself to the horses, whose jostling and neighing seemed to Darcy a fitting accompaniment to an enterprise he was beginning to think ill advised. Thrusting their way through the almost impenetrable bushes, they walked in single file, the colonel leading, slowly casting their lanterns from side to side and halting at every sign that someone might recently have passed that way, while Alveston manoeuvred the long poles of the stretcher with difficulty under the low-hanging branches of the trees. Every few steps they halted, called out and then listened in silence, but there was no reply. The wind, which had been hardly heard, suddenly dropped and in the calm it seemed that the secret life of the woodland was stilled by their unwonted presence.

At first, from the torn and hanging twigs of some of the bushes and a few smudges which could be footprints, there was hope that they were on the right trail, but after five minutes the trees and bushes became less thick, their calls were still un-answered and they stopped to consider how best to proceed. Afraid to lose contact in case one or other of them got lost, they had kept within yards of each other, moving west. Now they decided to return to the chaise by turning eastward towards Pemberley. It was impossible for three men to cover the whole extensive woodland; if this change of direction produced no results they would go back to the house and, if Wickham and Denny had not returned by daylight, call in estate workers and perhaps the police to institute a more thorough search.

They trudged on, when suddenly the barrier of tangled bushes was less dense and they glimpsed a moonlit glade formed by a ring of slender silver birch trees. They pressed forward with renewed energy, crashing through the undergrowth, glad to break free of the imprisonment of the tangled shrubs and the thick unyield-ing trunks into freedom and light. Here there was no overhanging canopy of boughs and the moonlight silvering the delicate trunks made this a vision of beauty, more chimera than reality.

And now the glade was before them. Passing slowly, almost in awe, between two of the slender trunks, they stood as if physic-ally rooted, speechless with horror. Before them, its stark colours a brutal contrast to the muted light, was a tableau of death. No one spoke. They moved slowly forward as one, all three holding their lanterns high; their strong beams, outshining the gentle radiance of the moon, intensified the bright red of an officer's tunic and the ghastly blood-smeared face and mad glaring eyes turned towards them.

Captain Denny lay on his back, his right eye caked with blood, his left, glazed, fixed unseeing on the distant moon. Wickham was kneeling over him, his hands bloody, his own face a splattered mask. His voice was harsh and guttural but the words were clear. 'He's dead! Oh God, Denny's dead! He was my friend, my only friend, and I've killed him! I've killed him! It's my fault.'

Before they could reply, he slumped forward and began a wild sobbing which tore at his throat, then collapsed over Denny's body, the two bloody faces almost touching.

The colonel bent over Wickham, then straightened up. He said, 'He's drunk.'

Darcy said, 'And Denny?'

'Dead. No, better not touch him. I know death when I see it. Let us get the body onto the stretcher and I'll help carry it. Alveston, you are probably the strongest among us, can you support Wickham back to the chaise?'

'I think so, sir. He's not a heavy man.'

In silence Darcy and the colonel lifted Denny's body onto the canvas stretcher. The colonel then moved to help Alveston get Wickham to his feet. He staggered but made no resistance. His breath, which came in sobbing gasps, polluted the air of the glade with its stink of whisky. Alveston was the taller man and, once he had managed to raise Wickham's right arm and placed it over his shoulder, was able to support his inert weight and half-drag him a few steps.

The colonel had bent down again and now straightened up. There was a pistol in his hand. He examined the gun then said, 'Presumably this was the weapon which fired the shots.' Then he and Darcy grasped the poles of the stretcher and with some effort lifted it. The sad procession began its laboured way back to the chaise, the stretcher first and Alveston, burdened with Wickham, some yards behind. The evidence of their passing was plain and they had no difficulty in retracing their footsteps but the journey was slow and tedious. Darcy trudged behind the colonel in a desolation of spirit in which a dozen different fears and anxieties jostled in his mind making rational thought impossible. He had never let himself wonder how close Elizabeth and Wickham had been in the days of their friendship at Longbourn, but now jealous doubts, which he recognised as unjustified and ignoble, crowded his mind. For one terrible moment he wished that it was Wickham's body he was straining his shoulders to carry, and the realisation that he could wish, even for a second, that his enemy was dead appalled him.

Pratt's relief at their reappearance was apparent, but at the sight of the stretcher he began shaking with fear and it was only after the colonel's sharp command that he controlled the horses who, smelling blood, were becoming unmanageable. Darcy and the colonel lowered the stretcher to the ground and Darcy, taking a blanket from the chaise, covered Denny's body. Wickham had been quiet on the walk through the woodland but now was becoming belligerent and it was with relief that Alveston, helped by the colonel, managed to get him into the chaise and took his seat next to him. The colonel and Darcy again grasped the stretcher poles, and with aching shoulders took up their burden. Pratt at last had the horses under control and in silence and a great weariness of body and spirit Darcy and the colonel, following the chaise, began the long trudge back to Pemberley.

3

As soon as Lydia, now grown calmer, had been persuaded into bed Jane felt able to leave her in Belton's care and joined Elizabeth. Together they hurried to the front door to watch the departure of the rescue party. Bingley, Mrs Reynolds and Stoughton were already there, and the five of them stared into the darkness until the chaise had become two distant and wavering lights and Stoughton turned to shut and bolt the door.

Mrs Reynolds turned to Elizabeth, 'I will sit with Mrs Wickham until Dr McFee arrives, madam. I expect he will give her something to calm her and make her sleep. I suggest that you and Mrs Bingley go back to the music room to wait; you will be comfortable there and the fire has been made up. Stoughton will stay at the door and keep watch, and he will let you and Mrs Bingley know as soon as the chaise comes into sight. And if Mr Wickham and Captain Denny are discovered on the road, there will be room in the chaise for the whole party, although it will not perhaps be the most comfortable of journeys. I expect the gentlemen will need something hot to eat when they do return, but I doubt, madam, whether Mr Wickham and Captain Denny will wish to stay for refreshments. Once Mr Wickham knows

that his wife is safe, he and his friend will surely want to continue their journey. I think Pratt said that they were on their way to
the King's Arms at Lambton.'

This was exactly what Elizabeth wanted to hear, and she
wondered whether Mrs Reynolds was being deliberately reassuring. The thought that either Wickham or Captain Denny could
have broken or sprained an ankle while struggling through the
woodland and would need to be taken in, perhaps even for the
night, was a deeply disturbing possibility. Her husband would
never refuse shelter to an injured man, but to have Wickham under Pemberley's roof would be abhorrent to him and could have
consequences which she feared to contemplate.

Mrs Reynolds said, 'I shall check, madam, and see that all the
staff working on the preparation for the ball have now gone to
bed. Belton, I know, is happy to stay up in case she is needed,
and Bidwell is still working but he is absolutely discreet. No one
need be told about this night's adventure until the morning, and
then only as much as is necessary.'

They were beginning to mount the stairs when Stoughton announced that the chaise sent for Dr McFee was returning and
Elizabeth waited to receive him and briefly explain what had
happened. Dr McFee never entered the house without being giv-
en a warm welcome. He was a middle-aged widower whose wife
had died young leaving him her considerable fortune, and although he could afford to use his carriage, he preferred to do his
rounds on horseback. With his square leather bag strapped to his
saddle, he was a familiar figure in the roads and lanes of Lambton and Pemberley. Years of riding in all weathers had coarsened
his features but, although he was not considered a handsome

man, he had an open and clever face in which authority and benevolence were so united that he seemed destined by nature to be a country doctor. His medical philosophy was that the human body had a natural tendency to heal itself if patients and doctors did not conspire to interfere with its benign processes but, recognising that human nature demands pills and potions, he relied on draughts prepared by himself in which his patients had absolute faith. He had early learned that a patient's relatives are less trouble if they are kept busy in the sufferer's interest and had devised concoctions whose efficacy was in proportion to the time taken to prepare them. He was already known to his patient, as Mrs Bingley would call him in if husband, child, visiting friends or servants showed the slightest signs of indisposition and he had become a family friend. It was an immense relief to take him up to Lydia, who greeted him with a new outburst of recrimination and grief but became calmer almost as soon as he drew close to the bed.

Elizabeth and Jane were now free to begin their watch in the music room where the windows gave a clear view of the road to the woodland. Although both she and Jane tried to relax on the sofa, neither could resist walking ceaselessly to the window or moving restlessly about the room. Elizabeth knew they were making the same silent calculations and at last Jane put them into words.

'My dear Elizabeth, we cannot expect them to return very quickly. Let us suppose it takes them as long as fifteen minutes for Pratt to identify the trees where Captain Denny and Mr Wickham disappeared into the wood. They might then have to search for fifteen minutes or longer if the two gentlemen are indeed lost, and we should allow some time for returning to the chaise and making the return journey. And we must remember that one of them will need to call at Woodland Cottage to check that Mrs Bidwell and Louisa are safe. There are so many incidents which could hamper their journey. We must try to be patient; I calculate that it could be an hour before we see the chaise. And, of course, it is possible that Mr Wickham and Captain Denny finally found their way to the road and have decided to walk back to the inn.'

Elizabeth said, 'I think they would hardly do that. It would be a long walk and they told Pratt that after Lydia was left at Pemberley they were proceeding to the King's Arms at Lambton. Besides, they would need their luggage. And surely Wickham would want to ensure that Lydia had arrived here safely. But we can know nothing until the chaise returns. There is every hope that the two will be found on the road and we shall see the chaise soon. In the mean time, we had better get such rest as we can.'

But rest was impossible and they found themselves constantly walking to and from the window. After half an hour they lost hope of a quick return of the rescue party but still stood in a silent agony of apprehension. Above all, remembering the gunshots, they dreaded to see the chaise moving as slowly as a hearse with Darcy and the colonel following on foot with the loaded stretcher. At best it could be carrying Wickham or Denny, not seriously injured but unable to tolerate the jolting of the chaise. Both tried resolutely to put out of their minds the vision of a shrouded body and the appalling task of explaining to a distraught Lydia that her worst fears had been realised and that her husband was dead.

They had been waiting an hour and twenty minutes and,

weary with standing, had turned away from the window when Bingley appeared with Dr McFee.

The doctor said, 'Mrs Wickham was exhausted both with anxiety and with prolonged weeping and I have given her a sedative. She should soon be sleeping peacefully, I hope for some hours. The maid Belton and Mrs Reynolds are with her. I can make myself comfortable in the library and check on her condition later. There is no need for anyone to attend me.'

Elizabeth thanked him warmly and said that, indeed, that was what she would wish. And when the doctor accompanied by Jane had left the room, she and Bingley went again to the window.

Bingley said, 'We should not give up hope that all is well. The shots could have been a poacher after rabbits, or perhaps Denny fired his gun as a warning to someone lurking in the woods. We must not allow our imagination to conjure up images which reason must surely tell us are imaginary. There can be nothing in the woodland to tempt anyone with evil intent towards either Wickham or Denny.'

Elizabeth did not reply. Now even the familiar and well-loved landscape looked alien, the river winding like molten silver under the moon until a sudden gust of wind set it trembling into life. The road stretched in what seemed an eternal emptiness in a phantom landscape, mysterious and eerie, where nothing human could ever live or move. And it was just as Jane returned that, at last, the chaise came into sight, at first no more than a moving shape defined by the faint flicker of the distant lights. Resisting the temptation to dash to the door, they stood intently waiting.

Elizabeth could not keep the despair from her voice. She said, 'They are moving slowly. If all were well they would come at speed.'

At that thought she could wait at the window no longer but ran downstairs, Jane and Bingley at her side. Stoughton must have seen the chaise from the ground floor window for the front door was already ajar. He said, 'Would it not be wise, madam, to return to the music room? Mr Darcy will bring you the news as soon as they arrive. It is too cold to wait outside and there is nothing any of us can do until the chaise arrives.'

Elizabeth said, 'Mrs Bingley and I would prefer to wait at the door, Stoughton.'

'As you wish, madam.'

Together with Bingley they went out into the night and stood waiting. No one spoke until the chaise was a few yards from the door and they saw what they had feared, the shrouded shape on the stretcher. There was a sudden gust of wind, tossing Elizabeth's hair around her face. She felt herself falling but managed to clutch at Bingley who put a supporting arm round her shoulders. At that moment the wind lifted the corner of the blanket and they saw the scarlet of an officer's jacket.

Colonel Fitzwilliam spoke directly to Bingley. 'You can tell Mrs Wickham that her husband is alive. Alive but unfit to be seen. Captain Denny is dead.'

Bingley said, 'Shot?'

It was Darcy who replied. 'No, not shot.' He turned to Stoughton, 'Fetch the outdoor and indoor keys to the gunroom. Colonel Fitzwilliam and I will carry the body across the north courtyard and lay it on the gunroom table.' He turned again to Bingley. 'Please take Elizabeth and Mrs Bingley inside. There is nothing they can do here and we need to bring Wickham in from the chaise. It would be distressing for them to see him in his present condition. We need to get him to a bed.'

Elizabeth wondered why her husband and the colonel seemed unwilling to lower the stretcher to the ground, but they stood as if rooted until Stoughton came back within minutes and handed over the keys. Then almost ceremoniously, with Stoughton preceding them like an undertaker's mute, they made their way through the courtyard and round to the rear of the house and the gunroom.

The chaise was now rocking violently and between the gusts of wind Elizabeth could hear Wickham's wild, incoherent shouting, railing against his rescuers and the cowardice of Darcy and the colonel. Why hadn't they caught the murderer? They had a gun. They knew how to use it. By God, he'd tried a shot or two, and he would be there now had they not lugged him away. Then came a stream of oaths, the worst of them borne away by the wind, followed by an outburst of weeping.

Elizabeth and Jane went inside. Wickham had now fallen and Bingley and Alveston together managed to pull him to his feet and began half-dragging him into the hall. Elizabeth had one glimpse at the wild-eyed, blood-besmirched face and then retreated out of sight while Wickham tried to fight himself free of Alveston's grasp.

Bingley said, 'We need a room with a strong door and a key. What do you suggest?'

Mrs Reynolds, who had now returned, looked at Elizabeth.

She said, 'The blue room, madam, at the end of the north corridor would be the most secure. There are only two small windows and it's the furthest from the nursery.'

Bingley was still helping to control Wickham. He called to Mrs Reynolds, 'Dr McFee is in the library. Tell him he is needed now. We cannot manage Mr Wickham in his present state. Tell him that we shall be in the blue bedroom.'

Bingley and Alveston grasped Wickham's arms and began half-pulling him up the stairs. He was quieter now but still sobbing; as they reached the last step, he wrestled himself free and, glaring down, hurled his final imprecations.

Jane turned to Elizabeth. She said, 'I had better return to Lydia. Belton has been there for a long time and may need some relief. When I left Lydia she was becoming sleepy, but I will hurry now to give her the good news that Wickham is alive before Dr McFee's draught takes full effect. At least we have something to be grateful for. Dear Lizzy, if only I could have spared you this.'

The two sisters clung together for a moment and then Jane was gone. And now the hall was quiet. Elizabeth was shivering and, feeling suddenly faint, sat down on the nearest chair. She felt bereft, longing for Darcy to appear, and soon he was with her, coming from the gunroom through the back of the house. He came to her immediately and, raising her up, drew her gently to him.

'My dear, let us get away from here and I will explain what happened. You have seen Wickham?'

'Yes, I saw him carried in. He was a dreadful sight. Thank God Lydia did not see.'

'How is she?'

'Asleep, I hope. Dr McFee gave her something to calm her. And now he has gone with Mrs Reynolds to help with Wickham. Mr Alveston and Charles are taking Wickham to the blue bed-room in the north corridor. It seemed the best place for him.'

'And Jane?'

'She is with Lydia and Belton. She will spend the night in Lydia's room with Mr Bingley in the dressing room next door. Lydia would not tolerate my company. It has to be Jane.'

'Then let us go to the music room. I must have some moments with you alone. Today we have scarcely seen each other. I will tell you as much as I know, but it isn't good. Then I must go tonight to notify Sir Selwyn Hardcastle of Captain Denny's death. He is the nearest magistrate. I cannot have any part in this; it will be for Hardcastle to take over from now on.'

'But can it not wait, Fitzwilliam? You must be exhausted. And it will be after midnight if Sir Selwyn comes back tonight with the police. He cannot hope to do anything until morning.'

'It is right that Sir Selwyn should be told without delay. He will expect it, and he is right to expect it. He will want to remove Denny's body and probably see Wickham, if he is sober enough to be questioned. In any case, my love, Captain Denny's body should be moved as soon as possible. I do not want to seem cal-lous or irreverent but it will be convenient to have it out of the house before the servants wake. They will have to be told what has happened but it will be easier for all of us, particularly for the servants, if the body is no longer here.'

'But you could at least stay and have something to eat and drink before you go. It is hours since dinner.'

'I will stay for five minutes to take some coffee and to make sure Bingley is aware of my plans, but then I must be off.'

'And Captain Denny, tell me what happened? Anything is better that this suspense. Charles is talking about an accident. Was this an accident?'

Darcy said gently, 'My love, we must wait until the doctors have examined the body and can tell us how Captain Denny died. Until then it is all conjecture.'

'So it could have been an accident?'

'It is comforting to hope so, but I believe what I believed when I first saw his body – that Captain Denny was murdered.'

4

Five minutes later Elizabeth waited with Darcy at the front door for his horse to be brought round, and did not re-enter the house until she saw him break into a gallop and melt into the moonlit darkness. It would be an uncomfortable journey. The wind, which had spent its worst fury, had been succeeded by a heavy slanting rain, but she knew that the ride was necessary. Darcy was one of the three magistrates serving Pemberley and Lambton but he could have no part in this investigation and it was right that one of his colleagues should be informed of Denny's death without delay. She hoped, too, that the body would be removed from Pemberley before morning when the waking household would have to be told by Darcy and herself something of what had happened. The presence of Mrs Wickham would have to be explained and Lydia herself was unlikely to be discreet. Darcy was a fine horseman and even in poor weather a night ride away from the house would hold no terror for him, but straining her eyes to see the last flashing shadow of the galloping horse, she had to fight down an irrational fear that something terrible would happen before he reached Hardcastle and that she was destined never to see him again.

For Darcy the gallop into the night was a release into temporary freedom. Although his shoulders still ached from the weight of the stretcher and he knew he was exhausted in mind and body, the smack of the wind and the cold rain stinging his face were a liberation. Sir Selwyn Hardcastle was the only magistrate known to be always at home and living within eight miles of Pemberley who would be able to take the case and would indeed be glad to do so, but he was not the colleague Darcy would have chosen. Unfortunately Josiah Clitheroe, the third member of the local magistrates, was incapacitated by gout, an affliction as painful as it was undeserved since the doctor, although known to be partial to a good dinner, never touched port wine, which was commonly believed to be the chief cause of this disabling complaint. Dr Clitheroe was a distinguished lawyer respected beyond the borders of his native Derbyshire, and accordingly regarded as an asset to the bench despite his garrulity which arose from a belief that the validity of a judgment was in proportion to the length of time spent in arriving at it. Every nuance of a case with which he was concerned was scrutinised in meticulous detail, previous cases researched and discussed and the relevant law propounded. And if the dictates of an ancient philosopher – particularly Plato or Socrates – could be seen as adding weight to the argument, they were produced. But despite the circuity of the journey, his eventual decision was invariably reasonable and there were few defendants who would not have felt unfairly discriminated against if Dr Clitheroe had not paid them the compliment of at least one hour's incomprehensible dissertation when they appeared before him.

For Darcy, Dr Clitheroe's illness was particularly inconvenient. He and Sir Selwyn Hardcastle, although they respected each other as magistrates, were not comfortable colleagues and until Darcy's father succeeded to the Pemberley estate the two houses had been at enmity. The disagreement dated back to the time of Darcy's grandfather, when the young servant from Pemberley, Patrick Reilly, had been found guilty of stealing a deer from the then Sir Selwyn's deer park and was subsequently hanged.

The hanging had produce outrage among the Pemberley villagers but it was accepted that Mr Darcy had at least done his best to save the boy, and Sir Selwyn and he became set in their publicly prescribed roles of the compassionate magistrate and the harsh upholder of the law, the distinction helped by Hardcastle's seemingly appropriate name. The servants followed the example of their masters and resentment and animosity between the two houses were bequeathed from father to son. Only with the succession of Darcy's father to the Pemberley estate was any attempt made to heal the breach, and then not until he was on his deathbed. He asked his son to do what he could to restore accord, pointing out that it was neither in the interests of the law nor of good relations between the two estates for the present hostility to continue. Darcy, inhibited by his reserve and a belief that openly to discuss a quarrel might only confirm its existence, took a more subtle path. Invitations to shooting parties and occasionally to family dinners were given and were accepted by

Hardcastle. Perhaps he too had become increasingly aware of the dangers of the long-standing animosity, but the rapprochement had never developed into intimacy. Darcy knew that in the present trouble he would find in Hardcastle a conscientious and honest magistrate, but not a friend.

His horse seemed as glad of the fresh air and exercise as was its rider, and Darcy dismounted at Hardcastle House within half an hour. Sir Selwyn's ancestor had received his baronetcy in the time of James I when the family house had been built. It was a large, rambling and complicated edifice, its seven high chimneys a landmark above the tall elms which surrounded the house like a barricade. Inside, the small windows and low ceilings gave little light. The present baronet's father, impressed by some of the building by his neighbours, had added an elegant but discordant extension, now rarely used except as servant accommodation, Sir Selwyn preferring the original building despite its many inconveniences.

Darcy's tug on the iron bell-pull produced a clanging loud enough to awaken the whole house, and the door was opened within seconds by Sir Selwyn's elderly butler, Buckle, who like his master apparently managed without sleep since he was known to be on duty whatever the hour. Sir Selwyn and Buckle were inseparable and the position of butler to the Hardcastle family was generally regarded as being hereditary since Buckle's father had held it before him, as had his grandfather. The family resemblance between the generations was remarkable, every Buckle being squat, heavily built and long-armed, with the face of a benevolent bulldog. Buckle divested Darcy of his hat and riding jacket and, although the visitor was well known to him, asked him his name and, as was his invariable custom, instructed him to wait while his arrival was announced. The delay seemed interminable but eventually his heavy footsteps were heard approaching and he announced, 'Sir Selwyn is in his smoking room, sir, if you will follow me.'

They went through the great hall with its high vaulted roof, many-paned window, impressive collection of armour and the mounted head of a stag, somewhat mouldy with age. It also housed the family portraits and down the generations the Hardcastles had gained a reputation among the neighbouring families for the impressive number and size of them, a reputation founded more on quantity than quality. Every baronet had bequeathed at least one strong prejudice or opinion to instruct or inconvenience his successors, among them being the belief, first formed by a seventeenth-century Sir Selwyn, that it was a waste of money to employ an expensive artist to paint the women of the family. All that was necessary to satisfy the pretensions of husbands and the vanity of wives was that the painter make a plain face pretty, a pretty face beautiful, and spend more time and paint on the sitter's clothes than on the features. Since the Hardcastle men shared a propensity to admire the same type of female beauty, Buckle's three-branch candelabrum, held high, illumined a line of poorly painted identical disapproving pursed lips and hostile protruding eyes, as satin and lace succeeded velvet, silk replaced satin, and silk gave way to muslin. The male Hardcastles had fared better. The strongly inherited, slightly hooked nose, the bushy eyebrows much darker than the hair, a wide mouth with almost bloodless lips looked down on Darcy with confident assurance. Here, one could believe, was the present Sir Selwyn, immortalised down the centuries by distinguished painters, in his various roles: responsible landowner and master, paterfamilias, benefactor of the poor, captain of the Derbyshire Volunteers, richly uniformed with his sash of office, and last of all the magistrate, stern, judicial but fair. There were few lowly visitors to Sir Selwyn who were not deeply impressed and suitably intimidated by the time they reached the Presence.

Darcy now followed Buckle into a narrow corridor towards the back of the house at the end of which Buckle, without knocking, opened a heavy oak door and announced in a stentorian voice, 'Mr Darcy of Pemberley to see you, Sir Selwyn.'

Selwyn Hardcastle did not get up. He was sitting in a high-backed chair beside the fire wearing his smoking cap, his wig on a round table beside him which also held a bottle of port and a half-filled glass. He was reading from a heavy book which lay open in his lap and which he now closed with obvious regret after placing a bookmark carefully on the open page. The scene was almost a live reproduction for his portrait as magistrate and Darcy could imagine that he had a glimpse of the painter flitting tactfully through the door, the sitting over. The fire had obviously been recently tended and was now burning fiercely; against its small explosions of sound and the crackling of the logs, Darcy apologised for the lateness of his visit.

Sir Selwyn said, 'It is no matter. I seldom end my reading for the day before one o'clock in the morning. You seem discomposed. I take it that this is an emergency. What trouble now is affecting the parish – poaching, sedition, mass insurrection? Has Boney at last landed, or has Mrs Phillimore's poultry been raided once again? Please sit. That chair with the carved back is said to be comfortable and should hold your weight.'

Since it was the chair Darcy usually occupied he had every confidence that it would. He seated himself and told his story fully but succinctly, giving the salient facts without comment. Sir Selwyn listened in silence, then said. 'Let me see if I have understood you correctly. Mr and Mrs George Wickham and Captain Denny were being driven by hired chaise to Pemberley where Mrs Wickham would spend the night before attending Lady Anne's ball. Captain Denny at some stage left the chaise while it was in the Pemberley woodland, apparently after a disagreement, and Wickham followed him calling him to return. There was anxiety when neither gentleman reappeared. Mrs Wickham and Pratt, the coachman, said that they heard shots some fifteen minutes later and, naturally fearing foul play, Mrs Wickham, becoming overwrought, instructed the chaise to proceed at speed to Pemberley. After she arrived in considerable distress you initiated a search of the woodland by yourself, Colonel the Viscount Hartlep and the Honourable Henry Alveston, and together discovered the body of Captain Denny with Wickham kneeling over him apparently drunk and weeping, his face and hands bloodied.' He paused after the exertion of this feat of memory and took some sips of his port before speaking. 'Had Mrs Wickham been invited to the ball?'

The change in the line of questioning was unexpected but Darcy took it calmly. 'No. She would of course be received at Pemberley had she arrived unexpectedly at any time.'

'Not invited, but received, unlike her husband. It is common knowledge that George Wickham is never received at Pemberley.'

89

Darcy said, 'We are not on those terms.'

Sir Selwyn placed his book with some ceremony on the table. He said, 'His character is well known locally. A good beginning in childhood but thereafter a decline into wildness and dissolution, a natural result of exposing a young man to a lifestyle he could never hope to achieve by his own efforts, and companions of a class to which he could never aspire to belong. There are rumours that there could be another reason for your antagonism, something to do with his marriage to your wife's sister?'

Darcy said, 'There are always rumours. His ingratitude and lack of respect for my father's memory and the differences in our dispositions and interests are sufficient to explain our lack of intimacy. But are we not forgetting the reason for my visit? There can be no link between my relationship with George Wickham and the death of Captain Denny.'

'Forgive me, Darcy, but I disagree. There are links. The murder of Captain Denny, if murder it is, took place on your property and the person responsible could be a man who, in law, is your brother and with whom you are known to be at variance. When matters of importance come to mind I tend to express them. Your position is one of some delicacy. You understand that you cannot take part in this investigation?'

'That is why I am here.'

'The High Constable will have to be informed, of course. I take it that this has not yet been done.'

'I thought it more important to notify you immediately.'

'You were correct. I shall notify Sir Miles Culpepper myself and shall, of course, give him a full report of the state of the investigation as it proceeds. I doubt, however, that he will take much personal interest. Since marrying his new young wife he seems to spend more time enjoying the various divertissements of London than he does on local affairs. I have no criticism of this. The position of High Constable is in some sense invidious. His duties, as you know, are to enforce statutes and carry out the executive decisions of the justices, and also to oversee and direct the petty constables under his jurisdiction. Since he has no formal authority over them it is difficult to see how this can be done effectively but, as with so much in our country, the system works satisfactorily as long as it is left to local people. You remember Sir Miles, of course. You and I were two of the justices who swore him in at the quarter sessions two years ago. I will also get in touch with Dr Clitheroe. He may not be able to take an active part but he is usually invaluable on questions of law and I am reluctant to take all the responsibility. Yes, I think between the two of us we shall manage very well. I shall now accompany you back to Pemberley in my coach. It will be necessary to collect Dr Belcher before the body is moved and I shall bring the mortuary wagon and two petty constables. You know them both – Thomas Brownrigg, who likes to be known as a headborough to distinguish his seniority, and young William Mason.'

Without waiting for Darcy to comment, he got up and, moving to the bell-cord, gave it a vigorous tug.

Buckle arrived with a promptness which suggested to Darcy that he had been waiting outside the door. His master said, 'My greatcoat and hat, Buckle, and rouse Postgate if he is in bed, which I doubt. I want my carriage ready. I shall be driven to Pemberley, but calling en route to collect two petty constables and Dr Belcher. Mr Darcy will ride alongside us.'

Buckle disappeared into the gloom of the corridor, clanging the heavy door closed with what seemed unnecessary force.

Darcy said, 'I regret that my wife may be unable to receive you. I hope that she and Mrs Bingley will have retired for the night, but the upper servants are still on duty and Dr McFee is in the house. Mrs Wickham was in a state of considerable anguish when she arrived at Pemberley and Mrs Darcy and I thought it right that she should have immediate medical attention.'

Sir Selwyn said, 'And I think it right that Dr Belcher, as the doctor called in to advise the police on medical matters, should be involved at this early stage. He will be used to having his nights interrupted. Is Dr McFee examining your prisoner? I take it that George Wickham is under lock and key.'

'Not under lock and key but continually guarded. When I left, my butler, Stoughton, and Mr Alveston were with him. He also has been attended by Dr McFee and may now be asleep and unlikely to wake for some hours. It might be more convenient if you arrived after daybreak.'

Sir Selwyn said, 'Convenient for whom? The inconvenience will be largely mine, but that is no matter when it is a question of duty. And has Dr McFee in any way interfered with Captain Denny's body? I take it that you have ensured that it is inaccessible to anyone until my arrival.'

'Captain Denny's body is laid out on a table in the gunroom and is under lock and key. I thought that nothing should be done to ascertain the cause of death until your arrival.'

'You were right. It would be unfortunate if anyone could suggest that there had been any interference with the body. Of course ideally it should have been left in the woodland where it

92

lay until it could be seen by the police, but I can understand that that seemed impractical at the time.'

Darcy was tempted to say that he had never considered leaving the body where it lay, but thought it prudent to say as little as possible.

Buckle had now returned. Sir Selwyn put on his wig, which he invariably wore when on official duty as a justice of the peace, and was helped into his greatcoat and handed his hat. Thus clad and obviously empowered for any activity expected of him, he seemed both taller and more magisterial, the embodiment of the law.

Buckle led them to the front door and Darcy could hear the sound of three heavy bolts being shot while they waited in the darkness for the carriage. Sir Selwyn showed no impatience at the delay. He said, 'Did George Wickham say anything when you came upon him, kneeling, as you say, beside the body?'

Darcy knew that the question would be asked sooner or later, and not only of himself. He said, 'He was greatly agitated, weeping even, and hardly coherent. It was apparent that he had been drinking, possibly heavily. He seemed to believe that he was in some way responsible for the tragedy, presumably by not dissuading his friend from leaving the carriage. The woodland is dense enough to provide cover for any desperate fugitive and a prudent man would not walk there alone after dark.'

'I would prefer, Darcy, to hear his exact words. They must have impressed themselves on your mind.'

They had, and Darcy repeated what he had remembered. 'He said, "I have killed my best friend, my only friend. It is my fault." I may have got the words in the wrong order but that is the sense of what I heard.'

Hardcastle said, 'So we have a confession?'

'Hardly that. We can't be sure to what precisely he was admitting, nor the condition in which he was at the time.'

The old and cumbersome but impressive carriage was now rattling round the corner of the house. Turning for a last word before he got in, Sir Selwyn said, 'I do not look for complications. You and I have worked together for some years now as magistrates and I think we understand each other. I have every confidence that you know your duty, as I know mine. I am a simple man, Darcy. When a man confesses, one who is not under duress, I tend to believe him. But we shall see, we shall see, I must not theorise in advance of the facts.'

Within minutes Darcy's horse had been brought to him, he mounted and the carriage creaked into motion. They were on their way.

5

It was now after eleven o'clock. Elizabeth had no doubt that Sir Selwyn would set out for Pemberley the moment he had been told of the murder and thought that she should check on Wickham. It was extremely unlikely that he would be awake but she was anxious to satisfy herself that all was well.

But within four feet of the door she hesitated, gripped by a moment of self-knowledge which honesty compelled her to accept. The reason she was here was both more complex and compelling than her responsibility as hostess and, perhaps, more difficult to justify. She had no doubt that Sir Selwyn Hardcastle would remove Wickham under arrest and she had no intention of seeing him taken away under police escort and possibly in fetters. He could at least be spared that humiliation. Once gone it was unlikely that they would ever meet again; what she now found unbearable was the prospect of having that last image of him forever imprinted on her mind, the handsome agreeable and gallant George Wickham reduced to a shameful blood-spattered drunken figure shouting expletives as he was half-urged, half-dragged over the threshold of Pemberley.

She moved forward resolutely and knocked on the door. It was opened by Bingley and she saw with surprise that Jane and Mrs Reynolds were in the room standing by the bed. On a chair was a basin of water, pink with blood and, as she watched, Mrs Reynolds finished drying her hands on a cloth and hung it over the side of the bowl.

Jane said, 'Lydia is still asleep but I know she will insist on being united with Mr Wickham as soon as she is awake and I did not want her to see him as he was when he was brought here. Lydia has every right to see her husband even if he is unconscious, but it would be too horrible if his face were still smeared with Captain Denny's blood. Some of it may be his own; there are two scratches on his forehead and some on his hands, but they are slight and probably due to his trying to find a way through the bushes.'

Elizabeth wondered whether washing Wickham's face had been wise. Wasn't it possible that Sir Selwyn, when he arrived, would expect to see Wickham in the same state as he had been when discovered stooped over the body? But she wasn't surprised at Jane's action or at Bingley's being present to show his support. For all her gentleness and sweetness there was a core of determination in her sister and once she had decided that an action was right, no arguments were likely to deflect her from her purpose.

Elizabeth asked, 'Has Dr McFee seen him?'

'He checked on him about half an hour ago and will do so again if Mr Wickham wakes up. We hope that by then he will be quiet and able to have something to eat before Sir Selwyn arrives but Dr McFee thinks that unlikely. He was only able to persuade Mr Wickham to take a little of the draught but, given its strength, Dr McFee thinks it should be enough to ensure some hours of restorative sleep.'

Elizabeth moved over to the bed and stood looking down at Wickham. Dr McFee's draught had certainly been effective, the stertorous stinking breath was no more and he was sleeping as deeply as a child, his breathing so shallow that he could have been dead. With his face cleaned, his dark hair tumbled on the pillow, his shirt open to show the delicate line of the throat, he looked like a young wounded knight exhausted after battle. Gazing down on him, Elizabeth was visited by a tumble of emotions. Her mind unwillingly jerked back to memories so painful that she could recall them only with self-disgust. She had been so close to falling in love with him. Would she have married him if he had been rich instead of penniless? Surely not, she knew now that what she had then felt had never been love. He, the darling of Meryton, the handsome newcomer with whom every girl was besotted, had sought her out as his favourite. It had all been vanity, a dangerous game played by them both. She had accepted and – worse – had passed on to Jane his allegations about

96

the perfidy of Mr Darcy, the spoiling of all his chances in life, Darcy's betrayal of their friendship and the callous neglect of the responsibilities towards Wickham laid on him by his father. Only much later had she realised how inappropriate those revelations, made to a comparative stranger, had been.

Looking down on him now, she felt a resurgence of shame and humiliation at having been so lacking in sense and judgement and the discernment of the character of others on which she had always prided herself. But something remained, an emotion close to pity which made it appalling to contemplate what his end might be, and even now, when she knew the worst of which he was capable, she couldn't believe that he was a murderer. But whatever the outcome, with his marriage to Lydia he had become part of her family, part of her life, as her marriage had made him part of Darcy's. And now every thought of him was besmirched by terrifying images: the howling crowd suddenly silenced as the handcuffed figure emerged from prison, the high gallows and the noose. She had wanted him out of their lives, but not that way – dear God, not that way.

Book Three

Police at Pemberley

1

When Sir Selwyn's carriage and the mortuary wagon drew up at the main entrance to Pemberley the door was immediately opened by Stoughton. There was a little delay until one of the grooms arrived to take Darcy's horse, and he and Stoughton, after a brief discussion, agreed that Sir Selwyn's carriage and the wagon would be less visible by any watcher from the window if they were taken from the front of the house and through to the stables and the back courtyard, from which Denny's body could eventually be swiftly and, it was hoped, discreetly removed. Elizabeth had thought it right formally to receive this late and hardly welcome guest, but Sir Selwyn quickly made it obvious that he was anxious to set to work immediately and paused only for the customary bow on his part and curtsey on Elizabeth's and his brief apology for the lateness and inconvenience of his visit, before he announced that he would begin by seeing Wickham and would be accompanied by Dr Belcher and the two policemen, Headborough Thomas Brownrigg and Petty Constable Mason.

Wickham was being guarded by Bingley and Alveston, who opened the door to Darcy's knock. The room could have been designed as a guardroom. It was simply and sparsely furnished with a single bed under one of the high windows, a washbasin, a small wardrobe and two upright wooden chairs. Two additional and more comfortable chairs had been brought in and placed one each side of the door to provide some ease for whoever would be keeping watch during the night. Dr McFee, who was sitting to the right of the bed, stood up at Hardcastle's arrival. Sir Selwyn had met Alveston at one of the Highmarten dinner parties and was, of course, familiar with Dr McFee. He gave both men a brief bow and nod of acknowledgement, and then approached the bed. Alveston and Bingley, after a glance at each other, recognised that they were expected to leave the room and quietly did so, while Darcy remained standing a little apart. Brownrigg and Mason took up positions one on each side of the door, and stared ahead as if to demonstrate that, although it was not at present appropriate for them to take a more active part in the investigation, the room and the guarding of its occupant would now be their responsibility.

Dr Obadiah Belcher was the medical adviser called in by the High Constable or magistrate to help with inquiries and, not surprisingly for a man accustomed to dissecting the dead rather than treating the living, had acquired a sinister reputation not helped by his unfortunate appearance. His hair, almost as fine as a child's, was so fair as to be almost white, drawn back from a sallow skin, and he looked at the world through small suspicious eyes under the thin line of the brow. His fingers were long and carefully manicured and the public reaction to him was fairly summed up by the cook at Highmarten. 'I'll never let that Dr Belcher put his hands on me. Who's to know where they've been last?'

His reputation as a sinister eccentric was also not helped by his having a small upstairs room equipped as a laboratory where it was rumoured that he conducted experiments on the time taken for blood to clot under different circumstances and on the speed with which changes took place in the body after death. Although nominally he was in general practice, he had only two patients, the High Constable and Sir Selwyn Hardcastle, and as neither had ever been known to be ill, their status did nothing to enhance his medical reputation. He was highly thought of by Sir Selwyn and other gentlemen concerned with administering the law, since in court he gave his opinion as a medical man with authority. He was known to be in communication with the Royal Society and exchanged letters with other gentlemen who were engaged in scientific experiments, and in general the most knowledgeable of his neighbours were more proud of his public reputation than afraid of the occasional minor explosion which shook his laboratory. He seldom spoke except after deep thought, and now he drew close to the bed and stood looking down at the sleeping man in silence.

Wickham's breathing was so gentle that it could hardly be heard, his lips slightly parted. He was lying on his back, his left arm flung out, his right curved on the pillow.

Hardcastle turned to Darcy. 'He is obviously not in the state in which you gave me to understand he was brought here. Someone has washed his face.'

There were seconds of silence, then Darcy looked Hardcastle in the eyes and said, 'I take responsibility for everything that has happened since Mr Wickham was brought into my house.'

Hardcastle's response was surprising. His long mouth

twitched momentarily into what could, in any other man, be thought of as an indulgent smile. He said, 'Very chivalrous of you, Darcy, but I think we can look to the ladies for this. Isn't that what they see as their function, to clean up the mess we make of our rooms and sometimes of our lives? No matter, there will be evidence enough from your servants of Wickham's state when he was brought into this house. There appear to be no obvious signs of injury on his body except small scratches on his forehead and hands. Most of the blood on his face and hands will have been Captain Denny's.'

He turned to Belcher. 'I take it, Belcher, that your clever scientific colleagues have not yet found a way of distinguishing one man's blood from another's? We would welcome such assistance although, of course, it would deprive me of my function and Brownrigg and Mason of their jobs.'

'I regret not, Sir Selwyn. We do not set out to be gods.'

'Do you not? I am glad to hear it. I rather thought that you did.' As if aware that the conversation had become inappropriately light, Hardcastle turned to Dr McFee, magisterial and sharp-voiced. 'What have you given him? He looks unconscious, not asleep. Did you not know that this man could be the principal suspect in a murder inquiry and that I would want to question him?'

McFee said quietly, 'To me, sir, he is my patient. When I first saw him he was obviously drunk, violent and becoming out of control. Later, before the draught I gave him had time to take full effect, he became incoherent with fear, calling out in terror but none of it making sense. Apparently he had a vision of bodies hanging on gibbets, their necks stretched. He was a man inhabiting a nightmare even before he slept.'

Hardcastle said, 'Gibbets? Hardly surprising given his situation. What was the medication? I assume it was some kind of sedative.'

'One I mix myself and have used in a number of cases. I persuaded him to take it to lessen his distress. You could have had no hope of getting sense out of him in that state.'

'Nor in his present state. How long before you expect him to be awake and sober enough to be questioned?'

'That is difficult to say. Sometimes after a shock the mind takes refuge in unconsciousness and sleep is deep and prolonged. Judging from the dose I administered, he should be conscious by nine tomorrow morning, possibly earlier, but I cannot be precise, I had difficulty in persuading him to take more than a few mouthfuls. With Mr Darcy's consent I propose to stay until my patient is conscious. I have also Mrs Wickham under my care.'

'And no doubt also sedated and unfit to be questioned?'

'Mrs Wickham was hysterical with shock and distress. She had convinced herself that her husband was dead. I was attending a grievously disturbed woman who needed the relief of sleep. You would have got nothing out of her until she became calmer.'

'I might have got the truth. I think you and I understand each other, Doctor. You have your responsibilities and I have mine. I am not an unreasonable man. I have no wish to disturb Mrs Wickham until the morning.' He turned to Dr Belcher. 'Have you any observation to make, Belcher?'

'None, Sir Selwyn, except to say that I concur with Dr McFee's action in administering a sedative to Wickham. He could not usefully have been questioned in the state described and, if he were later committed for trial, anything he did say might be challenged in court.'

Hardcastle turned to Darcy. 'Then I shall return at nine o'clock tomorrow morning. Until then, Headborough Brownrigg and Petty Constable Mason will be on guard and will take possession of the key. If Wickham requires attention from Dr McFee they will call for him, otherwise no one will be admitted to this room until I return. The constables will need blankets, and some food and drink to see them through – cold meats, bread, the usual.'

Darcy said shortly, 'Everything necessary will be attended to.'

It was then that Hardcastle seemed for the first time to take note of Wickham's greatcoat slung over one of the chairs and the leather bag on the floor beside it. 'Is this all the baggage there was in the chaise?'

Darcy said, 'Apart from a trunk, a hatbox and a bag belonging to Mrs Wickham there were two other bags, one marked GW and one with Captain Denny's name. As I was told by Pratt that the chaise had been hired to take the gentlemen on to the King's Arms at Lambton, the bags were left in the chaise until we returned with Captain Denny's body, when they were brought into the house.'

Hardcastle said, 'They will, of course, need to be handed over. I will confiscate all the bags except those of Mrs Wickham. In the mean time, let us see what he had on his person.'

He took the heavy greatcoat in his hands and shook it vigorously. Three dried leaves caught in one of the capes fluttered to the floor and Darcy saw that there were a few adhering to the sleeves. Hardcastle handed the coat to Mason and himself dug his hands into the pockets. From the left-hand pocket he drew out the usual minor possessions which a traveller might be expected to carry: a pencil, a small notebook but with no entries, two handkerchiefs, a flask which Hardcastle, after unscrewing the top, said had contained whisky. The right-hand pocket yielded a more interesting object, a leather notecase. Opening it Hardcastle drew out a wad of notes, carefully folded, and counted them.

'Thirty pounds precisely. In notes, obviously new, or at least recently issued. I'll give you a receipt for them, Darcy, until we can discover their legal owner. I'll place the money in my safe tonight. Tomorrow morning I may get an explanation of how he came by such a sum. One possibility is that he took it from Denny's body and, if so, we may have a motive.'

Darcy opened his mouth to protest but, deciding that he would only make matters worse, said nothing.

Hardcastle said, 'And now I propose to view the body. I take it that the corpse is under guard?'

Darcy said, 'Not under guard. Captain Denny's body is in the gunroom, the door of which is locked. The table there seemed convenient. I have in my possession the keys both to the room and to the cupboard containing the weapons and ammunition; it hardly seemed necessary to arrange any additional safeguards. We can go there now. If you have no objection, I would like Dr McFee to accompany us. You may feel a second opinion on the state of the body would be an advantage.'

After a moment's hesitation, Hardcastle said, 'I can see no objection. You yourself will doubtless wish to be present and I shall need Dr Belcher and Headborough Brownrigg but no others will be necessary. Let us not make a public spectacle of the dead. We shall, of course, need plenty of candles.'

Darcy said, 'I had foreseen that. Extra candles have been placed in the gunroom ready to be lit. I think you will find that the light is as adequate as it can be at night.'

Hardcastle said, 'I need someone to watch with Mason while Brownrigg is away. Stoughton would seem an appropriate choice. Can you call him back, Darcy?'

Stoughton, as if expecting the summons, was waiting close to the door. He entered the room and stood silently next to Mason. Picking up their candles, Hardcastle and the party left, and Darcy heard the key being turned in the lock behind them.

The house was so quiet that it could have been deserted. Mrs Reynolds had ordered any servants still preparing food for the morrow to go to their beds and of the staff only she, Stoughton and Belton remained on duty. Mrs Reynolds was waiting in the hall beside a table which held a group of new candles in high silver candlesticks. Four had been lit and the flames, burning steadily, seemed to emphasise rather than illuminate the surrounding darkness of the great entrance hall.

Mrs Reynolds said, 'There may be more than needed, but I thought you might want additional light.'

Each man took up and lit a fresh candle. Hardcastle said, 'Leave the others where they are at present. The constable will fetch them if necessary.' He turned to Darcy. 'You said you have the key to the gunroom and that you have already provided an adequate number of candles?'

'There are fourteen already there, Sir Selwyn. I took them in myself with Stoughton. Apart from that visit no one has entered the gunroom since Captain Denny's body was placed there.'

'So let us get started. The sooner the body is examined the better.'

Darcy was relieved that Hardcastle had accepted his right to be one of the party. Denny had been brought to Pemberley and it was fitting that the master of the house should be there when his body was viewed although he could think of no way in which he could be of particular use. He led the candlelit procession towards the rear of the house and, taking two keys on a ring from his pocket, used the larger to unlock the door to the gunroom. It was surprisingly large with pictures of old shooting parties and their spoils and a shelf with the bright leather spines of records going back at least a century, a mahogany desk and chair and a locked cupboard containing the guns and ammunition. The narrow table had obviously been moved out from the wall and was now in the middle of the room with the body covered by a clean sheet.

Before setting off to inform Sir Selwyn of Denny's death, Darcy had instructed Stoughton to provide candlesticks of equal size and the best tall wax candles, an extravagance which he guessed would be the cause of some muttering between Stoughton and Mrs Reynolds. These were candles normally reserved for the dining room. Together he and Stoughton had set them up in two rows on the desktop, taper to hand. Now he lit them and as the taper found each candle-tip the room brightened, suffusing the watching faces with a warm glow and softening even Hardcastle's strong bony features into gentleness, while each trail of smoke rose like incense, its transitory sweetness lost in the smell of beeswax. It seemed to Darcy that the desktop with its glittering rows of light had become an over-decorated altar, the sparsely furnished and functional gunroom a chapel, and that the five of them were secretly engaged in the obsequies of some alien but exacting religion.

As they stood like inappropriately clad acolytes round the body, Hardcastle folded back the sheet. The right eye was blackened with blood which had been smeared over a large part of the face, but the left eye was wide open, the pupil turned upward so that Darcy, standing behind Denny's head, felt that it was fixed on him, not with the blankness of death, but holding in its sticky gaze a lifetime of reproach.

Dr Belcher placed his hands on Denny's face, arms and legs, then said, 'Rigor mortis is already present in the face. As a preliminary estimate I would say he has been dead about five hours.'

Hardcastle did a brief calculation, then said, 'That confirms what we have already surmised, that he died shortly after he left the chaise and approximately at the time the shots were heard. He was killed at about nine o'clock last evening. What about the wound?'

Dr Belcher and Dr McFee moved closer, handing their candles to Brownrigg who, placing his own candle on the desktop, raised them high as the two doctors peered closely at the dark patch of blood.

Dr Belcher said, 'We need to wash this away before we can ascertain the depth of the blow but, before doing so, we should note the fragment of a dead leaf and the small smear of dirt both above the effusion of blood. At some point after the infliction of the wound he must have fallen on his face. Where is the water?' He looked round as if expecting it to materialise out of the air.

Darcy put his head outside the door and instructed Mrs Reynolds to bring a bowl of water and some small towels. They were so quick in coming that Darcy thought that she must have anticipated the request and been waiting at the tap in the adjoining cloakroom. She handed the bowl and towels to Darcy without entering the room and Dr Belcher went over to his case of instruments, took out some small balls of white wool and firmly wiped the skin clean, then tossed the reddened wool into the water. He and Dr McFee in turn looked closely at the wound and again touched the skin around it.

It was Dr Belcher who finally spoke. 'He was hit with something hard, possibly round in shape, but as the skin has been broken I can't be specific about the shape and size of the weapon. What I am sure of is that the blow didn't kill him. It produced a considerable effusion of blood, as head wounds often do, but the blow could not have been fatal. I don't know whether my colleague agrees.'

Dr McFee took his time prodding the skin round the wound, and after about a minute said, 'I agree. The wound is superficial.'

Hardcastle's hard voice broke the silence. 'Then turn him over.'

Denny was a heavy man, but Brownrigg, with the help of Dr McFee, turned him in one movement. Hardcastle said, 'More light, please,' and Darcy and Brownrigg moved over to the desk and each took one of the cluster of candles and, holding a candle in each hand, approached the body. There was silence as if no one present wished to state the obvious. Then Hardcastle said, 'There, gentlemen, you have the cause of death.'

They saw a gash some four inches long across the base of the skull, but its full extent obscured by the matting of hair, some of which had been forced into the wound. Dr Belcher went over to his bag and, returning with what looked like a small silver knife, carefully lifted the hair away from the skull, revealing a gash about a quarter of an inch wide. The hair beneath it was stiff and matted, but it was difficult to see whether this was with blood or some exudation from the wound. Darcy made himself look closely but a mixture of horror and pity made the sickness rise in his throat. There was a sound like a low involuntary groan and he wondered whether it was he who had made it.

Both doctors bent closely over the body. Dr Belcher again took his time, then said, 'He has been bludgeoned but there is no ragged laceration, which suggests that the weapon was heavy but smooth-edged. The wound is characteristic of severe head wounds with strands of hair, tissue and blood vessels impacted into the bone, but even if the skull has remained intact, the haemorrhaging of the blood vessels beneath the bone will have resulted in internal bleeding between the skull and the membrane covering the brain. The blow was struck with extraordinary force, either by an assailant taller than the victim or one equal in size. I would say that the attacker was right-handed and that the weapon was something like the back of an axe, that is, it was heavy but blunt. If it had been the blade of an axe or sword, the wound would have been deeper, the body almost decapitated.'

Hardcastle said, 'So the murderer first attacked from the front, disabling his victim, then when he staggered away, blinded by blood which he instinctively tried to wipe from his eyes, the killer attacked again, this time from the rear. Could the weapon have been a large sharp-edged stone?'

Belcher said, 'Not sharp-edged, the wound is not jagged. Certainly it could be a stone, heavy but smooth-edged, and no doubt there were some lying about in the woodland. Do not the stones and wood for repairs to the estate come down that path? Some stones could have fallen from a cart and later been kicked into the undergrowth, possibly to lie there half-concealed for years. But if it was a stone, it would need an exceptionally strong man to deliver such a blow. Much more likely the victim had fallen on his face and the stone was brought down with force while he was lying prone and helpless.'

Hardcastle asked, 'How long could he have lived with this wound?'

'That is difficult to say. Death may have occurred within a matter of seconds but certainly could not have been long delayed.'

He turned to Dr McFee, who said, 'I have known cases where a fall on the head has produced few symptoms other than a headache, and the patient has continued with the business of his life only to die some hours later. That could not have been the case here. The wound is too serious to be survived for more than a very short time, if at all.'

Dr Belcher lowered his head still nearer the wound. He said, 'I shall be able to report on the damage to the brain when I have made my examination post-mortem.'

Darcy knew that Hardcastle very much disliked post-mortem examinations and although Dr Belcher invariably won when they had a dispute on the matter, he now said, 'Will that really be necessary, Belcher? Is the cause of death not apparent to us all? What appears to have happened is an assailant made the original blow to the forehead while facing his victim. Captain Denny, blinded by blood, then tried to escape only to be dealt from the back the fatal blow. We know from the debris on his forehead that he fell face-downwards. I believe you said when you reported the crime, Darcy, that you found him on his back.'

'We did, Sir Selwyn, and that is how he was lifted onto the stretcher. This is the first time I have seen this wound.'

Again there was silence, then Hardcastle addressed Belcher. 'Thank you, doctor. You will, of course, undertake any further examination of the body that you feel to be necessary, I have no wish to curb the progress of scientific knowledge. We have done as much as we can here. We shall now remove the body.' He turned to Darcy, 'You may expect me at nine o'clock tomorrow morning when I hope to speak to George Wickham and to members of the family and household, so that alibis for the estimated time of death can be established. I am sure you will accept the necessity for this. As I have ordered, Headborough Brownrigg and Constable Mason will remain on duty and will be responsible for guarding Wickham. The room will be kept locked from the inside and only opened in case of necessity. At all times there will be two watchers. I would like your assurance that these instructions will be complied with.'

Darcy said, 'Naturally they will. Is there any refreshment I can offer you or Dr Belcher before you leave?'

'None, thank you.' He added, as if aware that something more should be said, 'I'm sorry that this tragedy should have occurred on your land. Inevitably it will be a cause of distress, particularly to the ladies of the family. The fact that you and Wickham were not on good terms will not make it easier to bear. As a fellow magistrate you will understand my responsibility in this matter. I shall send a message to the coroner and I hope that the inquest will be held at Lambton within the next few days. There will be a local jury. You will, of course, be required to attend with the other witnesses to the finding of the body.'

'I shall be there, Sir Selwyn.'

Hardcastle said, 'I shall need help with the stretcher to convey the victim to the mortuary wagon.' He turned to Brownrigg. 'Can you take over the duty of watching Wickham and send Stoughton down? And, Dr McFee, since you are here and would no doubt wish to be helpful, perhaps you could assist in conveying the body.'

Within five minutes Denny's corpse, with some panting on Dr McFee's part, was carried from the gunroom and placed in the mortuary wagon. The driver was woken from sleep, Sir Selwyn and Dr Belcher got back into the coach and Darcy and Stoughton waited at the open door until the vehicles clattered out of sight.

As Stoughton turned to go back into the house, Darcy said, 'Hand me the keys, Stoughton. I'll see to the locks. I want some fresh air.'

The wind had dropped now but heavy dollops of rain were falling into the pitted surface of the river under the full moon. How many times had he stood here in solitude, escaping for a few minutes from the music and chatter of the ballroom? Now, behind him, the house was silent and dark, and the beauty which had been a solace all his life could not touch his spirit. Elizabeth must be in bed, but he doubted that she was asleep. He needed the comfort of being with her but he knew that she must be exhausted, and even in his longing for her voice, her reassurance, her love, he would not wake her. But when he had entered and turned the key, then stretched to thrust back the heavy bolts, he was aware of a faint light behind him and, turning, he saw Elizabeth, candle in hand, coming down the stairs and moving into his arms.

After some minutes of blessed silence she gently freed herself and said, 'My love, you have not eaten since dinner and you look exhausted. You must take some nourishment before what remains of the night. Mrs Reynolds has provided hot soup in the small dining room. The colonel and Charles are already there.'

But the comfort of a shared bed and Elizabeth's loving arms were denied him. In the small dining room he found that Bingley and the colonel had already eaten and that the colonel was determined once again to take command.

He said, 'I propose, Darcy, to spend the night in the library, which is close enough to the front door to provide some assurance that the house will be secure. I have taken the liberty of instructing Mrs Reynolds to provide pillows and some blankets. It is not necessary for you to join me if you need the greater comfort of your bed.'

Darcy thought the precaution of being near the locked and bolted front door was unnecessary, but he could not allow a guest to sleep in some discomfort while himself in bed. Feeling he had no choice, he said, 'I cannot suppose that whoever killed Denny will be so audacious as to attack Pemberley, but I shall, of course, join you.'

Elizabeth said, 'Mrs Bingley is sleeping on a couch in Mrs Wickham's room, and Belton will be on call, as shall I. I will check that all is well there before retiring. I can only wish you gentlemen an uninterrupted night and I hope some hours of sleep. As Sir Selwyn Hardcastle will be here by nine, I shall order an early breakfast. For now I wish you goodnight.

2

Entering the library, Darcy saw that Stoughton and Mrs Reynolds had done their best to ensure that the colonel and he were made as comfortable as possible. The fire had been replenished, lumps of coal wrapped in paper for quietness and added logs lay ready in the grate, and there was a sufficiency of pillows and blankets. A covered dish of savoury tarts, carafes of wine and water and plates, glasses and napkins were on a round table some distance from the fire.

Privately Darcy thought a watch unnecessary. The main door to Pemberley was well secured with double locks and bolts and even if Denny had been murdered by a stranger, perhaps an army deserter who had been challenged and responded with deadly violence, the man would hardly present a physical threat to Pemberley House itself or anyone in it. He was both tired and restless, an uneasy state in which to sink into a deep sleep which, even were it possible, would seem like an abdication of responsibility. He was troubled by a premonition that some danger threatened Pemberley without being able to form any logical idea of what that danger could be. Dozing in one of the armchairs in the library with the colonel for company would probably give him as good a rest as he could expect for the remaining hours of the night.

As they settled themselves in the two high buttoned and well-padded chairs, Fitzwilliam taking the one by the fire and he a little distant, the thought occurred to him that his cousin might have suggested this vigil because he had something to confide. No one had questioned him about his ride just before nine and he knew that, like him, Elizabeth, Bingley and Jane must be expecting him to provide an explanation. Since it had not yet been forthcoming a certain delicacy prohibited any questions, but no such delicacy would inhibit Hardcastle when he returned; Fitzwilliam must know that he was the only member of the family and guests who had not yet put forward an alibi. Darcy had never for a moment considered that the colonel was in any way involved in Denny's death, but his cousin's silence was worrying and, what was more surprising in a man of such formal manners, it smacked of discourtesy.

To his surprise he felt himself falling into sleep much more quickly than he had expected, and it was an effort even to answer a few commonplace remarks which came to him as at a remote distance. There were brief moments of half-consciousness as he shifted in his chair and his mind took hold of where he was. He glanced briefly at the colonel stretched out in the chair, his handsome face ruddied by the fire, his breathing deep and regular, and watched for a moment the dying flames licking at a blackened log. He urged his stiffened limbs out of his chair and, with infinite care, added a few more logs and some lumps of coal and waited until they were alight. Then he returned to his chair, pulled a blanket over him and slept.

His next awakening was curious. It was a sudden and complete return to consciousness in which all his senses were so acutely alert that it was as if he had been subconsciously expecting this moment. He was huddled on his side and it was through eyelids almost entirely closed that he saw the colonel moving in front of the fire, momentarily blocking out its glow which provided the only light in the room. Darcy wondered whether it was this change which had awakened him. He had no difficulty in feigning sleep, looking through almost closed eyes. The colonel's jacket was hanging on the back of his chair, and now he fumbled for a pocket and pulled out an envelope. Still standing, he took out a document and spent some time in perusing it. Then all that Darcy could see was the colonel's back, a sudden movement of his arm and a spurt of flame; the paper was being burnt. Darcy gave a little grunt and turned his face further from the fire. Normally he would have made it apparent to his cousin that he was awake and would have enquired if the colonel had managed to get some sleep, and the small deceit seemed ignoble. But the shock and horror of the moment when he had first seen Denny's body, the disorientating moonlight, had struck him like a mental earthquake in which he no longer stood on firm ground and in which all the comfortable conventions and assumptions which since boyhood had ruled his life lay in rubble round him. Compared with that disruptive moment the colonel's strange behaviour, his still unexplained ride into the night, and now the apparently surreptitious burning of some document, were small aftershocks but they were still disconcerting.

He had known his cousin since boyhood and the colonel had always seemed the most uncomplicated of men, the one least given to subterfuge or deceit. But there had been a change since he had become an elder son and the heir to an earl. What had become of that gallant, light-hearted young colonel, that easy and confident sociability so different from Darcy's own sometimes paralysing shyness? He had seemed the most affable and popular of men. But even then he had been conscious of his family responsibilities, of what was expected of a younger son.

He would never have married an Elizabeth Bennet, and Darcy occasionally felt that he had lost some respect in his cousin's eyes because he had placed his desire for a woman above the responsibilities of family and class. Certainly Elizabeth seemed to have sensed some change, although she had never discussed the colonel with Darcy except to warn him that his cousin was about to seek a meeting to request Georgiana's hand. Elizabeth had felt it right to prepare him for the meeting but it had not, of course, taken place, and now it never would; he had known from the moment when the drunken Wickham was almost carried through the door of Pemberley that the Viscount Hartlep would be looking elsewhere for his future countess. What surprised him now was not that the offer would never be made, but that he who had harboured such high ambitions for his sister was content that this offer at least was one she would never be tempted to accept.

It was not surprising that his cousin should feel oppressed by the weight of his coming responsibilities. Darcy thought of the great ancestral castle, the miles of pitheads above the black gold of his coalfields, the manor house in Warwickshire with its square miles of fertile earth, the possibility that the colonel, when he succeeded, might feel that he had to relinquish the career he loved and take his seat in the House of Lords. It was as if he were making a disciplined attempt to change the very core of his personality and Darcy wondered whether this was either possible or wise. Was he perhaps facing some private obligation or problem, different in kind from the responsibilities of inheritance? He thought again how strange it was that his cousin should have been so anxious to spend the night in the library.

If he wanted to destroy a letter there were sufficient fires already lit in the house for him to seize a private moment, and why destroy it now and in such secrecy? Had something happened that made the destruction of the document imperative? Trying to make himself comfortable enough for sleep, Darcy told himself that there were enough mysteries without adding to them, and eventually he slid again into unconsciousness.

He was awoken by the colonel noisily drawing the curtains then, after a glance, he pulled them back again, saying, 'Hardly light yet. You slept well, I think.'

'Not well, but adequately.' Darcy reached for his watch.

'What is the time?'

'Just on seven.'

'I think I ought to go and see if Wickham is awake. If so, he'll need something to eat and drink and the watchers may need some food. We can't relieve them, Hardcastle's instructions were adamant, but I think someone should look into that room. If Wickham is awake and in the same state that Dr McFee described when he was first brought here, Brownrigg and Mason may have difficulty in restraining him.'

Darcy got up. 'I'll go. You ring for breakfast. It won't be served in the dining room until eight.'

But the colonel was already at the door. He turned and said, 'Better leave it to me. The less you have to do with Wickham the better. Hardcastle is on the alert for any interference on your part. He is in charge. You can't afford to antagonise him.'

Privately Darcy admitted that the colonel was right. He was still determined to regard Wickham as a guest in his house, but it would have been foolish to ignore the reality. Wickham was the prime suspect in a murder inquiry and Hardcastle had the right to expect that Darcy would keep away from him, at least until Wickham had been interrogated.

The colonel had hardly left before Stoughton arrived with coffee, followed by a housemaid to attend to the fire accompanied by Mrs Reynolds to enquire whether they would like breakfast to be served. A log smouldering in the acrid ash crackled into life as fresh fuel was added, the leaping flames illuminating the corners of the library but emphasising the darkness of the autumnal morning. The day, which for Darcy presaged nothing but disaster, had begun.

The colonel returned within ten minutes as Mrs Reynolds was leaving, and went straight to the table to pour himself coffee. Settling again into the chair, he said, 'Wickham is restless and muttering but still asleep and likely to remain so for some time. I'll visit him again before nine and prepare him for Hardcastle's arrival. Brownrigg and Mason have been well supplied with food and drink during the night. Brownrigg was dozing in his chair and Mason complained that his legs were stiff and he needed to exercise them. What he probably needed was to visit the water closet, that new-fangled apparatus you have had installed here which, I understand, has caused much ribald interest in the neighbourhood, so I gave him directions and waited on guard until he returned. As far as I can judge, Wickham will be sufficiently awake to be questioned by Hardcastle by nine. Do you intend to be present?'

'Wickham is in my house and Denny was murdered on my property. It is obviously right that I should take no part in the investigation, which will of course be under the direction of the High Constable when Hardcastle reports to him; he is unlikely to take an active part. I'm afraid this is going to be an inconvenient business for you, Fitzwilliam; Hardcastle will want an inquest as soon as possible. Luckily the coroner is at Lambton, so there shouldn't be a delay in selecting the twenty-three members from which to provide the jury. They will be local men but I'm not sure that will be an advantage. It is well known that Wickham is not received at Pemberley and I have no doubt the gossips have been busy speculating why. Obviously both of us will be needed to give evidence, which I suppose will have to take precedence over your recall to duty.'

Colonel Fitzwilliam said, 'Nothing can take precedence over that, but if the inquest is held soon, there should be no problem. Young Alveston is more fortuitously placed; he seems to have no difficulty in leaving what is said to be a very busy London career to enjoy the hospitality of Highmarten and Pemberley.'

Darcy didn't reply. After a short silence, Colonel Fitzwilliam said, 'What is your programme for today? I suppose the staff will need to be told what is happening and prepared for Hardcastle's interrogation.'

'I shall go now and see if Elizabeth is awake, as I think she will be, and together we will speak to all the staff. If Wickham is conscious, Lydia will be demanding to see him, and indeed that is her right; then, of course, we must all prepare ourselves to be questioned. It is opportune that we have alibis, so Hardcastle need not waste much time on anyone who was at Pemberley yesterday evening. He will no doubt enquire of you when you started on your ride and when you returned.'

The colonel said briefly, 'I hope I shall be able to satisfy him.'

Darcy said, 'When Mrs Reynolds comes back will you please

inform her that I am with Mrs Darcy and shall take breakfast as usual in the small dining room.' With that he was gone. It had been an uncomfortable night in more ways than one and he was glad that it was over.

3

Jane, who had never since her marriage spent a night away from her husband's side, spent restless hours on the couch by Lydia's bed, her brief periods of slumber broken by the need to check that Lydia was sleeping. Dr McFee's sedative had been effective and Lydia slept soundly, but at half-past five stirred into life and demanded that she be taken at once to her husband. For Jane this was a natural and reasonable request, but she felt it wise to warn Lydia gently that Wickham was unlikely to be yet awake. Lydia was not prepared to wait, so Jane helped her to dress – a lengthy process since Lydia insisted on looking her best, and considerable time was taken in rummaging through her trunk and in holding up different gowns to demand Jane's opinion, discarding others in a heap on the floor and fussing over her hair. Jane wondered whether she would be justified in waking Bingley but, going out to listen, she could hear no sound from the next room and was reluctant to disturb his sleep. Surely being with Lydia when she first saw her husband after his ordeal was women's work, and she should not presume on Bingley's unfailing good nature for her own comfort. Eventually Lydia was satisfied with her appearance and, taking their lighted candles, they made their way along dark passages to the room where Wickham was being held.

It was Brownrigg who let them in, and at their entrance Mason, who was asleep in his chair, woke with a start. After that there was chaos. Lydia rushed to the bed where Wickham was still asleep, flung herself over him as if he were dead and began weeping in apparent anguish. It was minutes before Jane could gently draw her from the bed and murmur that it would be better if she came back later when her husband would be awake and able to speak to her. Lydia, after a final burst of crying, allowed herself to be led back to her room where Jane was at last able to calm her and ring for an early breakfast for them both. It was promptly brought in by Mrs Reynolds, not by the usual servant, and Lydia, viewing the carefully chosen delicacies with evident satisfaction, discovered that grief had made her hungry and ate avidly. Jane was surprised that she appeared unconcerned about Denny, who had been her favourite among the officers stationed with Wickham at Meryton, and the news of his brutal death, which Jane had broken to her as gently as possible, seemed hardly to have penetrated her understanding.

Breakfast over, Lydia's mood fluctuated with outbursts of weeping, self-pity, terror of the future for herself and her dearest Wickham, and resentment against Elizabeth. If Lydia and her husband had been invited to the ball, as they should have been, they would have arrived the next morning by the proper approach. They had only come through the woodland because her arrival had to be a surprise, otherwise Elizabeth would probably never have let her in. It was Elizabeth's fault that they had to hire a hackney chaise and stay at the Green Man, which was not at all the kind of inn she and dear Wickham liked. If Elizabeth had been more generous in helping them they could have afforded to stay on Friday night at the King's Arms at Lambton, one of the Pemberley carriages would have been sent the next day to take them to the ball, Denny wouldn't have travelled with them and none of this trouble would have happened. Jane had to hear it all, and with pain; as was usual, she tried to soothe away resentment, counsel patience and encourage hope, but Lydia was in too full enjoyment of her grievance to listen to reason or to welcome advice.

None of this was surprising. Lydia had disliked Elizabeth from childhood and there could never have been sympathy or close sisterly affection between such disparate characters. Lydia, boisterous and wild, vulgar in speech and behaviour, unresponsive to any attempts to control her, had been a continual embarrassment to the two elder Miss Bennets. She was her mother's favourite child and they were, in fact, much alike, but there were other reasons for the antagonism between Elizabeth and the younger sister. Lydia suspected, and with reason, that Elizabeth had attempted to persuade her father to forbid her to visit Brighton. Kitty had reported that she had seen Elizabeth knocking at the library door and being admitted to the sanctum, a rare privilege since Mr Bennet was adamant that the library was the one room in which he could hope for solitude and peace. To attempt to deny Lydia any pleasure on which she had set her heart ranked high in the catalogue of sisterly offences and it was a matter of principle for Lydia that it should never be forgiven or forgotten.

And there was another cause for a dislike close to enmity: Lydia knew that her elder sister had been singled out by Wickham as his acknowledged favourite. On one of Lydia's visits to Highmarten, Jane had heard her talking to the housekeeper. It was the same Lydia, self-serving and indiscreet. 'Of course, Mr

Wickham and I will never be invited to Pemberley. Mrs Darcy is jealous of me and everyone at Meryton knows why. She was wild for Wickham when he was stationed at Meryton and would have had him if she could. But he chose elsewhere – lucky me! And anyway, Elizabeth would never have taken him, not without money, but if there had been money she would be Mrs Wickham by choice. She only married Darcy – a horrid, conceited, bad-tempered man – because of Pemberley and all his money. Everyone at Meryton knows that too.'

This involvement of her housekeeper in the family's private concerns, and the mixture of untruths and vulgarity with which Lydia passed on her heedless gossip caused Jane to reconsider the wisdom of accepting so readily her sister's usually unannounced visits, and she resolved to discourage them in future for Bingley's and her children's sakes as well as for her own. But one further visit must be endured. She had promised to convey Lydia to Highmarten when, as arranged, she and Bingley left Pemberley on Sunday afternoon, and she knew how greatly Elizabeth's difficulties would be eased without Lydia's constant demands for sympathy and attention and her erratic outbursts of noisy grief and querulous complaining. Jane had felt helpless in the face of the tragedy overshadowing Pemberley but this small service was the least she could do for her beloved Elizabeth.

4

Elizabeth slept fitfully with brief periods of blessed unconsciousness broken by nightmares which jolted her into wakefulness and to an awareness of the real horror which lay like a pall over Pemberley. Instinctively she reached out for her husband, only to recall that he was spending the night with Colonel Fitzwilliam in the library. The impulse to get out of bed and pace about the room was almost uncontrollable, but she tried again to settle into sleep. The linen sheets, usually so cool and comforting, had been twisted into a confining rope and the pillows, filled with the softest down feathers, seemed hard and hot, requiring constant shaking and turning to make them comfortable.

Her thoughts turned to Darcy and Fitzwilliam. It was absurd that they were sleeping, or attempting to sleep, in what must be some discomfort, especially after such an appalling day. And what had Colonel Fitzwilliam had in mind to propose such a scheme? She knew that it had been his idea. Did he have something important to communicate to Darcy and needed a few uninterrupted hours with him? Could he be providing some explanation of that mysterious ride into the night, or had the confidence something to do with Georgiana? Then it occurred to her that his motive might have been to prevent her and Darcy having some time in private together; since the return of the search party with Denny's body, she and her husband had hardly had a chance for more than a few minutes' confidential talk. She thrust the idea aside as ridiculous and tried again to settle herself for sleep.

Although she knew that her body was exhausted, her mind had never been more active. She thought of how much had to be done before the arrival of Sir Selwyn Hardcastle. Fifty households would have to be notified of the cancellation of the ball and it would have been pointless to deliver letters last night when most of the recipients would undoubtedly have been in bed; perhaps she should have stayed up even later and at least made a start on the task. But there was a more immediate responsibility which she knew must be the earliest to be faced. Georgiana had gone early to bed and would know nothing of the night's tragedy. Since his attempted seduction of her seven years earlier, Wickham had never been received at Pemberley or his name mentioned. The whole incident was treated as if it had never taken place. She knew that Denny's death would increase the pain of the present while rekindling the unhappiness of the past. Did Georgiana retain any affection for Wickham? How, especially now with two suitors in the house, would she cope with seeing him again and in such circumstances of suspicion and horror? Elizabeth and Darcy planned to see all members of the household together as soon as the servants' breakfast was over to break the news of the tragedy, but it would be impossible to keep the arrival of Lydia and Wickham secret from the maids who, from five o'clock onwards, would be busy cleaning and tidying the rooms and lighting fires. She knew that Georgiana woke early and that her maid would draw back the curtains and bring in her morning tea promptly at seven. It was she, Elizabeth, who must speak to Georgiana before someone else inadvertently blurted out the news.

She looked at the small gilt clock on her bedside table and saw that the time was fifteen minutes past six. Now, when it was important not to fall asleep, she felt that sleep could at last come, but she needed to be fully awake before seven and, ten minutes before the hour, she lit her candle and made her way quietly along the passageway to Georgiana's room. Elizabeth had always woken early to the familiar sounds of the house coming alive, greeting each day with the sanguine expectation of happiness, the hours filled with the duties and pleasures of a community at peace with itself. Now she could hear soft distant noises like the scratching of mice, which meant that the housemaids were already busy. She was unlikely to encounter them on this floor, but if she did, they would smile and flatten themselves against the wall as she passed.

She knocked quietly on Georgiana's door and, entering, found that she was already in her dressing gown, standing at the window and looking out into the dark emptiness. Almost immediately her maid arrived; Elizabeth took the tray from her and placed it on the bedroom table. Georgiana seemed to sense that something was wrong. As soon as the maid had left she came quickly across to Elizabeth and said with concern, 'You look tired, my dear Elizabeth. Are you unwell?'

'Not unwell but worried. Let us sit down together, Georgiana, there is something I have to tell you.'

'Not Mr Alveston?'

'No, not Mr Alveston.'

And then Elizabeth gave a brief account of what had happened the previous night. She described how, when Captain Denny was found, Wickham was kneeling by the body, deeply distressed, but she did not report what Darcy had told her had been his words. Georgiana sat quietly while she spoke, her hands in her lap. Looking at her, Elizabeth saw that two tears were glistening in her eyes and rolled unchecked down her cheeks. She put out her hand and grasped Georgiana's.

After a moment's pause, Georgiana dried her eyes and said

calmly, 'It must seem strange to you, my dear Elizabeth, that I should be weeping for a young man I have never even met, but I cannot help remembering how happy we were together in the music room and even as I was playing and singing with Mr Alveston Captain Denny was being brutally done to death less than two miles from us. How will his parents bear this terrible news? What loss, what grief for his friends.' Then, perhaps seeing surprise on Elizabeth's face, she said, 'My dear sister, did you think I was weeping for Mr Wickham? But he is alive and Lydia and he will soon be reunited. I am happy for them both. I don't wonder that Mr Wickham was so distraught at his friend's death and being unable to save him but, dearest Elizabeth, please don't think that I am distressed that he has come back into our lives. The time when I thought I was in love with him has long passed and I know now that it was only the memory of his kindness to me as a child and gratitude for his affection, and perhaps loneliness, but it was never love. And I know too that I would never have gone away with him. Even at the time it seemed more like a childish adventure than reality.'

'Georgiana, he did intend to marry you. He has never denied it.'

'Oh yes, he was perfectly serious about that.' She blushed and added, ' But he promised that we would live only as brother and sister until the marriage took place.'

'And you believed him?'

There was a note of sadness in Georgiana's voice. 'Oh yes, I believed him. You see, he was never in love, it was the money he wanted, it was always the money. I have no bitterness except for the pain and trouble he caused my brother, but I would prefer not to see him.'

Elizabeth said, 'It will be much the best, and there is no need.' She did not add that unless George Wickham were extremely fortunate he would very likely be leaving Pemberley later that morning under police escort.

They drank the tea together almost in silence. Then as Elizabeth rose to leave, Georgiana said, 'Fitzwilliam will never mention Mr Wickham or what happened all those years ago. It would be easier if he would. Surely it is important that people who love each other should be able to speak openly and truly about matters which touch them.'

Elizabeth said, 'I think that it is, but sometimes it can be difficult. It depends on finding the right moment.'

'We shall never find the right moment. The only bitterness I feel is shame that I disappointed a dearly loved brother, and the certainty that he will never again trust my judgement. But Elizabeth, Mr Wickham is not an evil man.'

Elizabeth said, 'Only perhaps a dangerous and a very foolish one.'

'I have spoken about what happened to Mr Alveston and he believes that Mr Wickham could have been in love, although he was always motivated by his need for money. I can talk freely to Mr Alveston so why not to my brother?'

Elizabeth said, 'So the secret is known to Mr Alveston.'

'Of course, we are dear friends. But Mr Alveston will understand, as do I, that we cannot be more while this terrible mystery hangs over Pemberley. He has not declared his wishes and there is no secret engagement. I would never keep such a secret from you, dear Elizabeth, or from my brother, but we both know what is in our hearts and we shall be content to wait.'

So there was yet another secret in the family. Elizabeth thought she knew why Henry Alveston would not yet propose to Georgiana or to make his intentions clear. It would seem as if he were taking advantage of any help he might be able to give Darcy, and both Alveston and Georgiana were sensitive enough to know that the great happiness of successful love cannot be celebrated under the shadow of the gallows. She could only kiss Georgiana and murmur how much she liked Mr Alveston and express her good wishes for them both.

Elizabeth felt it was time now to get dressed and start the day. She was oppressed by the thought of how much had to be done before the arrival of Sir Selwyn Hardcastle at nine o'clock. The most important was to send the letters to the invited guests explaining, but not in detail, why the ball had to be cancelled. Georgiana said that she had ordered breakfast in her room but would join the rest of the party in the breakfast room for coffee and would very much like to help. Breakfast for Lydia had been served in her room with Jane to keep her company, and once both ladies were dressed and the room put to rights, Bingley, anxious as always to be with his wife, would join them.

As soon as Elizabeth had dressed and Belton had left her to see if any help was needed by Jane, Elizabeth sought Darcy and together they went to the nursery. Usually this daily visit took place after breakfast, but both were gripped by an almost superstitious fear that the evil which overshadowed Pemberley might even infect the nursery, and they needed to reassure themselves that all was well. But nothing had changed in that secure, self-contained little world. The boys were delighted to see their parents so unexpectedly early and, after their hugs, Mrs Donovan drew Elizabeth to one side and said quietly, 'Mrs Reynolds was good enough to see me at first light to give me the news of Captain Denny's death. It is a great shock to us all but be assured that it will be kept from Master Fitzwilliam until Mr Darcy feels it right to talk to him and tell him as much as a child needs to know. Have no fear, madam; there will be no housemaids carrying gossip into the nursery.'

As they left, Darcy expressed his relief and gratitude that Elizabeth had broken the news to Georgiana and that his sister had received it with no more distress than was natural, but Elizabeth sensed that his old doubts and worries had resurfaced, and that he would have been happier if Georgiana could have been spared any news which would recall her to the past.

A little before eight Elizabeth and Darcy entered the breakfast room to find that the only guest at the largely untasted meal was Henry Alveston, and although a great deal of coffee was drunk, little of the usual breakfast of eggs, home cured bacon, sausages and kidneys left on the sideboard beneath their silver domes was touched.

It was an awkward meal and the air of constraint, so unusual when they were all together, was not helped by the arrival of the colonel and, minutes later, of Georgiana. She took her seat between Alveston and the colonel, and as Alveston was helping her to coffee, said, 'Perhaps after breakfast, Elizabeth, we could get started on the letters. If you would decide on the wording I can begin the copies. All the guests can have the same letter and surely it need only be brief.'

There was a silence which all felt to be uncomfortable, and then the colonel spoke to Darcy. 'Surely Miss Darcy should leave Pemberley, and soon. It is inappropriate that she should have any part in this affair, or in any way be submitted to Sir Selwyn's or the constables' presumptive questioning.'

Georgiana was very pale but her voice was firm. 'I would like to help.' She turned to Elizabeth. 'You will be needed later in the morning in so many ways but if you will give me the wording I can write for you and you would only need to sign the letters.'

Alveston broke in. 'An excellent plan. Only the briefest note will be necessary.' He turned to Darcy. 'Permit me to be of service, sir. If I could have a fast horse and a spare I could help deliver the letters. As a stranger to most of the guests I should better be able to avoid explanations which would delay a member of the family. If Miss Darcy and I could together consider a local map, we could work out the quickest and most rational route. Some houses with close neighbours who have also been invited might take responsibility for spreading the news.'

Elizabeth reflected that a number of them would undoubtedly take pleasure in the task. If anything could compensate for the loss of the ball it would be the drama that was unfolding at Pemberley. Some of their friends would certainly grieve at the anxiety everyone at Pemberley must be feeling and would hasten to write letters of condolence and assurances of support, and she told herself firmly that many of these would arise from a genuine affection and concern. She must not allow cynicism to disparage the impulses of compassion and love.

But Darcy was speaking, his voice cold. 'My sister will have no part in this. She is not concerned in any of it and it is totally inappropriate that she should be.'

Georgiana's voice was gentle but equally firm. 'But Fitzwilliam, I am concerned. All of us are.'

Before he could reply, the colonel broke in. He said, 'It is important, Miss Georgiana, that you should not remain at Pemberley until this matter has been fully investigated. I shall be writing by express to Lady Catherine this evening and I have no doubt she will speedily invite you to Rosings. I know that you do not particularly like the house and that the invitation will to some extent be unwelcome, but it is your brother's wish that you go where you will be safe and where neither Mr nor Mrs Darcy need have any anxiety about your safety and welfare. I am sure that with your good sense you will see the wisdom – indeed the propriety – of what is proposed.'

Ignoring him, Georgiana turned to Darcy. 'You need have no anxiety. Please do not ask me to leave. I only wish to be of use to Elizabeth and I hope I can be. I cannot see that there is any impropriety in that.'

It was then that Alveston intervened. 'Forgive me, sir, but I feel I must speak. You discuss what Miss Darcy should do as if she were a child. We have entered the nineteenth century; we do not need to be a disciple of Mrs Wollstonecraft to feel that women should not be denied a voice in matters that concern them. It is some centuries since we accepted that a woman has a soul. Is it not time that we accepted that she also has a mind?'

Fitzwilliam took a moment to control himself. He said, 'I suggest, sir, that you save your diatribe for the Old Bailey.'

Darcy turned to Georgiana. 'I was thinking only of your welfare and happiness. Of course, if you wish, you must stay; Elizabeth will, I know, be glad of your help.'

Elizabeth had been sitting quietly wondering whether she could speak without making matters worse. Now she said, 'Very

134

glad indeed. I must be available for Sir Selwyn Hardcastle when he arrives and I do not see how the necessary letters can be delivered in time unless I have help. So shall we make a start?'

Thrusting back his chair with some force, the colonel made a stiff bow to Elizabeth and Georgiana, then left the room.

Alveston stood up and spoke to Darcy. 'I must apologise, sir, for intervening in a family matter which is not my concern. I spoke inadvisably and with more force than was either courteous or wise.'

Darcy said, 'The apology is due to the colonel rather than to me. Your comments may have been inappropriate and presumptuous but that does not mean that they were not true.' He turned to Elizabeth. 'If you could settle the question of the letters now, my love, I think it is time for us to speak to the staff, both the indoor servants and those who may be working in the house. Mrs Reynolds and Stoughton will have told them only that there has been an accident and the ball has been cancelled, and there will be considerable alarm and anxiety. I will ring for Mrs Reynolds now and say that we will come down to speak to them in the servants' hall as soon as you have drafted the letter for Georgiana to copy.'

5

Thirty minutes later Darcy and Elizabeth entered the servants' hall to the sound of sixteen chairs being scraped back and a muttered 'Good morning sir' in reply to Darcy's greeting, spoken in a concerted murmur so low that it could hardly be heard. Elizabeth was struck by the expanse of newly starched and very white afternoon aprons and goffered caps before remembering that, under Mrs Reynolds's directions, all the staff were impeccably dressed on the morning of Lady Anne's ball. The air smelled of baking and a pervading savoury aroma; in the absence of orders to the contrary, some of the tarts and savouries must already be in the ovens. Passing an open door leading to the conservatory, Elizabeth had been almost overwhelmed by the sickly scent of the cut flowers; unwanted now, how many, she wondered, would be alive by Monday. She found herself thinking of what could best be done with the many birds plucked for roasting, the huge meat joints, the fruits from the greenhouses, the white soup and the syllabubs. Most would not yet be prepared but with no counter-instructions there would inevitably be a surplus which somehow must not be allowed to go to waste. It seemed an unreasonable anxiety at such a time, but it crowded in with a multitude of other concerns. Why did Colonel Fitzwilliam not mention his ride into the night and where he had been? He could hardly have taken merely a wind-blown ride by the river. And if Wickham were arrested and taken away, a possibility which no one had mentioned but each must know was almost certain, what would happen to Lydia? She was unlikely to want to stay at Pemberley, but it was necessary that she should be offered hospitality somewhere close to her husband. Perhaps the best plan and certainly the most convenient would be for her to be taken by Jane and Bingley to Highmarten, but would that be fair to Jane?

With these preoccupations crowding her mind, she was barely aware of her husband's words which were heard in absolute silence, and only the last few sentences fully penetrated her mind. Sir Selwyn Hardcastle had been summoned during the night and Mr Denny's body moved to Lambton. Sir Selwyn would be returning at nine o'clock that morning and would need to interview everyone who was at Pemberley last night. He and Mrs Darcy would be present when this happened. No one among the staff was in any way suspected but it was important that they answer Sir Selwyn's questions honestly. In the mean time they should continue with their duties without discussing the tragedy or gossiping together. The woods would be out of bounds for everyone except for Mr and Mrs Bidwell and their family.

The statement was met by a silence which Elizabeth felt she was expected to break. As she rose she was aware of sixteen pairs of eyes fixed on her, of worried and troubled people waiting to be told that all in the end would be well, that they personally had nothing to fear and that Pemberley would remain as it had always been, their security and their home. She said, 'Obviously the ball cannot now take place and letters are being sent to the invited guests, briefly explaining what has happened. Great tragedy has come to Pemberley but I know that you will carry on with your duties, remain calm and co-operate with Sir Selwyn Hardcastle and his investigation, as we must all do. If you have anything which particularly worries you, or any information to give, you should speak first to Mr Stoughton or Mrs Reynolds. I should like to thank you all for the many hours which, as ever, you have spent in preparing for Lady Anne's ball. It is the great regret of Mr Darcy and myself that, for so tragic a reason, it should be in vain. We rely, as always in good times and bad, on that mutual loyalty and devotion which is at the heart of our life at Pemberley. Have no fear for your safety and for the future, Pemberley has weathered many storms in its long history, and this too will pass.'

Her words were followed by brief applause, quickly suppressed by Stoughton, and he and Mrs Reynolds then said a few words expressing sympathy and co-operation with Mr Darcy's instructions before their audience was ordered to continue with the duties of the day; they would be called to reassemble when Sir Selwyn Hardcastle arrived. As Darcy and Elizabeth entered their part of the house, he said, 'I may have said much too little and you, my love, a little too much, but together, as usual, I think we got it right. And now we must brace ourselves for the majesty of the law in the person of Sir Selwyn Hardcastle.'

6

The visit of Sir Selwyn proved to be both less stressful and shorter than the Darcys had feared. The High Constable, Sir Miles Culpepper, had written to his butler the previous Thursday to say that he would be returning to Derbyshire in time for dinner on Monday and the butler had thought it prudent to pass on this information to Sir Selwyn. No explanation of this change of plan was vouchsafed but Sir Selwyn had little difficulty in divining the truth. The visit of Sir Miles and Lady Culpepper to London with its splendid shops and enticing variety of entertainments had exacerbated a disagreement common to marriages wherein an older husband believes that money should be used to make more of it, and a young and pretty wife is firmly of the view that it exists to be spent; how otherwise, as she frequently pointed out, would anyone know that you had it? After receiving the first bills for his wife's extravagant expenditure in the capital, the High Constable had discovered in himself a renewed commitment to the responsibilities of public life and had informed his wife that a return home was imperative. Although Hardcastle thought it unlikely that his express letter with the news of the murder had yet reached Sir Miles, he was well aware that as soon as the High Constable was informed of the tragedy he would demand a full report of the progress of the investigation. It was ridiculous to consider that either Colonel the Viscount Hartlep or any member of the Pemberley household could have had any part in Denny's death, and accordingly Sir Selwyn had no intention of spending more time at Pemberley than was necessary. Headborough Brownrigg had already checked, on his arrival, that no horse or carriage had left the Pemberley stables after Colonel Fitzwilliam departed for his ride. The suspect he was anxious to interrogate and urgently was Wickham, and he had arrived with the prison carriage and two officers with the intention of removing him to more appropriate accommodation in Lambton prison where he would obtain all the information necessary to produce for the High Constable a full and impressive account of his and the petty constables' activities.

The Darcys received an unusually affable Sir Selwyn who condescended to take refreshment before questioning the family, who, with Henry Alveston and the colonel, were interviewed together in the library. Only the colonel's account of his activities aroused any interest. He began by apologising to the Darcys for his previous silence. He had been to the King's Arms at Lambton by agreement with a lady who required his advice and help with regard to a delicate matter concerning her brother, formerly an officer under his command. She had been visiting a relative in the town and he had suggested that a meeting at the inn would be more private than at his London office. He had not disclosed this meeting earlier because he was anxious that the lady concerned should be able to leave Lambton before her stay at the inn became general knowledge and she was liable to become an object of curiosity to the locals. He could provide her name and London address if verification were required; he was confident, however, that the evidence of the innkeeper and customers who were drinking at the inn at the time of his arrival and departure would confirm his alibi.

Hardcastle said with a degree of self-satisfaction, 'That will hardly be necessary, Lord Hartlep. It was convenient for me to call at the King's Arms on the way here this morning to check whether there had been any strangers staying there on Friday, and I was told about the lady. Your friend made quite an impression at the inn; a very pretty coach, so they told me, and her own maid and a manservant. I imagine that she spent lavishly and the innkeeper was sorry to see her go.'

It was then time for Hardcastle to interview the staff, assembled as before in the servants' hall, the only one absent being Mrs Donovan who had no intention of leaving the nursery unprotected. Since guilt is more commonly felt by the innocent than by the culpable, the atmosphere was less of expectation than of anxiety. Hardcastle had resolved to make his discourse as reassuring and as brief as possible, an intention which was partly vitiated by his customary stern warnings of the terrible consequences for people who refused to co-operate with the police or who withheld information. In a gentler voice he continued, 'I have no doubt that all of you on the night before Lady Anne's ball had better things to do than make your way through the stormy night with the purpose of murdering a complete stranger in the wild woodland. I will now ask any of you who have information to give, or if you left Pemberley at any time last night between the hours of seven o'clock and seven o'clock this morning, to hold up your hands.'

Only one hand was held up. Mrs Reynolds whispered, 'Betsy Collard, sir, one of the housemaids.'

Hardcastle demanded that she stand up, which Betsy immediately did, and without apparent reluctance. She was a stout, confident girl and spoke clearly, 'I was with Joan Miller, sir, in the woodland last Wednesday and we saw the ghost of old Mrs Reilly plain as I see you. She were there hiding among the trees, wearing a black cloak and hood but her face were right plain in the moonlight. Joan and I were afraid and ran out of the wood quick as we could, and she never came after us. But we did see her, sir, and what I speak is God's truth.'

Joan Miller was commanded to stand up and, obviously terrified, muttered her timid agreement with Betsy's account. Hardcastle clearly felt that he was encroaching on feminine and uncertain ground. He looked to Mrs Reynolds, who took over. 'You know very well, Betsy and Joan, that you are not permitted to leave Pemberley unescorted after dark, and it is unchristian and stupid to believe that the dead walk the earth. I am ashamed that you allowed such ridiculous imaginings to enter your minds. I will see both of you in my sitting room as soon as Sir Selwyn Hardcastle has finished his questions.'

It was apparent to Sir Selwyn that this was a more intimidating prospect than he could produce. Both girls muttered, 'Yes, Mrs Reynolds,' and promptly sat down.

Hardcastle, impressed by the immediate effect of the housekeeper's words, decided that it would be appropriate for him to establish his status by a final admonition. He said, 'I am surprised that any girl who has the privilege of working at Pemberley can give way to such ignorant superstition. Have you not learned your catechism?' A murmured 'Yes sir' was the only response.

Hardcastle returned to the main part of the house and joined Darcy and Elizabeth, apparently relieved that all that remained was the easier task of removing Wickham. The prisoner, now in gyves, was spared the humiliation of having a group watching him taken away, and only Darcy felt it his duty to be there to wish him well and to see him put into the prison carriage by Headborough Brownrigg and Constable Mason. Hardcastle then prepared to enter his carriage but before the coachman had cracked the reins he thrust his head out of the window and called to Darcy, 'The catechism. It does contain an injunction, does it not, against entertaining idolatrous and superstitious beliefs?'

Darcy could recall being taught the catechism by his mother but only one law had remained in his mind, that he should keep his hands from picking and stealing, an injunction which had returned to memory with embarrassing frequency when, as a boy, he and George Wickham had ridden their ponies into Lambton and the ripe apples on the then Sir Selwyn's laden boughs were drooping invitingly over the garden wall. He said gravely, 'I think, Sir Selwyn, that we can take it that the catechism contains nothing contrary to the formularies and practices of the Church of England.'

'Quite so, quite so. Just as I thought. Stupid girls.'

Then Sir Selwyn, satisfied with the success of his visit, gave a command and the coach, followed by the prison carriage, rumbled down the wide drive, watched by Darcy until it was out of sight. It occurred to Darcy that seeing visitors come and go was becoming something of a habit, but the departure of the prison carriage with Wickham would lift a pall of recollected horror and distress from Pemberley and he hoped too that it would not now be necessary for him to see Sir Selwyn Hardcastle again before the inquest.

Book Four

The Inquest

1

It was taken for granted both by the family and the parish that Mr and Mrs Darcy and their household would be seen in the village church of St Mary at eleven o'clock on Sunday morning. The news of Captain Denny's murder had spread with extraordinary rapidity and for the family not to appear would have been an admission either of involvement in the crime or of their conviction of Mr Wickham's certain guilt. It is generally accepted that divine service affords a legitimate opportunity for the congregation to assess not only the appearance, deportment, elegance and possible wealth of new arrivals to the parish, but the demeanour of any of their neighbours known to be in an interesting situation, ranging from pregnancy to bankruptcy. A brutal murder on one's own property by a brother by marriage with whom one is known to be at enmity will inevitably produce a large congregation, including some well-known invalids whose prolonged indisposition had prohibited them from the rigours of church attendance for many years. No one, of course, was so ill bred as to make their curiosity apparent, but much can be learnt by the judicious parting of fingers when the hands are raised in prayer, or by a single glance under the protection of a bonnet during the singing of a hymn. The Reverend Percival Oliphant, who had before the service paid a private visit to Pemberley House to convey his condolences and sympathy, did all he could to mitigate the family's ordeal, firstly by preaching an unusually long, almost incomprehensible sermon on the conversion of St Paul, and then by detaining Mr and Mrs Darcy as they left the church in so protracted a conversation that the waiting queue, impatient for their luncheon of cold meats, contented themselves with a curtsey or a bow before making for their carriage or barouche.

Lydia did not appear, and the Bingleys stayed at Pemberley both to attend her and to prepare for their return home that afternoon. After the disarray that Lydia had made of her garments since her arrival, arranging her gowns in the trunk to her satisfaction took considerably longer than did the packing of the Bingleys' trunks. But all was finished by the time Darcy and Elizabeth returned for luncheon and by twenty minutes after two o'clock the Bingleys were settled in their coach. The final farewells were said and the coachman cracked the reins. The vehicle lurched into movement, then swayed down the broad path bordering the river, down the incline in the long drive and disappeared. Elizabeth stood looking after the coach as if she could conjure it back into sight, then the small group turned and re-entered the house.

In the hall Darcy paused, then said to Fitzwilliam and Alveston, 'I would be grateful if you would join me in the library in half an hour. We are the three who found Denny's body and we may all be required to give evidence at the inquest. Sir Selwyn sent a messenger after breakfast this morning to say that the coroner, Dr Jonah Makepeace, has ordered it for eleven o'clock on Wednesday. I want to be clear if our memories agree, particularly about what was said at the finding of Captain Denny's body, and it might be useful to discuss generally how we should proceed in this matter. The memory of what we saw and heard is so bizarre, the moonlight so deceptive, that occasionally I have to remind myself that it was real.'

There was a murmur of acquiescence and almost exactly on time Colonel Fitzwilliam and Alveston made their way to the library where they found Darcy already in possession. There were three upright chairs set at the rectangular map table and two high buttoned armchairs, one each side of the fireplace. After a moment's hesitation, Darcy gestured to the new arrivals to take those, then brought over a chair from the table and seated himself between them. It seemed to him that Alveston, sitting on the edge of his seat, was ill at ease, almost embarrassed, an emotion so at variance with his customary self-confidence that Darcy was surprised when Alveston spoke first, and to him.

'You will, of course, be calling in your own lawyer, sir, but if I can be of any help in the mean time, should he be at a distance, I am at your service. As a witness I cannot, of course, represent either Mr Wickham or the Pemberley estate, but if you feel I could be of use, I could impose on Mrs Bingley's hospitality for a little longer. She and Mr Bingley have been kind enough to suggest that I should do so.'

He spoke hesitantly, the clever, successful, perhaps arrogant young lawyer transformed for a moment into an uncertain and awkward boy. Darcy knew why. Alveston feared that his offer might be interpreted, particularly by Colonel Fitzwilliam, as a ploy to further his cause with Georgiana. Darcy hesitated for only a few seconds, but it gave Alveston a chance quickly to continue.

'Colonel Fitzwilliam will have had experience of army courts martial and you may feel that any advice I could offer would be redundant, particularly as the colonel has local knowledge, which I lack.'

Darcy turned to Colonel Fitzwilliam. 'I think you will agree, Fitzwilliam, that we should take any legal help available.'

The colonel said evenly, 'I am not and have never been a magistrate, and I can hardly claim that my occasional experience of courts martial qualifies me to claim expertise in civil criminal law. As I am not related to George Wickham, as is Darcy, I can have no *locus standi* in this matter except as a witness. It is for Darcy to decide what advice would be useful. As he himself admits, it is difficult to see how Mr Alveston could be of use in the present matter.'

Darcy turned to Alveston. 'It would seem an unnecessary waste of time to be riding daily between Highmarten and Pemberley. Mrs Darcy has spoken to her sister and we all hope that you will accept our invitation to remain here at Pemberley. Sir Selwyn Hardcastle may require you to defer your departure until the police investigation is finished although I hardly feel he would be justified after you have given evidence to the coroner. But will not your own practice suffer? You are reputed to be exceptionally busy. We should not accept help to your detriment.'

Alveston said, 'I have no cases requiring my personal attendance for another eight days, and my experienced partner could keep routine matters running smoothly until then.'

'Then I would be grateful for your advice when you feel it is appropriate to give it. The lawyers who act for the Pemberley estate deal mostly with family matters, chiefly wills, the purchase and sale of property, local disputes, and have as far as I know little if any experience of murder, certainly not at Pemberley. I have already written to tell them what has happened and will now send another express to let them know of your involvement. I must warn you that Sir Selwyn Hardcastle is unlikely to be co-operative. He is an experienced and just magistrate, minutely interested in the detective processes normally left to the village constables and watchful always for any intrusion on his powers.'

The colonel made no further comment.

Alveston said, 'It would be helpful – at least I would find it so – if we could first discuss our initial response to the crime, particularly having regard to the defendant's apparent confession. Do we believe Wickham's assertion that he meant by his words that if he hadn't quarrelled with his friend, Denny would never have stepped out of the chaise to his death? Or did he follow Denny with murderous intent? It is largely a question of character. I have never known Mr Wickham but I understand that he is the son of your late father's steward and that you knew him well as a boy. Do you, sir, and the colonel believe him capable of such an act?'

He looked at Darcy who, after a moment's hesitation, replied, 'Before his marriage to my wife's younger sister we rarely met for many years and never afterwards. In the past I have found him ungrateful, envious, dishonest and deceitful. He has a

149

handsome face and an agreeable manner in society, especially with ladies, which procure him general favour; whether this lasts on longer acquaintance is a different matter but I have never seen him violent or heard that he has been guilty of violence. His offences are of the meaner kind and I prefer not to discuss them; we all have the capacity to change. I can only say that I cannot believe that the Wickham I once knew, despite his faults, would be capable of the brutal murder of a former comrade and a friend. I would say that he was a man averse to violence and would avoid it when possible.'

Colonel Fitzwilliam said, 'He confronted rebels in Ireland to some effect and his bravery has been recognised. We have to grant his physical courage.'

Alveston said, 'No doubt if there is a choice between killing or being killed he would show ruthlessness. I do not mean to disparage his bravery, but surely war and a first-hand experience of the realities of battle could corrupt the sensitivities of even a normally peaceable man so that violence becomes less abhorrent? Should we not consider that possibility?'

Darcy saw that the colonel was having difficulty in controlling his temper. He said, 'No man is corrupted by doing his duty to his King and country. If you had ever had experience of war, young man, I suggest you would be less disparaging in your reaction to acts of exceptional bravery.'

Darcy thought it wise to intervene. He said, 'I read some of the accounts of the 1798 Irish rebellion in the paper, but they were only brief. I probably missed most of the reports. Wasn't that when Wickham was wounded and earned a medal? What part exactly did he play?'

'He was involved, as was I, in the battle on 21st June at Enniscorthy when we stormed the hill and drove the rebels into retreat. Then, on 8th August, General Jean Humbert landed with a thousand French troops and marched south towards Castlebar. The French general encouraged his rebel allies to set up the so-called Republic of Connaught and on 27th August he routed General Lake at Castlebar, a humiliating defeat for the British Army. It was then that Lord Cornwallis requested reinforcements. Cornwallis kept his forces between the French invaders and Dublin, trapping Humbert between General Lake and himself. That was the end for the French. The British dragoons charged the Irish flank and the French lines, at which point Humbert surrendered. Wickham took part in that charge and was then engaged in rounding up the rebels and breaking up the Republic of Connaught. This was bloody work as rebels were hunted down and punished.'

It was obvious to Darcy that the colonel had given this detailed account many times before and took some pleasure doing so.

Alveston said, 'And George Wickham was part of that? We know what was involved in putting down a rebellion. Would not that be enough to give a man, if not a taste for violence, at least a familiarity with it? After all, what we are trying to do here is to arrive at some conclusion about the kind of man George Wickham had become.'

Colonel Fitzwilliam said, 'He had become a good and brave soldier. I agree with Darcy, I can't see him as a murderer. Do we know how he and his wife have lived since he left the army in 1800?'

Darcy said, 'He has never been admitted to Pemberley and we have never communicated, but Mrs Wickham is received at Highmarten. They have not prospered. Wickham became something of a national hero after the Irish campaign and that ensured that he was usually successful in obtaining employment, but not in keeping it. Apparently the couple went to Longbourn when Mr Wickham was unemployed and money was scarce, and no doubt Mrs Wickham enjoyed visiting old friends and boasting about her husband's achievements, but the visits seldom lasted beyond three weeks. Someone must have been helping them financially, and on a regular basis, but Mrs Wickham never explained further, and nor, of course, did Mrs Bingley ask. I am afraid that is all I know, or indeed wish to know.'

Alveston said, 'As I have never met Mr Wickham before Friday night, my opinion of his guilt or innocence is based not on his personality or record, but solely on my assessment of the evidence as it is so far available. I think he has an excellent defence. The so-called confession could mean nothing more than his guilt at provoking his friend to leave the chaise. He was in liquor, and that kind of maudlin sentimentality after a shock is not uncommon when a man is drunk. But let us look at the physical evidence. The central mystery of this case is why Captain Denny plunged into the woodland. What had he to fear from Wickham? Denny was the larger and stronger man and he was armed. If it was his intention to walk back to the inn, why not take the road? Admittedly the chaise could have overtaken him, but as I said, he was hardly in danger. Wickham would not have attacked him with Mrs Wickham in the chaise. It will probably be argued that Denny felt constrained to leave Wickham's company, and immediately, because of disgust for his companion's plan to leave Mrs Wickham at Pemberley without her having been invited to the ball, and without giving Mrs Darcy notice. The plan was certainly ill mannered and inconsiderate, but hardly warranted Denny's escape from the chaise in such a dramatic manner. The woodland was dark and he had no light; I find his action incomprehensible.

'And there is stronger evidence. Where are the weapons? Surely there must be two. The first blow to the forehead produced little more than an effusion of blood which prevented Denny from seeing where he was and left him staggering. The wound on the back of the head was made with a different weapon, something heavy and smooth-edged, perhaps a stone. And from the account of those who have seen the wound, including you Mr Darcy, it is so deep and long that a superstitious man might well say that it was made by no human hand, certainly not by Wickham's. I doubt whether he could easily have lifted a stone of that weight high enough to drop it precisely where aimed. And are we to suppose that by coincidence it lay conveniently close to hand? And there are those scratches on Wickham's forehead and hands. They certainly suggest that he could have lost himself in the woodland after first coming across Captain Denny's body.'

Colonel Fitzwilliam said, 'So you think if it goes to the assize he will be acquitted?'

'I believe on the evidence so far that he should be, but there is always a risk in cases where no other suspect is in question that the jury will ask themselves, if he did not do it, who did? It is difficult for a judge or defence counsel to warn a jury against this view without at the same time putting it into their minds. Wickham will need a good lawyer.'

Darcy said, 'That must be my responsibility.'

'I suggest that you try for Jeremiah Mickledore. He is brilliant with this kind of case and with a city jury, but he takes only cases in which he is interested and he hates leaving London.'

Darcy said, 'Is there a chance that the case could be remitted to London? Otherwise it won't be heard until it goes before the assize court at Derby next Lent or summer.' He looked at Alveston. 'Remind me of the procedure.'

Alveston said, 'Generally the state prefers defendants to be tried at the local assize town. The argument is that the people can themselves see that justice is done. If cases are removed, it is normally only as far as the next county assize court and there would have to be a good reason, something so serious that a fair trial could not be obtained in the local town, questions regarding fairness, jurors who might be nobbled, judges whom it was thought could be bribed. On the other hand there might be such local hostility to the defendant that it would prejudice a fair hearing. It is the attorney general who has powers to take control and terminate criminal prosecutions, which means for our purposes that trials can be moved elsewhere on his authority.'

Darcy said, 'So it will be in the hands of Spencer Perceval?'

'Exactly. Perhaps it could be argued that since the crime was committed on the property of a local magistrate, he and his family might be unreasonably involved, or there could be local gossip and innuendo about the relationship between Pemberley and the accused which could hamper the cause of justice. I do not think it would be easy to get the case transferred, but the fact that Wickham is related both to you and to Mr Bingley by marriage would be a complicating factor which might weigh with the Attorney General. His decision will be made not on any personal wishes, but on whether a transfer will best serve the cause of justice. Wherever the trial is held, I think it would certainly be worth trying to get Jeremiah Mickledore for the defence. I was his junior some two years ago and I think I may have some influence with him. I suggest you send an express setting out the facts and I follow this by discussing the case with him when I return to London, as I must after the inquest.'

Darcy said he was grateful and the proposal was agreed. Then Alveston said, 'I think, gentlemen, we should remind ourselves of the evidence we shall give when asked what words Wickham spoke when we came upon him kneeling over the body. They will undoubtedly be crucial to the case. Obviously we shall speak the truth but it will be interesting to know whether our memories agree on Wickham's exact words.'

Without waiting for either of the other two to speak, Colonel Fitzwilliam said, 'Not unnaturally they made a distinct impression on me and I believe I can repeat them exactly. Wickham said, "He's dead. Oh God, Denny's dead. He was my friend, my only friend, and I've killed him. It's my fault." It is, of course, a matter of opinion what he meant by Denny's death being his fault.'

Alveston said, 'My memory is precisely the same as the colonel's but, like him, I can attempt no interpretation of his words. So far we agree.'

It was Darcy's turn. He said, 'I cannot myself be as precise as to the exact order of his words, but I can with confidence state that Wickham said that he had killed his friend, his only friend, and that it was his fault. I too find those last words ambiguous and shall not attempt to explain them unless pressed, and possibly not then.'

Alveston said, 'We are unlikely to be pressed by the coroner. If the question is asked, he may point out that none of us can be sure of what is passing through another's mind. My own view, and it is speculative, is that he meant that Denny would not have gone into the woods and met his assailant had it not been for their quarrel, and that Wickham took responsibility for whatever it was that aroused Denny's repugnance. The case will undoubtedly rest on what Wickham meant by those few words.'

It seemed that the conference could now be considered over, but before they rose from their chairs, Darcy said, 'So Wickham's fate, life or death, will depend on twelve men influenced as they must be by their own prejudices and by the power of the accused's statement and the prosecuting counsel's eloquence.'

The colonel said, 'How else can it be dealt with? He will put himself on his countrymen and there can be no greater assurance of justice than the verdict of twelve honest Englishmen.'

Darcy said, 'And with no appeal.'

'How can there be? The decision of the jury has always been sacrosanct. What are you proposing, Darcy, a second jury, sworn in to agree or disagree with the first, and another jury after that? That would be the ultimate idiocy, and if carried on ad infinitum could presumably result in a foreign court trying English cases. And that would be the end of more than our legal system.'

Darcy said, 'Could it not be possible to have an appeal court

156

consisting of three, or perhaps five, judges to be convened if there were dissension over a difficult point of law?'

It was then that Alveston intervened. 'I can well imagine the reaction of an English jury to the proposal that their decision should be challenged by three judges. It must be for the trial judge to decide on points of law, and if he is unable to do so, then he has no right to be a judge. And there is to some extent a court of appeal. The trial judge can initiate the process for the granting of a pardon when he is unhappy with the outcome and a verdict which seems to the general public to be unjust will always result in a public outcry and sometimes violent protest. I can assure you there is nothing more powerful than the English when seized with righteous indignation. But as you may know, I am a member of a group of lawyers concerned with examining the effectiveness of our legal criminal system and there is one reform which we would like to see: the right of the prosecuting counsel to make a final speech before the verdict should be extended to the defence. I can see no reason against such a change, and we are hopeful that it may come before the end of this century.'

Darcy asked, 'What can be the objection to it?'

'Mostly time. The London courts are already overworked and too many cases are rushed through with indecent speed. The English are not so fond of lawyers that they wish to sit through hours of additional speeches. It is thought sufficient that the accused should speak for himself and that the cross-examination of prosecution witnesses by his defence counsel will be enough to ensure justice. I do not find these arguments entirely convincing but they are sincerely held.'

The colonel said, 'You sound like a radical, Darcy. I had not realised that you had such an interest in the law or were so dedicated to its reform.'

'Nor had I, but when one is faced, as we are now, by the reality of what awaits George Wickham, and how narrow the gap between life and death, it is perhaps natural to be both interested and concerned.' He paused, then said, 'If there is nothing else to be said, perhaps we can prepare to join the ladies for dinner.'

2

Tuesday morning promised to be a pleasant day with even the hope of autumn sunshine. Wilkinson, the coachman, had a well-deserved reputation for forecasting the weather and two days ago had prophesied that the wind and rain would be followed by some sun and occasional showers. It was the day when Darcy was to meet his steward, John Wooller, who would lunch at Pemberley, and in the afternoon he would ride to Lambton to see Wickham, a duty which he could be confident had no expectation of pleasure on either side.

While he was absent Elizabeth planned to visit Woodland Cottage with Georgiana and Mr Alveston, to enquire after Will's health and to carry wine and delicacies, which she and Mrs Reynolds hoped might tempt his appetite. She also wanted to satisfy herself that his mother and sister had not been made worried about being left alone when Bidwell was working at Pemberley. Georgiana had been eager to accompany her, and Henry Alveston had immediately offered to provide the male escort which Darcy thought essential and which he knew both ladies would find reassuring. Elizabeth was anxious to start as soon as possible after an early luncheon; the autumn sunshine was a benison which could not be expected to last, and Darcy had insisted that the party leave the woodland before the afternoon light began to fade.

But first there were letters to be written and, after an early breakfast, she settled to give some hours to this task. There were still replies outstanding to letters of sympathy and enquiry from friends who had been invited to the ball, and she knew that the family at Longbourn, who had received the news from Darcy by express post, would expect almost daily bulletins. There were also Bingley's sisters, Mrs Hurst and Miss Bingley, to be kept informed of progress, but here at least she could leave it to Bingley to write. They visited their brother and Jane twice a year but were so immersed in the delights of London that more than a month's stay in the country was intolerable. While at Highmarten they condescended to be entertained at Pemberley. To be able to boast about their visits, their relationship with Mr Darcy and the splendours of his house and estate was too valuable an indulgence to be sacrificed to disappointed hopes or resentment, but actually to see Elizabeth in possession as mistress of Pemberley remained an affront which neither sister could tolerate without a painful exercise of self-control and, to Elizabeth's relief, the visits were infrequent.

She knew that their brother would have tactfully discouraged them from visiting Pemberley during the present crisis and she had no doubt that they would stay away. A murder in the family can provide a frisson of excitement at fashionable dinner parties, but little social credit can be expected from the brutal despatch of an undistinguished captain of the infantry, without money or breeding to render him interesting. Since even the most fastidious among us can rarely escape hearing salacious local gossip, it is as well to enjoy what cannot be avoided, and it was generally known both in London and Derbyshire that Miss Bingley was particularly anxious at this time not to leave the capital. Her pursuit of a widowed peer of great wealth was entering a most hopeful phase. Admittedly without his peerage and his money he would have been regarded as the most boring man in London, but one cannot expect to be called 'your grace' without some inconvenience, and the competition for his wealth, title and anything else he cared to bestow was understandably keen. There were a couple of avaricious mamas, long-experienced in the matrimonial stakes, each working assiduously on her daughter's behalf, and Miss Bingley had no intention of leaving London at such a delicate stage of the competition.

Elizabeth had just finished letters to her family at Longbourn and to her Aunt Gardiner when Darcy arrived with a letter delivered the previous evening by express, which he had only recently opened.

Handing it to her, he said, 'Lady Catherine, as expected, has passed on the news to Mr Collins and Charlotte and has enclosed their letters with her own. I cannot suppose that they will give you either pleasure or surprise. I shall be in the business room with John Wooller but hope to see you at luncheon before I set out for Lambton.'

Lady Catherine had written:

My dear Nephew

Your express, as you will have realised, came as a considerable shock but, happily, I can assure you and Elizabeth that I have not succumbed. Even so, I had to call in Dr Everidge who congratulated me on my fortitude. You can be assured that I am as well as can be expected. The death of this unfortunate young man – of whom, of course, I know nothing – will inevitably cause a national sensation which, given the importance of Pemberley, can hardly be avoided. Mr Wickham, whom the police have very properly arrested, seems to have a talent for causing trouble and embarrassment to respectable people and I cannot help feeling that your parents' indulgence to him in childhood, about which I frequently expressed myself strongly to Lady Anne, has been responsible for many of his later delinquencies. However, I prefer to believe that of this enormity at least he is innocent and, as his disgraceful marriage to your wife's sister has made him your brother, you will no doubt wish to make yourself responsible for the expense of his defence. Let us hope it does not ruin both you and your sons. You will need a good lawyer. On no account employ someone local; you will get a nonentity who will combine inefficiency with unreasonable expectations in regard to remuneration. I would offer my own Mr Pegworthy, but I require him here. The long-standing boundary dispute with my neighbour, of which I have spoken, is now reaching a critical stage and there has been a lamentable rise in poaching in the last months. I would come myself to give advice – Mr Pegworthy said that were I a man and had taken to the law, I would have been an ornament to the English bar – but I am needed here. If I went to all the people who would benefit from my advice I would never be at home. I suggest you employ a lawyer from the Inner Temple. They are said to be a

gentlemanly lot in that Inn. Mention my name and you will be well
attended.

I shall convey your news to Mr Collins since it cannot long be
concealed. As a clergyman, he will wish to send his usual depress-
ing words of comfort, and I shall enclose his letter with mine but
will place an embargo on its length.

I send my sympathy to you and to Mrs Darcy. Do not hesitate
to send for me if events should turn ill with this affair and I will
brave the autumn mists to be with you.

Elizabeth expected to get nothing of interest from Mr Collins's
letter except the reprehensible pleasure of relishing his unique
mixture of pomposity and folly. It was longer than she expected.
Despite her proclamation, Lady Catherine de Bourgh had been
indulgent about length. He began by stating that he could find
no words to express his shock and abhorrence, and then proceeded to find a great number, few of them appropriate and
none of them helpful. As with Lydia's engagement, he ascribed
the whole of this dreadful affair to the lack of control over their
daughter by Mr and Mrs Bennet, and went on to congratulate
himself on having withdrawn an offer of marriage which would
have resulted in his being inescapably linked to their disgrace.
He went on to prophesy a catalogue of disasters for the afflicted
family ranging from the worst – Lady Catherine's displeasure
and their permanent banishment from Rosings – descending to
public ignominy, bankruptcy and death. It closed by mentioning that, within a matter of months, his dear Charlotte would be
presenting him with their fourth child. The Hunsford parsonage was becoming a little small for his increasing family, but he

trusted that Providence, in due time, would provide him with a valuable living and a larger house. Elizabeth reflected that this was a clear appeal, and not the first, to Mr Darcy's interest and would receive the same response. Providence had so far shown no inclination to help and Darcy certainly would not.

Charlotte's letter, unsealed, was what Elizabeth had expected, no more than brief and conventional sentences of distress and condolence and the reassurance that the thoughts of both herself and her husband were with the afflicted family. Undoubtedly Mr Collins would have read the letter and nothing warmer or more intimate could be expected. Charlotte Lucas had been Elizabeth's friend through the years of childhood and young womanhood, the only female except Jane with whom rational conversation had been possible, and Elizabeth still regretted that much of the confidence between them had subsided into general benevolence and a regular but not revealing correspondence. On Darcy's and her two visits to Lady Catherine since their marriage, a formal visit to the parsonage had been necessary and Elizabeth, unwilling to expose her husband to Mr Collins's presumptive civilities, had gone alone. She had tried to understand Charlotte's acceptance of Mr Collins's offer, made within a day of his proposal to her and her rejection, but it was unlikely that Charlotte had either forgotten or forgiven her friend's first amazed response to the news.

Elizabeth suspected that on one occasion Charlotte had taken her revenge. Elizabeth had often wondered how Lady Catherine had learned that she and Mr Darcy were likely to become engaged. She had never spoken of his first disastrous proposal to anyone but Jane and had come to the conclusion that it must have been Charlotte who had betrayed her. She recollected that evening when Darcy, with the Bingleys, had first made an appearance in the Meryton Assembly Rooms when Charlotte had somehow suspected that he might be interested in her friend and had warned Elizabeth, in her preference for Wickham, not to slight a man of Darcy's much greater importance. And then there had been Elizabeth's visit to the parsonage with Sir William Lucas and his daughter. Charlotte herself had commented on the frequency of the visits of Mr Darcy and Colonel Fitzwilliam during the visitors' stay and had said that it could only be a compliment to Elizabeth. And then there was the proposal itself. After Darcy had left, Elizabeth had walked alone to try to quieten her confusion and anger but Charlotte, on her return, must have seen that something untoward had happened during her absence.

No, it was impossible for anyone other than Charlotte to have guessed the cause of her distress, and Charlotte, in a moment of conjugal mischief, had passed on her suspicions to Mr Collins. He, of course, would have lost no time in warning Lady Catherine and had probably exaggerated the danger, making suspicion into certainty. His motives were curiously mixed. If the marriage took place he might have hoped to benefit from such a close relationship with the wealthy Mr Darcy; what livings might not be within his power to bestow? But prudence and revenge had probably been more powerful and sweeter motives. He had never forgiven Elizabeth for refusing him. Her punishment should have been a lonely indigent spinsterhood, not a glittering marriage which even an earl's daughter would not have scorned. Had not Lady Anne married Darcy's father? Charlotte, too, might have had cause for a more justified resentment. She was convinced, as was the whole of Meryton, that Elizabeth hated Darcy; she, her only friend, who had been critical of Charlotte's own marriage based on prudence and the need for a home, had herself accepted a man she was known to detest because she could not resist the prize of Pemberley. It is never so difficult to congratulate a friend on her good fortune than when that fortune appears undeserved.

Charlotte's marriage could be regarded as a success, as perhaps all marriages are when each of the couple gets exactly what the union promised. Mr Collins had a competent wife and housekeeper, a mother for his children and the approval of his patroness, while Charlotte took the only course by which a single woman of no beauty and small fortune could hope to gain independence. Elizabeth remembered how Jane, kind and tolerant as always, had cautioned her not to blame Charlotte for her engagement without remembering what it was she was leaving. Elizabeth had never liked the Lucas boys. Even in youth they had been boisterous, unkind and unprepossessing and she had no doubt that, as adults, they would have despised and resented a spinster sister, seeing her as an embarrassment and an expense, and would have made their feelings known. From the start Charlotte had managed her husband with the same skill as she did her servants and her chicken houses, and Elizabeth, on her first visit to Hunsford with Sir William and his daughter, had seen evidence of Charlotte's arrangements to minimise the disadvantage of her situation. Mr Collins had been assigned a room at the front of the rectory where the prospect of viewing passers-by, including the possibility of Lady Catherine in her carriage, kept him happily seated at the window while most of his free day-time hours, with her encouragement, were spent gardening, an activity for which he displayed enthusiasm and talent. To tend the soil is generally regarded as a virtuous activity and to see a gardener diligently at work invariably provokes a surge of sympathetic approval, if only at the prospect of freshly dug potatoes and early peas. Elizabeth suspected that Mr Collins had never been so acceptable a husband as when Charlotte saw him, at a distance, bent over his vegetable patch.

Charlotte had not been the eldest of a large family without acquiring some skill in the management of male delinquencies and her method with her husband was ingenious. She consistently congratulated him on qualities he did not possess in the hope that, flattered by her praise and approval, he would acquire them. Elizabeth had seen the system in operation when, at Charlotte's urgent entreaty, she had paid a short visit on her own some eighteen months after her marriage. The party was being driven back to the vicarage in one of Lady Catherine de Bourgh's carriages when the discussion turned to a fellow guest, a recently inducted clergyman from an adjoining parish who was a distant relation of Lady Catherine's.

Charlotte had said, 'Mr Thompson is no doubt an excellent young man, but he is too much a prattler for my liking. To praise every dish was unnecessarily fulsome and made him seem greedy. And once or twice, when in full flow of speech, I could see that Lady Catherine did not much like it. It is a pity he didn't take you, my love, as his example. He would then have said less, and that more to the point.'

Mr Collins's mind was not subtle enough to detect the irony

or suspect the stratagem. His vanity grasped at the compliment and, at their next dinner engagement at Rosings, he sat for most of the meal in such unnatural silence that Elizabeth was fearful that Lady Catherine would sharply tap her spoon on the table and enquire why he had so little to say for himself.

For the last ten minutes Elizabeth had laid down her pen and had let her mind wander back to the Longbourn days, to Charlotte and their long friendship. Now it was time to put away her papers and see what Mrs Reynolds had prepared for the Bidwells. Making her way to the housekeeper's room she remembered how Lady Catherine, on one of her visits the previous year, had accompanied Elizabeth in taking to Woodland Cottage nourishment suitable for a seriously ill man. Lady Catherine had not been invited to enter the sick room and had shown no disposition to do so, merely saying on the way back, 'Dr McFee's diagnosis should be regarded as highly suspect. I have never approved of protracted dying. It is an affectation in the aristocracy; in the lower classes it is merely an excuse for avoiding work. The blacksmith's second son has been reputedly dying for the last four years, yet when I drive past I see him assisting his father with every appearance of being in robust health. The de Bourghs have never gone in for prolonged dying. People should make up their minds whether to live or to die and do one or the other with the least inconvenience to others.'

Elizabeth had been too shocked and surprised to comment. How could Lady Catherine speak so calmly of protracted dying just three years after she had lost her only child following years of ill health? But after the first effusion of grief, controlled but surely genuine, Lady Catherine had regained her equanimity –

and with it much of her previous intolerance – with remarkable speed. Miss de Bourgh, a delicate, plain and silent girl, had made a negligible impact on the world while she lived and even less in dying. Elizabeth, then herself a mother, had done everything she could by warm invitations to visit Pemberley and by herself going to Rosings to support Lady Catherine in the first weeks of mourning, and both the offer and this sympathy, which perhaps the mother had not expected, had done its work. Lady Catherine was essentially the same woman that she had always been, but now the shades of Pemberley were less polluted when Elizabeth took her daily exercise under the trees, and Lady Catherine became fonder of visiting Pemberley than either Darcy or Elizabeth were anxious to receive her.

3

With each day there were duties to be attended to and Elizabeth found in her responsibility to Pemberley, her family and her servants at least an antidote to the worst horror of her imaginings. Today was one of duty both for her husband and for herself. She knew that she could no longer delay visiting Woodland Cottage. The shots in the night, the knowledge that a brutal murder had taken place within a hundred yards of the cottage and while Bidwell was at Pemberley must have left Mrs Bidwell with a legacy of pity and horror to add to her already heavy load of grief. Elizabeth knew that Darcy had visited the cottage last Thursday to suggest that Bidwell should be released from his duties on the eve of the ball so that he could be with his family at this difficult time, but both husband and wife had been adamant that this was not necessary and Darcy had seen that his persistence had only distressed them. Bidwell would always resist any suggestion that could carry the implication that he was not indispensable, even temporarily, to Pemberley and its master; since relinquishing his status as head coachman he had always cleaned the silver on the night before Lady Anne's ball and in his view there was no one else at Pemberley who could be trusted with the task.

During the past year, when young Will had grown weaker and hope of recovery gradually faded, Elizabeth had been regular in her visits to Woodland Cottage, at first being admitted to the small bedroom at the front of the cottage where the patient lay. Recently she had become aware that her appearance with Mrs Bidwell at his bedside was more of an embarrassment to him than a pleasure, could indeed be seen as an imposition, and she had remained in the sitting room giving what comfort she could to the stricken mother. When the Bingleys were staying at Pemberley, Jane would invariably accompany her together with Bingley, and she realised again how much she would today miss her sister's presence and what a comfort it had always been to have with her a dearly loved companion to whom she could confide even her darkest thoughts, and whose goodness and gentleness lightened every distress. In the absence of Jane, Georgiana and one of the upper servants had accompanied her, but Georgiana, sensitive to the possibility that Mrs Bidwell might find it a greater comfort to confide confidentially in Mrs Darcy, had usually paid her respects briefly and then sat outside on a wooden bench made some time ago by young Will. Darcy accompanied her rarely on these routine visits since the taking of a basket of delicacies provided by the Pemberley cook was seen as essentially women's work. Today, apart from the visit to Wickham, he was reluctant to leave Pemberley in case there were developments needing his attention, and it was agreed at breakfast that a servant would accompany Elizabeth and Georgiana. It was then that Alveston, speaking to Darcy, said quietly that it would be a privilege to accompany Mrs Darcy and Miss Georgiana if the suggestion were agreeable to them, and it was accepted with gratitude. Elizabeth glanced quickly at Georgiana and saw the look of joy, swiftly suppressed, which made her response to the proposal only too evident.

Elizabeth and Georgiana were driven to the woods in a landaulet, while Alveston rode his horse, Pompey, at their side. An early mist had cleared after a rain-free night and it was a glorious morning, cold but sunlit, the air sweet with the familiar tang of autumn – leaves, fresh earth and the faint smell of burning wood. Even the horses seemed to rejoice in the day, tossing their heads and straining at the bit. The wind had died but the detritus of the storm lay in swathes over the path, the dry leaves crackling under the wheels or tumbling and spinning in their wake. The trees were not yet bare, and the rich red and gold of autumn seemed intensified under the cerulean sky. On such a day it was impossible for her heart not to be lifted and for the first time since waking Elizabeth felt a small surge of hope. To an onlooker, she thought, the party must look as if they were on their way to a picnic – the tossing manes, the coachman in his livery, the basket of provisions, the handsome young man riding at their side. When they entered the wood the dark overreaching boughs, which at dusk had the crude strength of a prison roof, now let in shafts of sunlight which lay on the leaf-strewn path and transformed the dark green of the bushes into the liveliness of spring.

The landaulet drew to a stop and the coachman was given orders to return in precisely one hour, then the three of them, with Alveston leading Pompey and carrying the basket, walked between the gleaming trunks of the trees and down the trodden pathway to the cottage. The food was not brought as an act of charity – no member of the staff at Pemberley was without shelter, food or clothing – but they were the extras which the cook would contrive in the kitchens in the hope of tempting Will's appetite: consommés prepared with the best beef and laced with sherry, made to the recipe devised by Dr McFee, small savoury tartlets which melted in the mouth, fruit jellies and ripe peaches and pears from the glasshouse. Even these now could rarely be tolerated, but they were received with gratitude and if Will could not eat them, his mother and sister undoubtedly would.

Despite the softness of their footsteps, Mrs Bidwell must have heard them for she stood at the door to welcome them in. She was a slight, thin woman whose face, like a faded watercolour, still evoked the fragile prettiness and promise of youth but now anxiety and the strain of waiting for her son to die had made her an old woman. Elizabeth introduced Alveston who, without directly speaking of Will, managed to convey a genuine sympathy, said what a pleasure it was to meet her and suggested that he should wait for Mrs and Miss Darcy on the wooden bench outside.

Mrs Bidwell said, 'It was made by my son, William, sir, and finished the week before he was took ill. He was a clever carpenter, as you can see, sir, and liked designing and making pieces of furniture. Mrs Darcy has a nursery chair – have you not, madam? – which Will made the Christmas after Master Fitzwilliam was born.'

'Yes indeed,' said Elizabeth. 'We value it greatly and we always think of Will when the children clamber over it.'

Alveston made his bow, then went out and seated himself on the bench which was on the edge of the woodland and just visible from the cottage, while Elizabeth and Georgiana took their proffered seats in the living room. It was simply furnished with a central oblong table and four chairs, a more comfortable chair each side of the fireplace and a wide mantelpiece crowded with family mementoes. The window at the front was slightly open but the room was still too hot, and although Will Bidwell's bedroom was upstairs, the whole cottage seemed permeated with the sour smell of long illness. Close to the window was a cot on rockers with a nursing chair beside it and, at Mrs Bidwell's invitation, Elizabeth went over to peer down at the sleeping child and congratulate his grandmother on the health and beauty of the new arrival. There was no sign of Louisa. Georgiana knew that Mrs Bidwell would welcome the opportunity of talking alone to Elizabeth, and after making enquiries after Will and admiring the baby, accepted Elizabeth's suggestion, which had already been agreed between them, that she should join Alveston outside. The wicker basket was soon emptied, the contents gratefully received, and the two women settled themselves in the chairs beside the fire.

Mrs Bidwell said, 'There is not much he can keep down now, madam, but he does like that thin beef soup and I try him with some of the custards and, of course, the wine. It is good of you to call, madam, but I won't ask you to see him. It will only distress you and he hasn't the strength to say much.'

Elizabeth said, 'Dr McFee sees him regularly, does he not? Is he able to provide some relief?'

'He comes every other day, madam, busy as he is, and never a penny charged. He says Will has not long to go now. Oh madam, you knew my dear boy when you first arrived here as Mrs Darcy. Why should this happen to him, madam? If there was a reason or a purpose maybe I could bear it.'

Elizabeth put out her hand. She said gently, 'That is a question we always ask and we get no answer. Does Reverend Oliphant visit you? He said something after church on Sunday about coming to see Will.'

'Oh indeed he does, madam, and he is a comfort, to be sure. But Will has asked me not to send him in recently, so I make excuses, I hope without offence.'

Elizabeth said, 'I'm sure there would be no offence, Mrs Bidwell. Mr Oliphant is a sensitive and understanding man. Mr Darcy has great confidence in him.'

'So have we all, madam.'

For a few minutes they were silent, then Mrs Bidwell said, 'I have not spoken of the death of that poor young man, madam. It upset Will terribly that such a thing should happen in the woods so close to home and he unable to protect us.'

Elizabeth said, 'But you were not in danger I hope, Mrs Bidwell. I was told that you had heard nothing.'

'Nor had we, madam, except the pistol shots, but it brought home to Will how helpless he is and what a burden his father has to bear. But this tragedy is terrible for you and for the master, I know, and I should best not speak about matters of which I know nothing.'

'But you did know Mr Wickham as a child?'

'Indeed, madam. He and the young master used to play together in the woodland. They were boisterous like all young boys, but the young master was the quieter of the two. I know that Mr Wickham grew up very wild and was a grief to the master, but he has never been spoken of since your marriage, and no doubt it's for the best. But I cannot believe that the boy I knew grew up to be a murderer.'

For a minute they sat in silence. There was a sensitive proposal which Elizabeth had come to make and was wondering how best to introduce. She and Darcy were concerned that, since the attack, the Bidwells would feel at risk, isolated as they were in Woodland Cottage, particularly with a seriously ill boy in the house and Bidwell himself so often at Pemberley. It would be reasonable that they should feel nervous and Elizabeth and Darcy had agreed that she should suggest to Mrs Bidwell that the whole family move into Pemberley, at least until the mystery had been solved. Whether this was practicable would, of course, depend on whether Will could stand the journey, but he would be carried very carefully by stretcher all the way to avoid the jolting of a carriage, and would receive devoted care once he was settled in a quiet room at Pemberley. But when Elizabeth put forward this proposal, she was startled by Mrs Bidwell's response. For the first time the woman looked genuinely frightened and it was almost with a look of horror that she responded.

'Oh no, madam! Please don't ask this of us. Will couldn't be happy away from the cottage. We have no fear here. Even with

Bidwell absent, Louise and I were not afeared. After Colonel Fitzwilliam was good enough to check that we were all right, we did as he instructed. I bolted the door and locked the downstairs windows, and no one came near. It was just a poacher, madam, taken unawares and acting on impulse, he had no quarrel with us. And I'm sure that Dr McFee would say that Will couldn't stand the journey. Please tell Mr Darcy with our gratitude and compliments that it must not be thought of.'

Her eyes, her outstretched hands, were a plea. Elizabeth said gently, 'Nor shall it be, if that is your wish, but we can at least ensure that your husband is here most of the time. We shall miss him greatly, but others can manage his work while Will is so ill and requires your care.'

'He won't do it, madam. It will grieve him to think that others can take over.'

Elizabeth was tempted to say that, that being so, he would have to grieve, but she sensed that there was something here more serious than Bidwell's desire to feel perpetually needed. She would leave the question for the moment; no doubt Mrs Bidwell would discuss it with her husband and perhaps change her mind. And she was, of course, right; if Dr McFee was of the opinion that Will could not stand the journey it would be folly to attempt it.

They had made their goodbyes and were rising together when two chubby feet appeared above the rim of the cot, and the baby began to wail. With an anxious upward glance towards her son's room, Mrs Bidwell was at the cot's side and gathering the child into her arms. At that moment there were footsteps on the stair and Louisa Bidwell came down. For a moment Elizabeth failed to recognise the girl who, since she had been visiting the cottage as chatelaine of Pemberley, had been the picture of health and happy girlhood, pink-cheeked, clear-eyed and fresh as a spring morning in her newly ironed working clothes. Now she looked ten years older, pale and drawn, her uncombed hair pulled back from a face lined with tiredness and worry, her working dress stained with milk. She gave a quick bob to Elizabeth then, without speaking, almost grabbed the child from her mother and said, 'I'll take him to the kitchen in case he wakes Will. I'll put on the milk, Mother, for his feed, and some of that fine gruel. I'll try him with that.'

And then she was gone. Elizabeth, to break the silence, said, 'It must be a joy to have a new grandchild here, but also a responsibility. How long will he be staying? I expect his mother will want him back.'

'She will indeed, madam. It was a great pleasure for Will to see the new baby, but he doesn't like to hear the child wailing, although it's no more than natural if a baby is hungry.'

'When will he be going home?' Elizabeth asked.

'Next week, madam. My elder daughter's husband, Michael Simpkins – a good man, as you know madam – will meet them off the post-chaise at Birmingham, and take him home. We are waiting to hear which day will be convenient for him. He is a busy man and it isn't easy for him to leave the shop but he and my daughter are anxious to have Georgie back home.' It was impossible to miss the tension in her voice.

Elizabeth realised that it was time to leave. She said her goodbyes, listened again to Mrs Bidwell's thanks and immediately the door to Woodland Cottage closed behind her. Her spirits were depressed by the obvious unhappiness she had seen, and her mind confused. Why had the suggestion that the Bidwells should move to Pemberley been received with such distress? Had it perhaps been tactless, an unspoken implication that the dying boy would receive better care at Pemberley than a loving mother could give him in his home? Nothing could have been further from her intention. Had Mrs Bidwell genuinely felt the journey would kill her son, but was that really a risk when he would be carried, well wrapped, on a stretcher and attended every inch of the journey by Dr McFee? Nothing else had been envisaged. Mrs Bidwell had seemed more distressed by the thought of a move than she was by the possible presence of a murderer stalking the woods. And Elizabeth felt a suspicion, almost amounting to a certainty, which she could not discuss with her companions, which indeed she doubted whether it would be right to voice to anyone. She thought again how much she wished Jane were still at Pemberley; but it was right that the Bingleys should have left. Jane's place was with her children and Lydia would be closer to the local gaol where she could at least visit her husband. Elizabeth's feelings were complicated by the acknowledgement that Pemberley was a less distressing place without Lydia's violent swings of mood and continual complaints and lamentations.

For a moment, immersed in this jumble of thoughts and emotions, she had paid little attention to her two companions. Now she saw that they had been walking together on the fringes of the glade and were looking at her as if wondering when she would make a move. She shook off her preoccupations and joined them. Taking out her watch, she said, 'We have twenty minutes before the landaulet comes back. Now that we have the sunshine, however brief, shall we sit for a while before we go back?'

The bench faced away from the cottage towards a distant slope down to the river. Elizabeth and Georgiana seated themselves at one end and Alveston at the other, his legs stretched out before him, his hands clasped behind his head. Now that the autumn winds had stripped many of the trees it was just possible to see in the far distance the thin gleaming line which separated the river from the sky. Was it perhaps this glimpse of the water which had caused Georgiana's great-grandfather to choose this spot? The original bench had long gone, but the new one made by Will was sturdy and not uncomfortable. Beside it, as a half-shield, were a tangle of bushes with red berries and a shrub whose name Elizabeth could not remember, with tough leaves and white blossoms.

After a few minutes Alveston turned to Georgiana. 'Did your great-grandfather live here all the time, or was it an occasional retreat from the business of the great house?'

'Oh, all the time. He had the cottage built and then moved in without a servant or anyone to cook. Food would be left from time to time, but he and the dog, Soldier, wanted no one but each other. His life was a great scandal at the time, and even the family were unsympathetic. It seemed an abdication of responsibility for a Darcy to live anywhere other than Pemberley. And then, when Soldier became old and ill, Great-Grandfather shot him and then himself. He left a note saying that they were to be buried together in the same grave in the woodland, and there is a tombstone and a grave, but only for Soldier. The family were horrified by the thought that a Darcy would want to lie in unconsecrated ground and you can imagine what the parish clergyman thought of it. So Great-Grandfather is in the family plot and Soldier is in the woods. I always felt sorry for Great-Grandfather and, when I was a child, I would go with my governess and lay some blossoms or berries on the grave. It was just a childish imagining that Great-Grandfather was there with Soldier. But when my mother found out what was happening the governess was dismissed and I was told the woodland was out of bounds.'

Elizabeth said, 'For you, but not for your brother.'

'No, not for Fitzwilliam. But he is ten years older than I and was grown up when I was a child, and I don't think he felt the same about Great-Grandfather as I did.'

There was a silence, then Alveston said, 'Is the grave still there? You could take some flowers now, if you wish, now you are no longer a child.'

It seemed to Elizabeth that the words had a deeper implication than a visit to a dog's grave.

Georgiana said, 'I should like that. I have not visited the grave since I was aged eleven. I would like to see if anything has changed, but I cannot believe that it could. I know the way and it is not far from the path, so we shall not be late for the landaulet.'

They set off, Georgiana indicating the way and Alveston, with Pompey, walking a little in front to stamp down the nettles and hold any impeding branches out of their path. Georgiana was carrying a small posy which Alveston had plucked for her. It was surprising how much brightness, how many memories of spring, those few gatherings from a sunlit October day could provide. He had found a spray of white autumn blossom on tough stems, some berries, richly red but not yet ready to fall, and one or

179

two leaves veined with gold. No one spoke. Elizabeth, her mind already preoccupied with a tangle of worries, wondered if this short expedition was wise, without quite knowing in what way it could be thought inadvisable. It was a day in which any event out of the commonplace seemed mired in apprehension and potential danger.

It was then that she began to notice that the path must have been trodden in the recent past. In places the frailer branches and twigs had broken away, and at one point where the ground sloped slightly and the leaves were mushy she thought there were signs that they had been pressed down by a heavy foot. She wondered whether Alveston had noticed, but he said nothing and, within a few more minutes, they broke free of the undergrowth and found themselves in a small glade surrounded by beech trees. In the middle was a granite gravestone about two feet high with a slightly curved top. There was no raised grave and the stone, now gleaming in the frail sunlight, looked as if it had broken spontaneously through the earth. They read the engraved words in silence. *Soldier. Faithful unto death. Died here with his master, 3rd November 1735.*

Still without speaking, Georgiana approached to place her posy at the foot of the gravestone. As they stood for a moment regarding it, she said, 'Poor Great-Grandfather. I wish I had known him. No one ever talked about him when I was a child, even the people who could remember him. He was the family failure, the Darcy who dishonoured his name because he put private happiness before public responsibilities. But I shall not visit the grave again. After all, his body is not here; it was just a childish fantasy that he might somehow know that I cared about him. I hope he was happy in his solitude. At least he managed to escape.'

Escape from what? thought Elizabeth. And now she was anxious to return to the landaulet. She said, 'I think it is time we went home. Mr Darcy may soon be back from the prison and will be concerned if we are still in the woodland.'

They made their way down the narrow leaf-strewn path to join the lane where the landaulet would be waiting. Although they had been in the woodland for less than an hour, the bright promise of the afternoon had already faded and Elizabeth, who had never enjoyed walking in confined spaces, felt the shrubs and trees pressing on her like a physical weight. The smell of sickness was still in her nostrils, and her heart was oppressed by Mrs Bidwell's unhappiness and the loss of all hope for Will. When the main path was reached they walked together when the width permitted and, when it narrowed, Alveston took the lead and walked with Pompey a few feet ahead, looking at the ground and then from left to right as if in search of clues. Elizabeth knew that he would prefer to take Georgiana on his arm but would not let either lady walk alone. Georgiana, too, was silent, perhaps oppressed by the same feeling of foreboding and menace.

Suddenly Alveston stopped and moved quickly to an oak tree. Something had obviously caught his eye. They joined him and saw on its bark the letters F. D—Y carved about four feet from the ground.

Looking around, Georgiana said, 'Is there not a similar carving on that holly tree?'

A quick examination confirmed that there were indeed

initials carved on two other trunks. Alveston said, 'It does not seem like the usual carving of a lover. With lovers the initials are all that is necessary. Whoever carved these was anxious that there should be no doubt that the initials stand for Fitzwilliam Darcy.'

Elizabeth said, 'I wonder when it was cut. It looks quite recent to me.'

Alveston said, 'It was certainly done within the last month, and by two people. The F and the D are quite shallow and could have been made by a woman, but the dash that follows, and the Y are cut really deeply, almost certainly by a sharper implement.'

Elizabeth said, 'I do not believe that any sweetheart carved this memento. I think it was cut by an enemy and the intention was malignant. It was carved in hatred not in love.'

As soon as she had spoken she wondered whether she had been unwise to worry Georgiana, but Alveston said, 'I suppose it is possible that the initials stand for Denny. Do we know his Christian name?'

Elizabeth tried to remember if she had ever heard it at Meryton, and finally said, 'I think he was Martin, or perhaps Matthew, but I suppose the police will know. They must have been in touch with his relatives, if he had any. But Denny has never been in these woods before Friday as far as I know, and certainly he has never visited Pemberley.'

Alveston turned to go. He said, 'We will report it when we get back to the house and the police will have to be told. If the constables made the thorough search they should have made, they may already have seen the carving and reached some conclusion about its meaning. In the mean time I hope neither of you will worry too much. It could be a piece of mischief intending no particular harm; perhaps a lovesick girl from one of the cottages or a servant engaged in a foolish but harmless piece of foolery.'

But Elizabeth was not convinced. Without speaking she walked away from the tree and Georgiana and Alveston followed her example. It was in a silence which none of them was disposed to break that Elizabeth and Georgiana followed Alveston down the woodland path to the waiting landaulet. Elizabeth's sombre mood seemed to have infected her companions and when Alveston had handed the ladies into the carriage he closed the door, mounted his horse and they turned towards home.

4

The local prison at Lambton, unlike the county one at Derby, was more intimidating from the outside than it was within, presumably having been built on the belief that public money was better saved by discouraging would-be offenders than by disheartening them once they were incarcerated. The prison was not unknown to Darcy, who had occasionally visited in his capacity of magistrate, notably on one occasion eight years previously when a mentally disturbed inmate had hanged himself in his cell and the chief gaoler had called the only magistrate then available to view the body. It had been such a distressing experience that it had left Darcy with a permanent horror of hanging and he never visited the gaol without a vivid memory of that dangling body and the stretched neck. Today it was a more than usually potent vision. The keeper of the gaol and his assistant were humane men and although none of the cells could be called spacious, there was no active ill treatment, and prisoners who could pay well for food and drink to be brought in could entertain visitors in some comfort and had little of which to complain.

Since Hardcastle had strongly advised that it would be unwise for Darcy to meet Wickham before the inquest had been held, Bingley, with his usual good nature, volunteered for the task and he had visited on Monday morning, when the prisoner's immediate necessities had been dealt with and enough money passed to ensure that he could purchase the food and other comforts which could help make imprisonment bearable. But, after further thought, Darcy had decided that he had a duty to visit Wickham, at least once before the inquest. Not to do so would be taken throughout Lambton and Pemberley village to be a clear sign that he believed his brother-in-law to be guilty, and it was from the Lambton and Pemberley parishes that the inquest jury would be drawn. He might have no choice about being called as a witness for the prosecution, but at least he could demonstrate quietly that he believed Wickham to be innocent. There was, too, a more private concern: he was deeply concerned that there should be no open conjecture about the reason for the family estrangement which might put the matter of Georgiana's proposed elopement at risk of discovery. It was both just and expedient that he should go to the prison.

Bingley had reported that he had found Wickham sullen, uncooperative and prone to burst out in incivilities against the magistrate and the police, demanding that their efforts be redoubled to discover who had murdered his chief – indeed his only – friend. Why did he languish in gaol while the guilty went unsought? Why did the police keep interrupting his rest to harass him with stupid and unnecessary questions? Why had they asked why he had turned Denny over? To see his face, of course, it was a perfectly natural action. No, he had not noticed the wound on Denny's head, it was probably covered by his hair and, anyway, he was too distressed to notice details. And what, he was asked, had he been doing in the time between the shots being heard and the finding of Denny's body by the search party? He was stumbling through the woodland trying to catch a murderer, and that was what they should be doing, not wasting time pestering an innocent man.

Today Darcy found a very different man. Now, in fresh clothes, shaved and his hair combed, Wickham received him as if in his own home, bestowing a favour on a not particularly welcome visitor. Darcy remembered that he had always been a creature of moods and now he recognised the old Wickham, handsome, confident and more inclined to relish his notoriety than to see it as a disgrace. Bingley had brought the articles for which he had asked: tobacco, several shirts and cravats, slippers, savoury pies baked at Highmarten to augment the food purchased for him from the local bakery, and ink and paper with which Wickham proposed to write an account both of his part in the Irish campaign and of the deep injustice of his present imprisonment, a personal record which he was confident would find a ready market. Neither man spoke of the past. Darcy could not rid himself of its power but Wickham lived for the moment, was sanguine about the future and reinvented the past to suit his audience, and Darcy could almost believe that, for the present, he had put the worst of it completely out of his mind.

Wickham said that the Bingleys had brought Lydia from Highmarten to visit him the previous evening but she had been so uncontrolled in her complaints and weeping that he had found the occasion too dispiriting to be tolerated and had instructed that in future she should be admitted only at his request and for fifteen minutes. He was hopeful, however, that no further visit would be necessary; the inquest had been fixed for Wednesday at eleven o'clock and he was confident that he would then be released, after which he envisaged the triumphant return of Lydia and himself to Longbourn and the congratulations of his former friends at Meryton. No mention was made of Pemberley, perhaps because even in his euphoria he hardly expected to be welcomed there, nor wished to be. No doubt, thought Darcy, in the happy event of his release, he would first join Lydia at Highmarten before travelling on to Hertfordshire. It seemed unjust that Jane and Bingley should be burdened with Lydia's presence even for a further day, but all that could be decided if his release indeed took place. He wished he could share Wickham's confidence.

He stayed only for half an hour, was provided with a list of requirements to be brought the next day, and left with Wickham's request that his compliments should be paid to Mrs Darcy and to Miss Darcy. Leaving, he reflected that it was a relief to find Wickham no longer sunk in pessimism and incrimination, but the visit had been uncomfortable for him and singularly depressing.

He knew, and with bitterness, that if the trial went well he would have to support Wickham and Lydia, at least for the foreseeable future. Their spending had always exceeded their income, and he guessed that they had depended on private subventions from Elizabeth and Jane to augment an inadequate income. Jane occasionally still invited Lydia to Highmarten while Wickham, loudly complaining in private, amused himself by staying in a variety of local inns, and it was from Jane that Elizabeth had news of the couple. None of the temporary jobs Wickham had taken since resigning his commission had been a success. His latest attempt to earn a competence had been with Sir Walter Elliot, a baronet who had been forced by extravagance to rent his house to strangers and had moved to Bath with two of his daughters. The younger, Anne, had since made a prosperous and happy marriage with a naval captain, now a distinguished admiral, but the elder, Elizabeth, had still to find a husband. The baronet, disenchanted with Bath, had decided that he was now sufficiently prosperous to return home, gave his tenant notice and had employed Wickham as a secretary to assist with the necessary work occasioned by the move. Wickham had been dismissed within six months. When faced with depressing news of public discord or, worse, of family disagreements it was always Jane's reconciling task to find no party greatly at fault. But when the facts of Wickham's latest failure were passed on to her more sceptical sister, Elizabeth suspected that Miss Elliot had been worried by her father's response to Lydia's open flirtation, while Wickham's attempt to ingratiate himself with her had been met, at first with some encouragement born of boredom and vanity, finally with disgust.

Once away from Lambton, it was good to take deep breaths of cool fresh-smelling air, to be free of the unmistakable prison smell of bodies, food and cheap soap and the clank of turning keys, and it was with a surge of relief and a sense that he himself had escaped from durance that Darcy turned his horse's head towards Pemberley.

5

Pemberley was as quiet as if it were uninhabited, and it was apparent that Elizabeth and Georgiana had not yet returned. He had hardly dismounted when one of the stable boys came round the corner of the house to take his horse, but he must have returned earlier than expected and there was no one waiting at the door. He entered the silent hall and made for the library where he thought it likely that he would find the colonel impatient for news. But to his surprise he discovered Mr Bennet there alone, ensconced in a high-backed chair by the fire, reading the *Edinburgh Review*. It was clear from the empty cup and soiled plate on a small table at his side that he had been provided with refreshment after his journey. After a second's pause, occasioned by surprise, Darcy realised that he was exceedingly glad to see this unexpected visitor, and as Mr Bennet rose from his chair, shook hands with him warmly.

'Please don't disturb yourself, sir. It is a great pleasure to see you. I hope you have been attended?'

'As you see. Stoughton has been his usual efficient self and I have met Colonel Fitzwilliam. After greeting me he said he would take advantage of my arrival to exercise his horse; I had the impression that he was finding confinement to the house a little tedious. I have also been welcomed by the estimable Mrs

Reynolds who assures me that my usual room is always kept ready.'

'When did you arrive, sir?'

'About forty minutes ago. I hired a chaise. That is not the most comfortable way to travel far and I had it in mind to come by coach. Mrs Bennet, however, complained that she needs it to convey the most recent news of Wickham's unfortunate situation to Mrs Philips, the Lucases and the many other interested parties in Meryton. To use a hack-chaise would be demeaning, not only to her but to the whole family. Having proposed to abandon her at this distressing time I could not deprive her of a more valued comfort; Mrs Bennet has the coach. I have no wish to cause additional work by this unannounced arrival but I thought you might be glad to have another man in the house when you were concerned with the police or with Wickham's comfort. Elizabeth told me in her letter that the colonel is likely to be recalled soon to his military duties and young Alveston to London.'

Darcy said, 'They will depart after the inquest, which I heard on Sunday will be held tomorrow. Your presence here, sir, will be a comfort to the ladies and a reassurance to me. Colonel Fitzwilliam will have acquainted you with the facts of Wickham's arrest.'

'Succinctly, but no doubt accurately. He could have been giving me a military report. I almost felt obliged to throw a salute. I think that throwing a salute is the correct expression, I have no experience of military matters. Lydia's husband seems to have distinguished himself by this latest exploit in managing to combine entertainment for the masses with the maximum embarrassment for his family. The colonel told me you were at Lambton visiting the prisoner. How did you find him?'

'In good heart. The contrast between his present appearance and that in the day following the attack on Denny is remarkable, but then, of course, he was in liquor and deeply shocked. He has recovered both his courage and his looks. He is remarkably sanguine about the result of the inquest and Alveston thinks he has a right to be. The absence of any weapon certainly weighs in his favour.'

They both seated themselves. Darcy saw that Mr Bennet's eyes were straying towards the *Edinburgh Review* but he resisted the temptation to resume reading. He said, 'I wish Wickham would make up his mind how he wishes to be regarded by the world. At the time of his marriage he was an irresponsible but charming lieutenant in the militia, he made love to us all, simpering and smiling as if he had brought to his marriage three thousand a year and a desirable residence. Later, after taking his commission, he metamorphosed into a man of action and public hero, a change certainly for the better and one highly agreeable to Mrs Bennet. And now we are expected to see him as deep-dyed in villainy and at some risk, although I hope remote, of ending as a public spectacle. He has always sought notoriety, but hardly, I think, the final appearance now threatened. I cannot believe him guilty of murder. His misdemeanours, however inconvenient for his victims, have not, as far as I know, involved violence either to himself or others.'

Darcy said, 'We cannot look into another's mind, but I believe him to be innocent and I shall ensure that he has the best legal advice and representation.'

'That is generous of you, and I suspect – although I have no firm knowledge – that it is not the first act of generosity which my family owes to you.' Without waiting for a reply, he said quickly, 'I understand from Colonel Fitzwilliam that Elizabeth and Miss Darcy are engaged in some charitable enterprise, taking a basket of necessities to an afflicted family. When are they expected back?'

Darcy took out his watch. 'They should be on their way now. If you are inclined for exercise, sir, would you care to join me and we can walk towards the woodland to meet them.'

It was obvious that Mr Bennet, although known to be sedentary, was willing to relinquish the *Review* and the comfort of the library fire for the pleasure of surprising his daughter. It was then that Stoughton appeared, apologising that he had not been at the door when his master returned and quick to fetch the gentlemen's hats and greatcoats. Darcy was as eager as his companion to see the landaulet come into sight. He would have prevented the excursion had he thought it in any way dangerous, and he knew Alveston to be both trustworthy and resourceful, but since Denny's murder he had been consumed with an unfocused and perhaps irrational anxiety whenever his wife was not within his view, and it was with relief that he saw the landaulet slow and then come to a stop within fifty yards of Pemberley. He had not realised how profoundly he was glad to see Mr Bennet until he saw Elizabeth get hurriedly out and run towards her father and heard her delighted 'Oh Father, how good to see you!' as he enfolded her in his arms.

6

The inquest was held at the King's Arms in a large room built at the back of the inn some eight years previously to provide a venue for local functions, including the occasional dance dignified always as a ball. Initial enthusiasm and local pride had ensured its early success but in these difficult times of war and want there was neither money nor inclination for frivolity and the room, now used mostly for official meetings, was seldom filled to anything like capacity and had the slightly depressing and neglected atmosphere of any place once intended for communal activity. The innkeeper, Thomas Simpkins, and his wife Mary had made the usual preparations for an event which they knew would undoubtedly attract a large audience and subsequently profit for the bar. To the right of the door was a platform large enough to accommodate a small orchestra for dancing, and on this had been placed an impressive wooden armchair taken from the private bar, and four smaller chairs, two on each side, for justices of the peace or other local worthies who chose to attend. All other chairs available in the inn had been brought into use and the motley collection suggested that neighbours had also made their contribution. Latecomers were expected to stand.

Darcy was aware that the coroner took an elevated view of his status and responsibilities and would have been happy to see the owner of Pemberley arrive in state in his coach. Darcy would himself have preferred to have ridden, as the colonel and Alveston proposed to do, but compromised by using the chaise. When he entered the room he saw that it was already well filled and there was the usual anticipatory chat which to Darcy sounded more subdued than expectant. It fell silent on his appearance and there was much touching of forelocks and murmurings of greeting. No one, not even among his tenants, came forward to invite his notice as he knew they would normally have done, but he judged that this was less an affront than a feeling on their part that it was his privilege to make the first move.

He looked round to see if there was an empty seat somewhere at the back, preferably with others that he could reserve for the colonel and Alveston, but at that moment there was a commotion at the door and a large wicker bath chair with a small wheel at the front and two much larger at the back, was being manoeuvred with difficulty through the door. In it Dr Josiah Clitheroe sat in some state, his right leg supported by an obtruding plank, the foot turbaned in a bandage of white linen, intricately wound. Those sitting at the front quickly disappeared and Dr Clitheroe was pushed through, not without difficulty since the small wheel, snaking wildly, proved recalcitrant. The chairs each side of him were immediately vacated and on one he placed his tall hat and beckoned to Darcy to occupy the second. The circle of chairs round them was now empty and there was at least some chance of a private conversation.

Dr Clitheroe said, 'I don't think this will take all day. Jonah Makepeace will keep everything under control. It is a difficult business for you, Darcy, and of course for Mrs Darcy. I trust she is well.'

'She is, sir, I am happy to say.'

'Obviously you can take no part in the investigation of this crime but no doubt Hardcastle has kept you informed of developments.'

Darcy said, 'He has said as much as he thinks it prudent to reveal. His own position is one of some difficulty.'

'Well he need not be too cautious. He will in duty bound keep the High Constable informed and will also consult me as necessary, although I am doubtful that I can be of much assistance. He, Headborough Brownrigg and Petty Constable Mason seem to have things under control. I understand they have spoken to everyone at Pemberley and are satisfied that you all have alibis; hardly surprising – on the evening before Lady Anne's ball there are better things to do than trudge through the Pemberley woodland bent on murder. Lord Hartlep too, I am informed, has an alibi, so at least he and you can be relieved of that anxiety. As he is not yet a peer it would be unnecessary, in the event of his being charged, for him to be tried in the House of Lords, a colourful but expensive procedure. You will also be relieved to know that Hardcastle has traced Captain Denny's next of kin through the colonel of his regiment. It appears that he has only one living relative, an elderly aunt residing in Kensington whom he rarely visits but who supplies some regular financial support. She is nearly ninety and too old and frail to take a personal interest in events but has asked that Denny's body, now released by the coroner, should be sent to Kensington for burial.'

Darcy said, 'If Denny had died in the woodland by a known hand or by accident, it would be right for Mrs Darcy or myself to send her a letter of condolence, but in the circumstances that might be ill advised and even unwelcome. It is strange how even the most terrible and bizarre events have social implications and it is good of you to pass on this information, which will, I know, be a relief to Mrs Darcy. What about the tenants on the estate? I hardly like to question Hardcastle directly; have they all been cleared?'

'Yes, I gather so. The majority were at home and those who can never resist venturing forth even on a stormy night to fortify themselves at the local inn have produced a superfluity of witnesses, some of whom were sober when questioned and can be considered reliable. Apparently no one has seen or heard of any stranger in the neighbourhood. You know, of course, that when Hardcastle visited Pemberley two silly young girls employed as housemaids came forward with the story of seeing the ghost of Mrs Reilly wandering in the woodland. Appropriately, she chooses to manifest herself on the night of the full moon.'

Darcy said, 'That is an old superstition. Apparently, as we later heard, the girls were there as a result of a dare and Hardcastle did not take it seriously. I thought at the time that they were telling the truth and that there could have been a woman in the woodland that night.'

Clitheroe said, 'Headborough Brownrigg has spoken to them in Mrs Reynolds's presence. They were remarkably persistent in affirming that they had seen a dark woman in the woods two days before the murder, and that she made a threatening gesture before disappearing among the trees. They are adamant that this apparition was neither of the two women at Woodland Cottage, although it is difficult to see how they can assert this so confidently since the woman was in black and faded away as soon as one of the girls screamed. If there was a woman in the woodland it is hardly of much importance. This was not a woman's crime.'

Darcy asked, 'Is Wickham co-operating with Hardcastle and the police?'

'I gather that he is erratic; sometimes he will answer the questions reasonably and at other times begins protesting that he, an innocent man, is being badgered by the police. You know, of course, that thirty pounds in notes was found in his jacket pocket; he remains resolutely uncommunicative about how this sum came into his possession, except to say that it was a loan to enable him to discharge a debt of honour and that he has solemnly sworn he will reveal nothing more. Hardcastle, as might be expected, thought that he could have stolen the money from Captain Denny's body, but in that case it would hardly have been clean of any bloodstains, considering the blood on Wickham's hands; nor, I imagine, would it be folded so neatly in Wickham's notecase. I have been shown the notes and they are freshly minted. Apparently, Captain Denny told the landlord at the inn that he had no money.'

There was a moment in which neither spoke, then Clitheroe said, 'I can understand that Hardcastle feels some reluctance to share information with you, as much for your protection as his, but since he is satisfied that all the family, visitors and servants at Pemberley have satisfactory alibis, it seems unnecessarily discreet to keep you in ignorance of important developments. I have to tell you, therefore, that he thinks the police have found the weapon, a large smooth-edged stone slab which was discovered under some leaves about fifty yards from the glade where Denny's body was discovered.'

Darcy managed to conceal his surprise and, looking straight ahead, spoke in a low voice. 'What evidence is there that this was in fact the weapon?'

'Nothing definite since there were no incriminating marks either of blood or hair on the stone but that is hardly surprising. Later that night, as you will remember, the wind gave way to heavy rain and the ground and leaves must have been sodden, but I have seen the slab and it is certainly of the size and type to have produced the wound.'

Darcy kept his voice low. 'The woodland has been placed out of bounds to everyone on the Pemberley estate but I know that the police have been searching assiduously for the weapons. Do you know which officer made the discovery?'

'Not Brownrigg or Mason. They needed additional manpower so engaged petty constables from the next parish, including Joseph Joseph. Apparently his parents were so enamoured of their surname that they gave it to him also in baptism. He seems a conscientious and reliable man, but not, I surmise, particularly intelligent. He should have left the stone in place and called the other police as witnesses. Instead he carried it in triumph over to Headborough Brownrigg.'

'So there can be no proof that it was where he said it was found?'

'None, I imagine. There were, I am informed, a number of stones of different size at the site, all half-buried in the soil and under leaves, but no proof that this particular stone slab was among them. Someone years ago could have tipped out the contents of a barrow or accidently overturned it, probably as long ago as the building by your great-grandfather of Woodland Cottage when the building materials would have been carried through the woodland.'

'Will Hardcastle or the police be producing the stone slab this morning?'

'I understand not. Makepeace is adamant that, since it cannot be proved to be the weapon, it should not be part of the evidence. The jury will merely be informed that a stone has been found, and even this may not be mentioned; Makepeace is anxious that the inquest should not degenerate into a trial. He will make the duty of the jury plain, and it does not include usurping the powers of the assize court.'

'So you think they will commit him?'

'Undoubtedly, given what they will see as a confession. It would be remarkable if they did not. Ah, I see that Mr Wickham has arrived, looking surprisingly at ease for one in his invidious situation.'

Darcy had noticed that close to the platform there were three empty chairs guarded by petty constables, and Wickham, walking between two prison officers and with gyves on his wrists, was escorted to the middle chair and the two warders took their seats. His composure almost amounted to nonchalance as he surveyed his potential audience with little apparent interest, not fixing his eyes on any single face. The baggage containing his clothes had been delivered to the prison after Hardcastle had released it and he was wearing what was obviously his best jacket, while what could be seen of his linen bore witness to the care and skill of the Highmarten laundry maid. Smiling, he turned to one of the prison officers who responded with a nod. Glancing at him, Darcy could believe that he was seeing something of the handsome and charming young officer who had so enchanted the young ladies of Meryton.

Someone barked a command, the babble of conversation was hushed and the coroner, Jonah Makepeace, entered with Sir Selwyn Hardcastle and, after bowing to the jury, took his seat, inviting Sir Selwyn to take the one on his right. Makepeace was a slight man with a waxen face which in others might have been thought to denote illness. He had served now for twenty years as coroner and it was his pride that, at sixty, there had been no inquest, either in Lambton or at the King's Arms, at which he had not presided. He had a long thin nose and a curiously formed mouth with a very full upper lip, and his eyes, under eyebrows which were as thin as lines drawn by a pencil, were as keen as they had been at twenty. He was highly regarded as a lawyer with a successful practice in Lambton and beyond, and with increasing prosperity and with anxious private clients awaiting his counsel he was never indulgent to witnesses who could not give their evidence clearly and concisely. There was a wall-mounted clock at the far end of the room at which he now directed a long, intimidating stare.

At his entrance all present had risen to their feet, then seated themselves when he had taken the chair. Hardcastle was on his right and the two policemen in the front row beneath the dais. The jury, who had been chattering together in a group, took their chairs then immediately rose. As a magistrate Darcy had been present at a number of inquests and he saw that the usual group of local worthies had been collected for the jury: George Wainwright the apothecary, Frank Stirling who kept the general store in Lambton, Bill Mullins the blacksmith at Pemberley village and John Simpson the undertaker, dressed as usual in a suit of funeral black said to be inherited from his father. The rest were all farmers and most had arrived at the last minute looking flustered and over-heated. It was never a good time to leave their farms.

The coroner turned to the prison officer. 'You may remove the fetters from Mr Wickham. No prisoner has ever absconded from my jurisdiction.'

This was done in silence and Wickham, after massaging his wrists, stood quietly, his eyes occasionally scouring the room as if seeking a familiar face. The oath was administered, during which Makepeace regarded the jury with the sceptical intensity of a man contemplating the purchase of an obviously dubious horse before making his usual preliminary announcement. 'We have met before, gentlemen, and I think you know your duty. It is to listen to the evidence carefully and pronounce on the cause of death of Captain Martin Denny, whose body was found in the woodland of Pemberley on or about ten of the clock on the night of Friday 14th October. You are not here to take part in a criminal trial nor to teach the police how to conduct their inquiry. Of the options before you, you may well consider that neither death by accident nor misadventure is appropriate, and a man does not commit suicide by striking a vicious blow to the back of his neck. That may logically lead you to the conclusion that this death was homicide and you will then consider two possible verdicts. If there is no evidence to indicate who was responsible, you will return a verdict of wilful murder by a person or persons unknown. I have put the options before you but I must emphasise that the verdict on the cause of death is entirely for you. If the evidence leads you to the conclusion that you know the identity of the killer, you should then name him or her, and as with all felonies, the perpetrator will be held in custody and committed for trial at the next assize at Derby. If you have any questions to put to a witness, please raise your hand and speak clearly. We will now get started, and I propose to call first Nathaniel Piggott, landlord of the Green Man inn, who will give evidence about the beginning of this unfortunate gentleman's last journey.'

After that, to Darcy's relief, the inquest proceeded at considerable speed. Mr Piggott had obviously been advised that it was wise in court to say as little as possible and, having taken the oath, merely confirmed that Mr and Mrs Wickham and Captain Denny had arrived at the inn on Friday afternoon by hack-chaise shortly after four and had ordered the chaise which he kept at the inn to take the party to Pemberley that evening, where they would leave Mrs Wickham, and then to proceed with the two gentlemen to the King's Arms at Lambton. He had heard no quarrel between any of the party either during the afternoon or when they entered the chaise. Captain Denny had been quiet – he seemed a quiet gentleman – and Mr Wickham had been drinking steadily, but in his opinion could not be said to be drunk and incapable.

He was followed by George Pratt, the coachman, whose evidence was obviously keenly awaited and recounted at some length, always with reference to the behaviour of the horses, Betty and Millie. They had been working well until they entered the woodland, when they became so nervous that he had difficulty getting them to move. Horses always hated going into the woodland when there was a full moon because of the ghost of Mrs Reilly. The gentlemen might have been quarrelling inside the coach but he did not hear because he was controlling the horses. It was Captain Denny who had put his head out of the window and ordered him to stop, and who then left the chaise. He heard the captain say that Mr Wickham was now on his own and that he would have no part in it – or something like that.

And then Captain Denny ran into the woods and Mr Wickham after him. It was sometime after that they heard shots, he could not be sure when, and Mrs Wickham, who was in a proper state, screamed to him to drive on to Pemberley, which he did. The horses by then were in such terror that he could hardly hold them and he was afeared that the chaise would be overturned before he got to Pemberley. He then described what had happened on the return journey, including the stopping of the coach so that Colonel Fitzwilliam could check on the family in Woodland Cottage. He reckoned the colonel was away about ten minutes.

Darcy gained the impression that Pratt's story was already known to the jury, and probably to the whole of Lambton and Pemberley village and beyond, and his evidence was given with a background of sympathetic groans and sighs, particularly when he dwelt on the distress of Betty and Millie. There were no questions.

Colonel the Viscount Hartlep was then called and the oath administered with impressive authority. The colonel briefly but firmly recounted his part in the events of the evening, including the finding of the body, evidence which was later repeated, also without emotion or embellishment, by Alveston, and lastly by Darcy. All three were asked by the coroner whether Wickham had spoken, and his damaging admission was repeated.

Before anyone else had a chance to speak, Makepeace asked the vital question. 'Mr Wickham, you are resolutely maintaining your innocence of Captain Denny's murder. Why then, when found kneeling over his body, did you say more than once that you killed him and that his death was your fault?'

The answer came without hesitation. 'Because, sir, Captain Denny left the chaise out of disgust with my plan to leave Mrs

Wickham at Pemberley uninvited and unexpected. I also felt that, had I not been drunk, I might have prevented him leaving the chaise and charging into the woodland.'

Clitheroe whispered to Darcy, 'Totally unconvincing, the fool is overconfident. He will need to do better than this at the assizes if he is to save his neck. And how drunk was he?'

No questions were, however, asked, and it appeared that Makepeace was content to let the jury come to their opinion without his comments and was wary of encouraging the witnesses to speculate at length on what, precisely, Wickham had meant by his words. Headborough Brownrigg followed and had obvious pleasure in taking his time over his account of the police activity, including the search of the woodland. No information had been received of any strangers in the vicinity, the occupants of Pemberley House and of all the cottages on the estate had alibis and the investigation was still proceeding. Dr Belcher gave his evidence largely in medical terms, to which his audience listened with respect and the coroner with obvious irritation, before delivering his opinion in plain English that the cause of death was a heavy blow to the back of the head and that Captain Denny could not have survived such an injury for more than a few minutes, if that, although it was impossible to give an accurate estimate of the time of death. A slab of stone which could have been used by the assailant had been discovered and which, in his view, could in size and weight have produced such a wound if delivered by force, but there was no evidence to link this particular stone with the crime. Only one hand was raised before he left the witness box.

Makepeace said, 'Well Frank Stirling, we usually hear from you. What is it you want to ask?'

'Just this, sir. We understand that Mrs Wickham was to be left at Pemberley House to attend the ball the next night, but not with her husband. I take it that Mr Wickham would not be received as a guest by his brother and Mrs Darcy.'

'And what is the relevance of Mrs Darcy's guest list for Lady Anne's ball to the death of Captain Denny, or indeed to the evidence just given by Dr Belcher?'

'Only this, sir, that if relations was so bad between Mr Darcy and Mr Wickham, and it might be that Mr Wickham was not a proper person to be received at Pemberley, then that would have some bearing on his character, as I see it. It is a powerful strange thing for a man to forbid his house to a brother unless it might be that the brother was a violent man or given to quarrelling.'

Makepeace appeared briefly to consider his words before replying that the relationship between Mr Darcy and Mr Wickham, whether or not it was the usual one between brothers, could have no relevance to the death of Captain Denny. It was Captain Denny not Mr Darcy who had been murdered. 'Let us try to keep to the relevant facts. You should have raised the question when Mr Darcy was giving evidence if you thought it relevant. However, Mr Darcy can be recalled to the witness stand and asked whether Mr Wickham was in general a violent man.'

This was immediately done and in reply to Makepeace's question, Darcy, after being reminded that he was still on oath, said that, as far as he knew, Mr Wickham had never had that reputation and that he personally had never seen him violent. They had not met for some years but at that time Mr Wickham had been generally known as a peaceable and socially affable man.

'I take it that satisfies you, Mr Stirling. A peaceable and affable man. Are there any further questions? No? Then I suggest that the jury now consider their verdict.'

After some conferring they decided to do this in private and, being dissuaded from entering their choice of venue, the bar, disappeared into the yard and stood for ten minutes at a distance in a whispering group. On their return they were formally asked for their verdict. Frank Stirling then stood up and read from a small notebook, obviously determined to deliver the words with the necessary accuracy and confidence. 'We find, sir, that Captain Denny died from a blow to the back of the skull and that this fatal blow was delivered by George Wickham and, accordingly, Captain Denny was murdered by the said George Wickham.'

Makepeace said, 'And that is the verdict of you all?'

'It is, sir.'

Makepeace took off his spectacles after glaring at the clock and replaced them in their case. He said, 'After the necessary formalities Mr Wickham will be committed for trial at the next Derby assize. Thank you, gentlemen, you are dismissed.'

Darcy reflected that a process he had expected to be fraught with linguistic pitfalls and embarrassment had proved almost as much a matter of routine as the monthly parish meeting. There had been interest and commitment but no obvious excitement or moments of high drama, and he had to accept that Clitheroe was right, the outcome had been inevitable. Even if the jury had decided for murder by a person or persons unknown, Wickham would still be in custody as prime suspect and the police inquiries, centred on him, would have continued with almost certainly the same result.

Clitheroe's servant now reappeared to take control of the wheelchair. Consulting his watch, Clitheroe said, 'Three-quarters of an hour from start to finish. I imagine it went exactly as Makepeace planned, and the verdict could hardly be otherwise.'

Darcy said, 'And the verdict at the trial will be the same?'

'By no means, Darcy, by no means. I could mount a very effective defence. I suggest you find him a good lawyer and if possible get the case transferred to London. Henry Alveston will be able to advise you on the appropriate procedure, my information is probably out of date. That young man is something of a radical, I hear, despite being heir to an ancient barony, but he is undoubtedly a clever and successful lawyer, although it is time he found himself a wife and settled on his estate. The peace and security of England depends on gentlemen living in their houses as good landlords and masters, considerate to their servants, charitable to the poor, and ready, as justices of the peace, to take a full part in promoting peace and order in their communities. If the aristocrats of France had lived thus, there would never have been a revolution. But this case is interesting and the result will depend on the answers to two questions: why did Captain Denny run into the woodland, and what did George Wickham mean when he said it was all his fault? I shall watch further developments with interest. *Fiat justitia ruat caelum.* I wish you good day.'

And with this the wicker bath chair was manoeuvred, again with some difficulty, through the door and out of sight.

7

For Darcy and Elizabeth the winter of 1803–4 stretched like a black slough through which they must struggle, knowing that spring could only bring a new ordeal, and perhaps an even greater horror, the memory of which would blight the rest of their lives. But somehow those months had to be lived through without letting their anguish and distress overshadow the life of Pemberley or destroy the peace and confidence of those who depended on them. Happily this anxiety was to prove largely unfounded. Only Stoughton, Mrs Reynolds and the Bidwells had known Wickham as a boy, and the younger servants had little interest in anything that happened outside Pemberley. Darcy had given orders that the trial should not be spoken of and the approach of Christmas was a greater source of interest and excitement than was the eventual fate of a man of whom the majority of the servants had never even heard.

Mr Bennet was a quiet and reassuring presence in the house, rather like a benign, familiar ghost. He spent some of the time when Darcy was able to be free in conversation with him in the library; Darcy, himself clever, valued high intelligence in others. From time to time Mr Bennet would visit his eldest daughter at Highmarten to ensure that the volumes in Bingley's library were safe from the housemaids' overzealous attention and to make a list of books to be acquired. He stayed at Pemberley, however, for only three weeks. A letter was received from Mrs Bennet complaining that she could hear stealthy footsteps outside the house every night and was suffering from continual palpitations and fluttering of the heart. Mr Bennet must come home at once to provide protection. Why was he concerning himself with other people's murders when there was likely to be one at Longbourn if he did not immediately return?

His loss was felt by the whole household, and Mrs Reynolds

was overheard saying to Stoughton, 'It is strange, Mr Stoughton, that we should miss Mr Bennet so much now that he has left when we seldom set eyes on him when he was here.'

Darcy and Elizabeth both found solace in work, and there was much to be done. Darcy had in hand some plans already formed for the repair of certain cottages on the estate, and was busier than he had ever been engaged in parish matters. The war with France, declared the previous May, was already producing unrest and poverty; the cost of bread had risen and the harvest was poor. Darcy was much engaged in the relief of his tenants and there was a regular stream of children calling at the kitchen to collect large cans of nourishing soup, thick and meaty as a stew. There were few dinner parties and those only for close friends, but the Bingleys came regularly to give encouragement and help, and there were frequent letters from Mr and Mrs Gardiner.

After the inquest Wickham had been transferred to the new county prison at Derby where Mr Bingley continued to visit him and reported that he generally found him in good spirits. In the week before Christmas they finally heard that the application to transfer the trial to London had been agreed and that it would take place at the Old Bailey. Elizabeth was determined that she would be with her husband on the day of the trial, although there was no question of her being present in the courtroom. Mrs Gardiner wrote with a warm invitation that Darcy and Elizabeth should spend their time in London at Gracechurch Street, and this was gratefully accepted. Before the New Year George Wickham was transferred to Coldbath Prison in London and Mr Gardiner took over the duty of making regular visits and of paying the sums from Darcy which ensured Wickham's comfort and his status with the turnkeys and his fellow prisoners. Mr Gardiner reported that Wickham remained optimistic and that one of the chaplains at the prison, the Reverend Samuel Cornbinder, was seeing him regularly. Mr Cornbinder was known for his skill at chess, a game which he had taught Wickham and which was now occupying much of the prisoner's time. Mr Gardiner thought that the reverend gentleman was welcomed more as a chess opponent than as an admonisher to repentance but Wickham seemed genuinely to like him and chess, at which he was becoming interested to the point of obsession, was an effective antidote to his occasional outbursts of anger and despair.

Christmas came and the annual children's party, to which all the children on the estate were invited, was held as usual. Both Darcy and Elizabeth felt that the young should not be deprived of this yearly treat, especially in such difficult times. Gifts had to be chosen and delivered to all the tenants as well as the indoor and outdoor staff, a task which kept both Elizabeth and Mrs Reynolds occupied, while Elizabeth tried to keep her mind busy by a planned programme of reading, and by improving her performance at the pianoforte with Georgiana's help. With fewer social obligations Elizabeth had time to spend with her children or in visiting the poor, the elderly and the infirm, and both Darcy and Elizabeth were to find that, with days so filled with activity, even the most persistent nightmares could occasionally be kept at bay.

There was some good news. Louisa was much happier since Georgie had gone back to his mother and Mrs Bidwell was finding life easier now that the child's crying was not causing Will distress. After Christmas the weeks suddenly seem to pass far more quickly as the date set for the trial rapidly approached.

Book Five

The Trial

1

The trial was scheduled to take place on Thursday 22nd March at eleven o'clock at the Old Bailey. Alveston would be at his rooms near the Middle Temple and had suggested that he wait upon the Gardiners at Gracechurch Street the day before, together with Jeremiah Mickledore, Wickham's defence counsel, to explain the next day's procedure and to advise Darcy on the evidence he would give. Elizabeth was anxious to take two days on the road so they proposed to stop at Banbury overnight, arriving in the early afternoon of Wednesday 21st March. Usually when the Darcys left Pemberley a group of the more senior staff would be at the door to wave goodbye and express their good wishes, but this departure was very different and only Stoughton and Mrs Reynolds were there, their faces grave, to wish them a safe journey and assure the Darcys that life at Pemberley would continue as it should while they were away.

To open the Darcy townhouse entailed considerable domestic disruption, and when visiting London for a short period for shopping, to view a new play or exhibition, or because Darcy had business with his lawyer or tailor, they would stay with the Hursts when Miss Bingley would join the party. Mrs Hurst preferred any visitor to none and took pride in exhibiting the splendour of her house and the number of her carriages and servants, while Miss Bingley could artfully drop the names of her distinguished friends and pass on the current gossip about scandals in high places. Elizabeth would indulge the amusement she had always taken in the pretensions and absurdities of her neighbours, provided no compassion was called for, while Darcy took the view that if family amity required him to meet people with whom he had little in common, it were best done at their expense not his. But on this occasion no invitation from the Hursts or Miss Bingley had been received. There are some dramatic events, some notoriety, from which it is prudent to distance oneself and they did not expect to see either the Hursts or Miss Bingley during the trial. But the invitation from the Gardiners had been immediate and warm. Here in that comfortable, unostentatious family house they would find the reassurance and security of familiarity, quietly speaking voices that would make no demands, require no explanations, and a peace which might prepare them for the ordeal ahead.

But when they reached the centre of London and the trees and green expanse of Hyde Park were behind them, Darcy felt that he was entering an alien state, breathing a stale and sour-smelling air, and surrounded by a large and menacing population. Never before had he felt so much a stranger in London. It was hard to believe that the country was at war; everyone seemed in a hurry, all walked as if preoccupied with their own concerns, but from time to time he saw envious or admiring glances cast at the Darcy coach. Neither he nor Elizabeth were disposed to comment as they passed into the wider and better-known streets where the coachman edged his careful way between the bright and gaudy shopfronts lit by flares, and the chaises, carts, wagons and private coaches which made the roads almost impassable. But at last they turned into Gracechurch Street and even as they approached the Gardiners' house the door was opened and Mr and Mrs Gardiner ran out to welcome them and to direct the coachman to the stables at the rear. Minutes later the baggage was unloaded and Elizabeth and Darcy walked into the peace and security which would be their refuge until the trial was over.

2

Alveston and Jeremiah Mickledore came after dinner to give Darcy brief instructions and advice, and, having expressed their hopes and best wishes, left in less than an hour. It was to be one of the worst nights of Darcy's life. Mrs Gardiner, unfailingly hospitable, had ensured that there was everything in the bedroom necessary for Elizabeth's and his comfort, not only the two longed-for beds but the table between them with the carafe of water, the books and the tin of biscuits. Gracechurch Street could not be completely quiet but the rumble and creaks of carriages and the occasional calling voices, a contrast to the total silence of Pemberley, would not normally have been enough to keep him awake. He tried to put the anxiety about tomorrow's ordeal out of his mind, but it was too occupied with even more disturbing thoughts. It was as if an image of himself were standing by the bed regarding him with accusatory, almost contemptuous eyes, rehearsing arguments and indictments which he had thought he had long disciplined into quiescence but which this unwanted vision had now brought forward with renewed force and reason. It was his own doing and no one else's that had made Wickham part of his family with the right to call him brother. Tomorrow he would be compelled to give evidence which could help send his enemy to the gallows or set him free. Even if the verdict were 'not guilty', the trial would bring Wickham closer to Pemberley, and if he were convicted and hanged, Darcy himself would carry a weight of horror and guilt which he would bequeath to his sons and to future generations.

He could not regret his marriage; it would have been like regretting that he himself had ever been born. It had brought him happiness which he had never believed possible, a love of which the two handsome and healthy boys sleeping in the Pemberley nursery was a pledge and an assurance. But he had married in defiance of every principle which from childhood had ruled his life, every conviction of what was owed to the memory of his parents, to Pemberley and to the responsibility of class and wealth. However deep the attraction to Elizabeth he could have walked away, as he suspected Colonel Fitzwilliam had walked away. The price he had paid in bribing Wickham to marry Lydia had been the price of Elizabeth.

He remembered the meeting with Mrs Younge. The rooming house was in a respectable part of Marylebone, the woman herself the personification of a reputable and caring landlady. He remembered their conversation. 'I accept only young men from the most respectable families who have left home to take work in the capital and to begin their careers of independence. Their parents know that the boys will be well fed and cared for, and a judicious eye kept on their behaviour. I have had, for many years, a more than adequate income, and now that I have explained my situation we can do business. But first may I offer you some refreshment?'

He had refused it with no attempt at civility and she had said, 'I am a woman of business and I never find it harmed by a little adherence to the formal rules of courtesy, but by all means let us dispense with them. I know what you want, the whereabouts of George Wickham and Lydia Bennet. Perhaps you will begin negotiations by stating the maximum you are prepared to pay for this information which, I can assure you, you will be unable to obtain from anyone but myself.'

His offer had, of course, not been enough, but in the end he had settled and had left the house as if it had been infected with the plague. And that had been the first of the large sums which it had been necessary to provide before George Wickham could be persuaded to marry Lydia Bennet.

Elizabeth, exhausted after the journey, retired to bed immediately after dinner. She was asleep when he came into the bedroom to join her, and he stood for some minutes quietly at her bedside, regarding with love her beautiful and peaceful face; for a few more hours at least she would be free of worry. Once in bed, he turned restlessly in search of a comfort which even the softness of the pillows could not provide, but at last felt himself drifting into sleep.

3

Alveston had gone early from his lodgings to the Old Bailey and Darcy was on his own when, shortly before half-past ten, he passed through the imposing hall which led to the courtroom. His immediate impression was that he had entered a birdcage of chattering humanity set down in Bedlam. The case was not due to be called for thirty minutes but the first seats were already packed with a gossiping crowd of fashionably dressed women, while the back rows were rapidly filling. All London seemed to be here, the poor crammed together in noisy discomfort. Although Darcy had presented his summons to the official at the door, no one showed him where he should sit or, indeed, took the least notice of him. The day was warm for March and the air was becoming hot and humid, a sickening mixture of scent and unwashed bodies. Near the judge's seat a group of lawyers stood talking together as casually as if in a drawing room. He saw that Alveston was among them and, catching Darcy's eye, he came immediately over to greet him and to show him the seats reserved for witnesses.

He said, 'The prosecution are calling only the colonel and you to testify to the finding of Denny's body. There is the usual pressure of time and this judge gets impatient if the same evidence is repeated unnecessarily. I will stay close; we may get a chance to talk during the trial.'

And now the hubbub died, as if noise could be cut with a knife. The judge had entered the court. Judge Moberley carried his honours with confidence but he was not a handsome man and his small-featured face, in which only his dark eyes were prominent, was almost extinguished by a large full-bottomed wig, giving him, to Darcy, the look of an inquisitive animal peering out of its lair. Groups of conferring lawyers separated and reformed as they and the clerk took their appointed places and the jury filed into the seats reserved for them. Suddenly the prisoner, with a police officer on either side of him, was standing in the dock. Darcy was shocked by his appearance. He was thinner, despite the food that had been regularly provided from outside, and his taut face was pale, less, Darcy thought, from the ordeal of the moment than from the long months in prison. Gazing at him Darcy was hardly aware of the preliminaries of the trial, the reading of the indictment in a clear voice, the selection of the jury and the administration of the oath. In the dock Wickham stood stiffly upright and, when asked how he pleaded to the charge, spoke the words 'Not guilty' in a firm voice. And even now, in fetters and pale, he was still handsome.

And then Darcy saw a familiar face. She must have bribed someone to keep her seat in the front row among the female spectators, and she had taken it quickly and silently. She now sat there, hardly moving, among the flutter of fans and the rise and fall of the fashionable headdresses. At first glance he saw only her profile, but then she turned her face and, although their eyes met without acknowledgement, he had little doubt that she was Mrs Younge; even that initial glimpse at her profile had been enough.

He was determined not to catch her eye but peering from time to time across the courtroom he could see that she was expensively dressed, with an elegance and simplicity at odds with the gaudy ostentation around her. Her hat, trimmed with purple and green ribbons, framed a face which seemed as youthful as when they had first met. So had she been dressed when he and Colonel Fitzwilliam had invited her to Pemberley to be interviewed for the post of Georgiana's companion, presenting before the two young men the picture of a well-spoken, reliable and well-born gentlewoman, deeply sympathetic to the young and aware of the responsibilities which would fall upon her. It had been different, but not so very different, when he had run her to ground in that respectable house in Marylebone. He wondered what power held her and Wickham together, strong enough to make her part of the audience of women who found entertainment in seeing a human being fight for his life.

4

Now, as the counsel for the prosecution was due to deliver his opening speech, Darcy saw that there was a change in Mrs Younge. She still sat upright, but was staring at the dock with an intensity and concentration of gaze, as if by silence and a meeting of their eyes, she could convey to the prisoner a message, perhaps of hope or of endurance. It lasted for a few seconds only, but it was a moment of time in which, for Darcy, the panoply of the court, the scarlet of the judge, the bright colours of the spectators, no longer existed and he was aware only of those two people and their absorption in each other.

'Gentlemen of the jury, the case before you is singularly distressing for us all, the brutal murder by a former army officer of his friend and erstwhile comrade. Although much of what happened will remain a mystery since the only person who can testify is the victim, the salient facts are plain and beyond conjecture, and will be put before you in evidence. The defendant, accompanied by Captain Denny and by Mrs Wickham, left the Green Man in Pemberley village, Derbyshire, at about nine o'clock on Friday 14th October to drive through the woodland path to Pemberley House where Mrs Wickham would spend the night and some indefinite period while her husband and Captain Denny were driven to the King's Arms at Lambton. You will hear evidence of a quarrel between the defendant and Captain Denny while they were at the inn, and of the words spoken by Captain Denny as he left the chaise and ran into the woodland. Wickham then followed him. Gunshots were heard, and when Wickham did not return a distraught Mrs Wickham was driven to Pemberley and a rescue expedition was mounted. You will hear evidence of the finding of the body by two witnesses who vividly recall this significant moment. The defendant, bloodstained, was kneeling beside his victim and twice in the clearest words confessed that he had murdered his friend. Among much that is perhaps unclear and mysterious about this case, that fact stands at its heart; there was a confession and it was repeated and, I suggest to you, was clearly understood. The rescue party did not pursue any other potential murderer, Mr Darcy was careful to keep Wickham under guard and immediately to call the magistrate, and despite an extensive and most conscientious search there is no evidence that any stranger was in the woodland that night. The people in Woodland Cottage, an elderly woman, her daughter and a man on the point of death, could not possibly have wielded the kind of heavy stone slab which is thought to have made the fatal wound. You will hear evidence that stones of this type can be found in the woodland, and Wickham, who was familiar with these woods from childhood, would have known where to look.

'This was a particularly vicious crime. A medical man will confirm that the blow to the forehead merely disabled the victim and was followed by a lethal attack, made when Captain Denny, blinded by blood, was attempting to escape. It is difficult to imagine a more cowardly and atrocious murder. Captain Denny cannot be brought back to life but he can have justice and I am confident that you, gentlemen of the jury, will have no hesitation in delivering a verdict of guilty. I shall now call the first of the witnesses for the prosecution.'

5

There was a bellow – 'Nathaniel Piggott' – and almost immediately the innkeeper of the Green Man took his place in the witness box and, holding the Testament aloft with some ceremony, pronounced the oath. He was carefully dressed in his Sunday suit in which he habitually appeared in church, but it was worn with the confidence of a man who feels at ease in his clothes, and he stood for a minute deliberately surveying the jury with the appraising look of one faced with unpromising candidates for a vacancy at the inn. Lastly he fixed his gaze on the prosecuting counsel as if confident to deal with anything that Sir

Simon Cartwright could throw at him. As requested, he gave his name and address: 'Nathaniel Piggott, innkeeper of the Green Man, Pemberley village, Derbyshire.'

His evidence was straightforward and took very little time. In reply to the counsel for the prosecution's questions, he told the court that George Wickham, Mrs Wickham and the late Captain Denny had arrived at the inn on Friday 14th October last by hack-chaise. Mr Wickham had ordered some food and wine and a chaise to take Mrs Wickham to Pemberley later that night. Mrs Wickham had told him when he was showing the party into the bar that she was going to spend the night at Pemberley to attend Lady Anne's ball the next day. 'She seemed right excited.' In reply to further questions, he said that Mr Wickham had told him that after calling at Pemberley he required the chaise to continue to the King's Arms at Lambton where he and Captain Denny would stay the night and, next morning, would be taking the London stage.

Mr Cartwright said, 'So there was no suggestion at that time that Mr Wickham should also stay at Pemberley?'

'Not that I heard, sir, it wasn't to be expected. Mr Wickham, as some of us know, is never received at Pemberley.'

There was a murmur in the court. Instinctively Darcy stiffened in his seat. They were venturing earlier than he had expected on dangerous ground. He kept his eyes on the prosecuting counsel but knew that those of the jury were fixed on him. But after a pause Simon Cartwright changed tack. 'Did Mr Wickham pay you for the food and wine, and for the hire of the chaise?'

'He did, sir, while they were in the bar. Captain Denny said to

Mr Wickham, "It's your show, you will have to pay. I have only enough to last me in London." '

'Did you see them leave in the chaise?'

'I did sir. It was about eight forty-five of the clock.'

'And when they set out, did you notice what humour they were in, the relationship between the two gentlemen?'

'I can't say that I noticed, sir. I was giving instructions to Pratt, the coachman. The lady was warning him to be careful putting her trunk into the chaise because it held her dress for the ball. I could see that Captain Denny was very quiet like he was when they was drinking in the inn.'

'Had either gentleman been drinking heavily?'

'Captain Denny only drank ale and no more than a pint. Mr Wickham had a couple of pints and then went on to whisky. By the time they set off he was red of face and none too steady on his feet, but he spoke clear enough, although loud, and got into the chaise without help.'

'Did you hear any conversation between them when they got into the chaise?'

'No sir, none as far as I remember. It was Mrs Piggott that heard the gentlemen quarrelling, as she told me, but that was earlier.'

'We shall be hearing from your wife. That is all I have to ask you, Mr Piggott, you may stand down unless Mr Mickledore has anything to ask you.'

Nathaniel Piggott turned to face the defence counsel with confidence, as Mr Mickledore rose. 'So neither gentleman was in a mood for conversation. Did you get the impression that they were content to be travelling together?'

'They never said they weren't, sir, and there was no argument-ing between them when they set out on the journey.'

'No sign of a quarrel?'

'None sir, that I noticed.'

There was no further cross-examination and Nathaniel Pig-gott left with the satisfied air of a man who is confident he has made a favourable impression.

Martha Piggott was then called and there was a small commo-tion in the far corner of the courtroom where a stout little woman disentangled herself from a crowd of supporters murmuring en-couragement and strutted her way to the stand. She was wearing a hat heavily trimmed with crisp pink ribbons which looked new, bought no doubt as a tribute to the importance of the occasion. It would have been more impressive had it not sat atop a bush of bright yellow hair and from time to time she touched it as if unsure whether it was still on her head. She fixed her eyes on the judge un-til the prosecuting counsel rose to address her, after bestowing on him an encouraging nod. She gave her name and address and took the oath in a clear voice and confirmed her husband's account of the arrival of the Wickhams and Captain Denny.

Darcy whispered to Alveston, 'She was not called to give evi-dence at the inquest. Is this something new?'

Alveston said, 'Yes, and it could be dangerous.'

Simon Cartwright asked, 'What was the general atmosphere in the inn between Mr and Mrs Wickham and Captain Denny? Would you say, Mrs Piggott, that this was a happy party?'

'I would not, sir. Mrs Wickham was in good spirits and laugh-ing. She is a free-speaking and pleasant lady, sir, and it was she who told me and Mr Piggott when we were in the bar that she was going to Lady Anne's ball and it was going to be a great lark because Mr and Mrs Darcy never even knew she was arriving and wouldn't be able to turn her away, not on a stormy night. Captain Denny was very quiet, but Mr Wickham was restless as if he wanted to be off.'

'And did you hear any quarrel, any words between them?'

Mr Mickledore was immediately on his feet to complain that the prosecution was leading the witness and the question was re-phrased. 'Did you hear any of the conversation between Captain Denny and Mr Wickham?'

Mrs Piggott quickly grasped what was wanted. 'Not while they were in the inn, sir, but after they had had their cold meat and drink Mrs Wickham asked for her trunk to be carried upstairs so that she could change her clothes before they set off for Pemberley. Not into her ball dress, she said, but something nice to arrive in. I sent Sally, my general maid, to help. After that I had occasion to go to the privy in the yard and when I opened the door – quietly like – to come out, I saw Mr Wickham and Captain Denny talking together.'

'Did you hear what they were saying?'

'I did sir. They were no more than a few feet away. I could see that Captain Denny's face was very white. He said, "It's been deceit from start to finish. You are utterly selfish. You have no idea how a woman feels." '

'You are certain about those words?'

Mrs Piggott hesitated. 'Well, sir, it could be that I got the order a bit mixed, but Captain Denny definitely said that Mr Wickham was selfish and didn't understand how women feel and that there had been deceit from start to finish.'

'And what happened then?'

'So, not wanting the gentlemen to see me leaving the privy, I closed the door until it was almost shut and kept watch through the gap until they went off.'

'And you are willing to swear that you heard those words?'

'Well, I am sworn, sir. I am giving evidence under oath.'

'So you are, Mrs Piggott, and I am glad you recognise the importance of that fact. What happened after you went back inside the inn?'

'The gentlemen came in soon after, sir, and Mr Wickham went up to the room I set aside for his wife. Mrs Wickham must have changed by then as he came down and said that the trunk had been re-strapped and was ready to be lifted into the chaise. The gentlemen put on their coats and hats and Mr Piggott called for Pratt to bring round the chaise.'

'What condition was Mr Wickham in then?'

There was a silence as if Mrs Piggott was uncertain of his meaning. He said a little impatiently, 'Was he sober or were there signs of drink in him?'

'I knew, of course, that he had been drinking, sir, and he looked as though he'd had more than enough. I thought his voice was slurred when he said goodbye. But he was still on his feet and got into the chaise without any help, and they were off.'

There was a silence. Prosecuting counsel studied his papers then said, 'Thank you, Mrs Piggott. Will you stay where you are for the moment, please?'

Jeremiah Mickledore rose to his feet. 'So, if there was this unfriendly talk between Mr Wickham and Captain Denny – let us call it a disagreement – it did not end in shouting or violence.

Did either of the gentlemen touch the other during the conversation you overheard in the yard?'

'No sir, not that I saw. Mr Wickham would be foolish to challenge Captain Denny to a fight. Captain Denny was taller than him by a couple of inches, I would say, and much the heavier man.'

'And did you see when they entered the coach whether either of them was armed?'

'Captain Denny was, sir.'

'So as far as you can say, Captain Denny, whatever his opinion of his companion's behaviour, could travel in the chaise with him without anxiety of any physical assault? He was the taller and heavier man and was armed. As far as you can remember, was that the situation?'

'I suppose it was, sir.'

'It is not what you suppose, Mrs Piggott. Did you see both gentlemen enter the chaise and Captain Denny, the taller of the two, with a firearm?'

'I did, sir.'

'So even if they had quarrelled, the fact that they were travelling together would have occasioned you no anxiety?'

'They had Mrs Wickham with them, sir. They wouldn't be starting a fight with a lady in the chaise. And Pratt is no fool. As like as not, if he had trouble, he would have whipped up the horses and come back to the inn.'

Jeremiah Mickledore rose with one last question. 'Why did you not give this evidence at the inquest, Mrs Piggott? Did you not realise its importance?'

I wasn't asked, sir. Mr Brownrigg came to the inn after the inquest and asked me then.'

'But surely you realised before Mr Brownrigg's talk with you that you had evidence which should be given at the inquest?'

'I thought, sir, that if they needed me to speak, they would have come and asked, and I wasn't going to have the whole of Lambton sniggering about me. It's a proper disgrace if a lady can't go to the privy without people asking in public about it. Put yourself in my position, Mr Mickledore.'

There was a small burst of quickly suppressed laughter. Mr Mickledore said he had no further questions and Mrs Piggott, clamping her hat more firmly on her head, stomped back to her seat in barely concealed satisfaction amid the congratulatory whispers of her supporters.

6

Simon Cartwright's management of the prosecution was now apparent and Darcy could appreciate its cleverness. The story would be told scene by scene, imposing both coherence and credibility on the narrative and producing in court as it unfolded something of the excited expectancy of a theatre. But what else, thought Darcy, but public entertainment was a trial for murder? The actors clothed for the parts assigned for them to play, the buzz of happy comment and anticipation before the character assigned to the next scene appeared, and then the moment of high drama when the chief actor entered the dock from which no escape was possible before facing the final scene: life or death. This was English law in practice, a law respected throughout Europe, and how else could such a decision be made, in all its terrible finality, with more justice? He had been subpoenaed to be present but, gazing round at the crowded courtroom, the bright colours and waving headdresses of the fashionable and the drabness of the poor, he felt ashamed to be one of them.

George Pratt was now called to give evidence. In the dock he looked older than Darcy had remembered. His clothes were clean but not new and his hair had obviously been recently washed and now stood up stiffly in pale spikes round his face, giving him the petrified look of a clown. He took the oath slowly, his eyes fixed on the paper as if the language were foreign to him, then gazed at Cartwright with something of the entreaty of a delinquent child.

The prosecution counsel had obviously decided that kindness would here be the most effective tool. He said, 'You have taken the oath, Mr Pratt, which means that you have sworn to tell the truth to this court both in reply to my questions and in anything you may say. I want you now to tell the court in your own words what happened on the night of Friday 14th October.'

'I was to take the two gentlemen, Mr Wickham and Captain Denny, and Mrs Wickham to Pemberley in Mr Piggott's chaise and then leave the lady at the house and go on to take the gentlemen to the King's Arms at Lambton. But Mr Wickham and the captain never got to Pemberley, sir.'

'Yes, we know that. How were you to get to Pemberley? By which gate to the property?'

'By the north-west gate, sir, and then through the woodland path.'

'And what happened? Was there any difficulty in getting through the gate?'

'No sir. Jimmy Morgan came to open it. He said no one was to pass through but he knew me and when I said I was to take Mrs Wickham to the ball he let us through. We was about half a mile or so down the path when one of the gentlemen – I think it was Captain Denny – knocked for me to stop, so I did. He got out of the chaise and made for the woodland. He shouted out that he wasn't going to have any more of it and that Mr Wickham was on his own.'

'Were those his exact words?'

Pratt paused. 'I can't be sure, sir. He may have said, "You are on your own now, Wickham. I'll have no more of it." '

'What happened next?'

'Mr Wickham got out of the chaise after him and called out that he was a fool and was to come back, but he didn't. So Mr Wickham followed him into the woodland. The lady got out of the chaise calling out for him to come back and not leave her, but he took no notice. When he disappeared into the woodland she got back into the chaise and began crying something pitiful. So there we stood, sir.'

'You didn't think yourself of going into the woods?'

'No sir. I couldn't leave Mrs Wickham, nor the horses, so I stayed. But after a time there were shots and Mrs Wickham began screaming and said to me that we would all be killed and that I was to drive to Pemberley as fast as I could.'

'Were the shots close?'

'I couldn't say, sir. But they was close enough to be heard plain.'

'And how many did you hear?'

'It could have been three or four. I can't be certain, sir.'

'So what happened then?'

'I whipped the horses into a gallop and we made our way to Pemberley, the lady screaming all the while. When we pulled up at the door she almost fell out of the chaise. Mr Darcy and some of the company were at the door. I can't rightly remember who but I think there was two gentlemen and Mr Darcy, and two ladies. The ladies helped Mrs Wickham into the house and Mr Darcy said I was to stay with the horses as he would want me to take him and some of the gentlemen back to the place where Captain Denny and Mr Wickham ran into the woods. So I waited, sir. And then the gentleman I now know is Colonel Fitzwilliam rode up the main drive very fast and joined the party. When someone had fetched a stretcher and some blankets and lanterns, the three gentlemen – Mr Darcy, the colonel and another man I didn't know – got into the coach and we went back into the woodland. Then the gentlemen got out and walked in front until we came to the path to Woodland Cottage and the colonel went to see that the family was safe and to tell them to lock their door. Then the three gentlemen walked on further until I saw where I thought Captain Denny and Mr Wickham had disappeared. Then Mr Darcy told me to wait there and they went into the wood.'

'That must have been an anxious time for you, Pratt.'

'It was, sir. I was sore afraid having no one with me and no weapon, and the wait seemed very long, sir. But then I heard them coming. They brought Captain Denny's body on a stretcher and Mr Wickham, who was unsteady on his feet, was helped into the chaise by the third gentleman. I turned the horses and we went slowly back to Pemberley with the colonel and Mr

Darcy walking behind carrying the stretcher and the third gentleman in the chaise with Mr Wickham. After that it's a muddle in my mind, sir. I know that the stretcher was carried away and Mr Wickham, who was shouting very loud and hardly standing on his feet, was taken into the house and I was asked to wait. At last the colonel came out and told me I should take the chaise on to the King's Arms and tell them that the gentlemen wouldn't be coming but to get away quick before they could ask any questions, and when I got back to the Green Man I was to say nothing to anyone about what happened otherwise I would be in trouble with the police. He said they would be coming to talk to me next day. I was worried in case Mr Piggott asked me questions when I got back, but he and Mrs Piggott had gone to bed. By then the wind had dropped and there was a driving rain. Mr Piggott opened his bedroom window and called out if everything was all right and if the lady had been left at Pemberley. I said that she had and he told me to see to the horses and get to bed. I was dead tired, sir, and next morning was asleep when the police arrived just after seven o'clock. I told them what had happened, same as I'm now telling you, sir, as far as I can remember and with nothing held back.'

Cartwright said, 'Thank you, Mr Pratt. That has been very clear.'

Mr Mickledore got to his feet immediately. He said, 'I have one or two questions to put to you, Mr Pratt. When you were called by Mr Piggott to drive the party to Pemberley, was that the first time you had seen the two gentlemen together?'

'It was, sir.'

'And how did their relationship appear to you?'

231

'Captain Denny was very quiet and Mr Wickham had obviously taken drink, but there was no quarrel or argumenting.'

'Was there reluctance on the part of Captain Denny to enter the chaise?'

'There was none, sir. He got in happy enough.'

'Did you hear any talk between them on the journey before the chaise was stopped?'

'No sir. It would not have been easy with the wind and the rough ground unless they had been shouting really loud.'

'And there was no shouting?'

'No sir, not that I could hear.'

'So the party, as far as you know, set off on good terms with each other and you had no reason to expect any problems?'

'No sir, I had not.'

'I understand that at the inquest you told the jury of the trouble you had in controlling the horses when they were in the woodland. It must have been a difficult journey for them.'

'Oh it were, sir. As soon as they entered the woodland they were right nervy, neighing and stamping.'

'They must have been difficult for you to control.'

'They was, sir, proper difficult. There's no horse likes going into the woodland in a full moon – no human neither.'

'Can you then be absolutely certain of the words Captain Denny spoke when he left the chaise?'

'Well sir, I did hear him say that he wouldn't go along with Mr Wickham any more and that Mr Wickham was now on his own, or something like that.'

'Something like that. Thank you Mr Pratt, that is all I have to ask.'

Pratt was released, considerably happier than when he had entered the dock. Alveston whispered to Darcy, 'No problem there. Mickledore has been able to cast doubt on Pratt's evidence. And now, Mr Darcy, it will be either you or the colonel.'

7

When his name was called, Darcy responded with a physical shock of surprise although he had known that his turn could not be long in coming. He made his way across the courtroom between what seemed rows of hostile eyes and tried to govern his mind. It was important that he keep both his composure and his temper. He was resolute that he would not meet the gaze of Wickham, Mrs Younge or the jury member who, every time his own eyes scoured the jury box, gazed at him with an unfriendly intensity. He would keep his own eyes on the prosecuting counsel when answering questions, with occasional glances either at the jury or the judge who sat immobile as a Buddha, his plump little hands folded on the desk, his eyes half-closed.

The first part of the interrogation was straightforward. In answer to questions he described the evening of the dinner party, who was present, the departure of Colonel Fitzwilliam and Miss Darcy, the arrival of the chaise with a distraught Mrs Wickham, and finally the decision to take the chaise back to the woodland path to discover what had happened and whether Mr Wickham and Captain Denny were in need of any assistance.

Simon Cartwright said, 'You were anticipating danger, perhaps tragedy?'

'By no means, sir. I had hoped, even expected, that the worst that had befallen the gentlemen would be that one had met with some minor but disabling accident in the woodland and that we should meet both Mr Wickham and Captain Denny making their slow way to Pemberley or back to the inn, one helping the other. It was the report by Mrs Wickham and subsequently confirmed by Pratt that there had been shooting which convinced me that it would be prudent to mount a rescue expedition. Colonel Fitzwilliam had returned in time to be part of the expedition and was armed.'

'The Viscount Hartlep will, of course, be giving his evidence later. Shall we continue? Will you please describe now the course of the journey into the woodland and the events leading to the discovery of Captain Denny's body.'

Darcy had had no need to rehearse this but had nevertheless spent some time selecting the actual words which he should use and the tone in which he would speak. He had told himself that he would be in a court of law, not recounting a story to a circle of friends. To dwell on the silence, unbroken except for their trudging feet and the creaking of the wheels, would be a dangerous indulgence; all that would be needed were facts, baldly and convincingly stated. He recounted now that the colonel had briefly left the party in order to warn Mrs Bidwell, her dying son and her daughter that there might be trouble and to instruct them to keep the door locked.

'Did Viscount Hartlep, in going to the cottage, inform you that that was his intention?'

'He did.'

'And for how long was he absent?'

'No more, I think, than fifteen or twenty minutes, but it seemed somewhat longer at the time.'

'And you then proceeded?'

'We did. Pratt was able with some certainty to indicate where Captain Denny had entered the woodland and my companions and I then did the same and attempted to discover the path that either one or both might have taken. After some minutes, perhaps as many as ten, we came upon the glade and found the body of Captain Denny with Mr Wickham bending over him and weeping. It was immediately apparent to me that Captain Denny was dead.'

'In what condition was Mr Wickham?'

'He was greatly distressed and I think from his speech and the smell on his breath that he had been drinking and probably heavily. Captain Denny's face was smeared with blood and there was blood on Mr Wickham's hands and face – probably, I thought, from touching his friend.'

'Did Mr Wickham speak?'

'He did.'

'And what did he say?'

So here at last was the dreaded question and for a few appalling seconds his mind was a blank. Then he looked at Cartwright and said, 'I think, sir, that I can recall the words with accuracy if not the precise order. As I remember, he said, "I have killed him. It is my fault. He was my friend, my only friend, and I have killed him." Then he repeated, "It is my fault."

'And what at the time did you think his words meant?'

Darcy was aware that the whole court was waiting for his answer. He shifted his gaze to the judge who now slowly opened his eyes and looked at him. 'Answer the question, Mr Darcy.'

It was only then that he realised with horror that he must have remained silent for seconds. He said, speaking to the judge, 'I was looking at a man in the greatest distress, kneeling over the body of his friend. I took Mr Wickham to mean that, had there not been some disagreement between them which caused Captain Denny to leave the chaise and run into the woods, his friend would not have been murdered. That was my immediate impression. I saw no weapons. I knew that Captain Denny was the heavier man and had been armed. It would have been the height of folly for Mr Wickham to follow his friend into the woodland without a light or a weapon with the intention of doing him to death. He could not even be sure that he would find Captain Denny in the dense bushes and trees with only moonlight to guide him. It seemed to me that this could not have been murder on Mr Wickham's part, either on impulse or premeditated.'

'Did you see or hear any person other than Lord Hartlep or Mr Alveston either when you were entering the woodland or at the scene of the murder?'

'No sir.'

'So you are saying on oath that you found the body of Captain Denny with a bloodstained Mr Wickham leaning over him and saying, not once but twice, that he was responsible for his friend's murder.'

And now the silence was longer. Darcy felt himself for the first time like a baited animal. At last he said, 'Those are the facts, sir. You asked me what I thought at the time those facts meant. I told you what I believed then and I believe now, that Mr Wickham was not confessing to murder but speaking what was in fact the truth, that had Captain Denny not left the chaise and entered the woodland he would not have met his murderer.'

But Cartwright had not finished. Changing his tack, he said, 'Had Mrs Wickham arrived at Pemberley House unexpectedly and without notice, would she have been admitted?'

'She would.'

'She, of course, is the sister of Mrs Darcy. Would Mr Wickham also be welcomed if he arrived in the same circumstances? Were he and Mrs Wickham invited to the ball?'

'That, sir, is a hypothetical question. There was no reason why they should be. We had not been in touch for some time and I did not know their address.'

'I suggest, Mr Darcy, that your answer is somewhat disingenuous. Would you have invited them had you known their address?'

It was then that Jeremiah Mickledore got up and addressed the judge. 'My lord, what relevance can Mrs Darcy's invitation list have to the murder of Captain Denny? We are surely all entitled to invite whom we wish into our homes, whether or not they are relations, without the necessity of explaining our reasons to a court of law in circumstances in which the invitation can have no possible relevance.'

The judge stirred himself, his voice unexpectedly firm. 'You have a reason for this line of questioning, Mr Cartwright?'

'I have, my lord: to throw some light on the possible relationship of Mr Darcy to his brother and therefore indirectly to give the jury some insight into Mr Wickham's character.'

The judge said, 'I doubt whether the absence of an invitation to a ball can give much insight into the man's essential nature.'

And now Jeremiah Mickledore rose. He turned to Darcy. 'You know something of Mr Wickham's conduct in the campaign in Ireland in August 1798?'

'I do, sir. I know he was decorated as a brave soldier and was wounded.'

'As far as you know, has he ever been imprisoned for a felony or, indeed, been in trouble with the police?'

'As far as I know he has not, sir.'

'And as he is married to Mrs Darcy's sister you would presumably know these things?'

'If they were serious or frequent I think I would.'

'Wickham has been described as being under the influence of drink. What steps were taken to control him when you arrived at Pemberley?'

'He was put to bed and Dr McFee was sent for, to help both Mrs Wickham and her husband.'

'But he was not locked up or guarded?'

'His door was not locked but there were two watchers.'

'Was that necessary since you believed him innocent?'

'He was drunk, sir, and could not be left to roam round the house, particularly as I have children. I was also uneasy about his physical condition. I am a magistrate, sir, and I knew that everyone who was concerned in this matter should be available for questioning when Sir Selwyn Hardcastle arrived.'

Mr Mickledore sat and Simon Cartwright resumed his examination. 'One last question, Mr Darcy. The search party consisted of three men, one of whom was armed. You also had Captain Denny's gun, which might have been usable. You had no reason to suspect that Captain Denny had been killed some time before you found him. The murderer might well have been close and hiding. Why did you not mount a search?'

'It seemed to me that the first action necessary was to return as quickly as possible to Pemberley with the body of Captain Denny. It would have been almost impossible to detect someone hiding in the dense woodland and I assumed that the killer had made his escape.'

'Some people might think that your explanation is a little un-convincing. Surely the first reaction to finding a murdered man is to attempt to arrest his killer.'

'In the circumstances, sir, it did not occur to me.'

'No indeed, Mr Darcy. I can understand that it did not occur to you. You were already in the presence of the man who, despite your protestations, you believed to have been the murderer. Why indeed should it occur to you to go searching for anyone else?'

Before Darcy could respond, Simon Cartwright consolidated his triumph by speaking his final words. 'I must congratulate you, Mr Darcy, on the acuity of your mind, which appears to have a remarkable facility for coherent thought even at mo-ments when most of us would be shocked into a less cerebral response. It was, after all, a scene of unprecedented horror. I asked what was your reaction to the words of the defend-ant when you and your companions discovered him kneeling with bloodstained hands over the body of his murdered friend. You were able to deduce without a second's delay that there must have been some disagreement which occasioned Captain Denny to leave the vehicle and escape into the woodland, re-call to mind the difference in height and weight of the two men and its significance, and note that there were no weapons at the scene which could have been used to inflict either wound. It is certain that the murderer had not been so helpful as to leave them conveniently at hand. Thank you. You may now step down.'

Somewhat to Darcy's surprise, Mr Mickledore did not again rise to cross-examine and he wondered whether this was because there was nothing the defence counsel could do to mitigate the damage he had done. He had no memory of returning to his seat. Once there he was filled with a despairing anger against himself. He cursed himself for an incompetent fool. Had not Alveston instructed him carefully how he should respond to examination? 'Pause to think before you reply, but not so long that you appear calculating, answer the questions simply and accurately, say no more than has been asked, never embroider; if Cartwright wants more he can ask for it. Disaster in the witness box is usually the result of saying too much not too little.' He had said too much, and disastrously. No doubt the colonel would be wiser, but the damage had been done.

He felt Alveston's hand on his shoulder. Darcy said miserably, 'I have done the defence harm, have I not?'

'By no means. You, a prosecution witness, have made a very effective speech for the defence which Mickledore cannot do. The jury have heard it, which is the important thing, and Cartwright cannot wipe it from their minds.'

Witness after witness for the prosecution gave their evidence. Dr Belcher testified to the cause of death and the constables described in some detail their fruitless attempts to identify the actual weapons, although slabs of stone were discovered under the leaves in the woodland; despite exhaustive searches and in-

240

quiries, no evidence had been discovered of a deserter or other person in the woodland at the relevant time.

And now the call for Colonel the Viscount Hartlep to take the witness stand was followed by an immediate silence, and Darcy wondered why Simon Cartwright had decided that this important witness should be the last to give evidence for the prosecution. Was it perhaps that he hoped the impression made would be more lasting and effective if it were the final evidence the jury heard? The colonel was in uniform and Darcy remembered that he had an appointment later that day at the War Office. He walked to the witness stand as normally as if taking a morning stroll, gave a short bow to the judge, took the oath and stood waiting for Cartwright to begin the examination with, Darcy thought, the slightly impatient air of a professional soldier with a war to be won, who was prepared to show proper respect for the court while distancing himself from its presumptions. He stood in the dignity of his uniform, an officer who had been described as among the most eligible and gallant in the British Army. There was a whispering, quickly hushed, and Darcy saw that the rows of fashionable women were leaning intently forward – rather, Darcy thought, like beribboned lapdogs quivering at the smell of a tasty morsel.

The colonel was questioned minutely about every detail of events, from the time he returned from his evening ride to join the expedition until the arrival of Sir Selwyn Hardcastle to take over the investigation. He had ridden earlier to the King's Arms inn at Lambton where he had been engaged in a private conversation with a visitor during the time Captain Denny was murdered. Cartwright then asked about the thirty pounds found in

Wickham's possession and the colonel said calmly that the money was given by him to enable the defendant to settle a debt of honour and that it was only the necessity to speak in court that had persuaded him to break a solemn promise between them that the transaction would be private. He did not intend to divulge the name of the intended benefactor, but it was not Captain Denny, nor had the money anything to do with Captain Denny's death.

Here Mr Mickledore briefly rose. 'Can you give the court an assurance, Colonel, that this loan or gift was not intended for Captain Denny or is in any way connected with the murder?'

'I can.'

And then Cartwright returned again to the meaning of Wickham's words spoken over his friend's body. What was the witness's impression of their meaning?

The colonel paused for a few seconds before speaking. 'I am not competent, sir, to look into another man's mind, but I agree with the opinion given by Mr Darcy. For me it was a question of instinct rather than of immediate and detailed consideration of the evidence. I do not despise instinct; it has saved my life on several occasions, and instinct is, of course, based on an appreciation of all the salient facts, which is not necessarily wrong because one is not conscious of it.'

'And the decision not to leave Captain Denny's body and immediately search for his murderer, was that ever considered? I take it that had it been, you, as a distinguished commander, would have taken the lead.'

'It was not considered by me, sir. I do not advance into hostile and unknown territory with an inadequate force, leaving my rear unprotected.'

There were no further questions and it was apparent that the evidence for the prosecution was now complete. Alveston whispered, 'Mickledore has been brilliant. The colonel has validated your evidence and doubt has been cast on the reliability of Pratt's. I am beginning to feel hopeful, but we still have Wickham's speech in his own defence and the judge's charge to the jury.

8

It was evident from occasional snores that the heat of the courtroom had induced sleep, but now there was nudging and whispering and a stir of interest as Wickham at last stood up in the dock to speak. His voice was clear and steady but without emotion, almost, Darcy thought, as if he were reading, not speaking, the words which could save his life.

'I am here charged with the murder of Captain Martin Denny and to that charge I have pleaded not guilty. I am indeed totally innocent of his murder and here I stand having put myself on my country. I served with Captain Denny in the militia over six years ago when he became a close friend as well as a comrade-in-arms. That friendship continued and his life was as dear to me as my own. I would defend to the death any attack on him and would have done so had I been present when the cowardly attack which caused his death was carried out. It has been said in evidence that there was a quarrel between us when we were at the inn before setting out on that fatal journey. It was no more than a disagreement between friends, but it was my fault. Captain Denny, who was a man of honour and had deep human sympathies, thought that I had been wrong to resign my commission without having a sound profession and a settled home for my wife. In addition he thought that my plan to leave Mrs Wickham at Pemberley to spend the night there and to attend the ball the next day was both inconsiderate and would be inconvenient for Mrs Darcy. I believe that it was his increasing impatience with my conduct that made my company intolerable to him, and that it was this reason that led him to stop the chaise and run into the woodland. I went after him to urge him to return. It was a stormy night and the woodland is in places impenetrable and could be dangerous. I do not deny that I spoke the words attributed to me, but I meant that my friend's death was my responsibility since it was our disagreement that had driven him into the woodland. I had been drinking heavily but, among much that I cannot recall, I remember clearly the abhorrence when I found him and saw his blood-smeared face. His eyes confirmed what I already knew, that he was dead. The shock, horror and pity of this unmanned me, but not so much that I neglected to take what action I could to apprehend his murderer. I took his pistol and fired several shots at what I thought was a fleeing figure and I pursued him deeper into the woodland. By then the drink I had imbibed had taken effect and I remember nothing more until I was kneeling by my friend and cradling his head. It was then that the rescue party arrived.

'Gentlemen of the jury, the case made out against me will not stand. If I struck my friend on the forehead and, more viciously, on the back of the neck, where are the weapons? After a most thorough search, neither weapon has been produced in court. If it is alleged that I followed my friend with murderous intent, how could I hope to prevail over a man taller and stronger than myself and armed with a weapon? And why should I do so? No motive has been alleged. The fact that there was no trace of a stranger lurking in the woodland cannot be taken to mean that no such man existed; he would hardly have waited at the scene of his crime. I can only swear, remembering that I am on oath, that I had no part in the murder of Captain Martin Denny and I put myself upon my country with confidence.'

There was a silence, then Alveston whispered to Darcy, 'It was not good.'

In a low voice Darcy said, 'How not good? I thought he had done enough. The main arguments were clearly made, no evidence produced of a serious quarrel, the absence of weapons, the irrationality of pursuing his friend with murderous intent, the lack of a motive. What was wrong?'

'It is difficult to explain but I have listened to so many speeches by the defendant and I fear this one may not succeed. For all the care in its construction it lacked that vital spark that comes from the assurance of innocence. The delivery, the lack of passion, the carefulness of it; he may have pleaded not guilty but he does not feel innocent. That is something that juries detect, don't ask me how. He may not be guilty to this murder but he is burdened by guilt.'

'So are we all sometimes; is not to feel guilt part of being human? Surely the jury must have been left with a reasonable doubt. That speech would have been enough for me.'

Alveston said, 'I pray it will be enough for the jury but I am not sanguine.'

'But if he was drunk?'

'He certainly claimed to be drunk at the time of the murder, but he was not too drunk to get into the chaise unaided at the inn. This question has not been pursued during the evidence, but in my view it is open to question how drunk he was at the time.'

During the speech Darcy had tried to focus on Wickham but now he couldn't resist glancing at Mrs Younge. There was no risk that their eyes would meet. Hers were fixed on Wickham, and sometimes he saw her lips moving as if she were listening to a recital of something she herself had written, or perhaps was silently praying. When he looked again at the dock Wickham was staring ahead; he turned towards the judge as Mr Justice Moberley began his charge to the jury.

9

Mr Justice Moberley had made no notes and now he leaned a little towards the jury as if the matter could have no concern to the rest of the court, and the beautiful voice which at first attracted Darcy was clear enough to be heard by everyone present. He went through the evidence succinctly but carefully, as if time had no importance. The speech ended with words that Darcy felt gave credence to the defence, and his spirits rose.

'Gentlemen of the jury, you have listened with patience and obviously close attention to the evidence given in this long trial, and it is now for you to consider the evidence and give your verdict. The accused was previously a professional soldier and has a record of conspicuous gallantry for which he has been awarded a medal, but this should not affect your decision, which should be based on the evidence which has been presented to you. Your responsibility is a heavy one but I know you will discharge your duty without fear or favour and in accordance with the law.

'The central mystery, if I can call it that, surrounding this case is why Captain Denny ran into the woodland when he could have safely and comfortably remained in the chaise; it is inconceivable that an attack would have been made on him in the presence of Mrs Wickham. The accused has given his explanation of why Captain Denny so unexpectedly stopped the chaise, and you will wonder whether you find this explanation satisfactory. Captain Denny is not alive to explain his action, and no evidence other than Mr Wickham's is available to elucidate the matter. Like much of this case, it has been supposition, and it is on sworn evidence, not on unsubstantiated opinions, that your verdict can safely be given: the circumstances under which members of the rescue party found Captain Denny's body and heard the words attributed to the accused. You have heard his explanation of their meaning and it is for you to decide whether or not you believe him. If you are certain beyond reasonable doubt that George Wickham is guilty of killing Captain Denny then your verdict will be one of guilty; if you have not that certainty the accused is entitled to be acquitted. I now leave you to your deliberations. If it is your wish to retire to consider your verdict, a room has been made available.

10

By the end of the trial Darcy felt as drained as if he himself had stood in the dock. He longed to ask Alveston for reassurance but pride and the knowledge that to badger him would be as irritating as it was futile kept him silent. There was nothing anyone could do now but hope and wait. The jury had chosen to retire to consider their verdict and in their absence the courtroom had again become as noisy as an immense parrots' cage as the audience discussed the evidence and made bets on the verdict. They had not long to wait After less than ten minutes the jury returned. He heard the loud authoritative voice of the clerk asking the jury, 'Who is your foreman?'

'I am, sir.' The tall dark man who had gazed at him so frequently during the trial and who was their obvious leader stood up.

'Have you arrived at a verdict?'

'We have.'

'Do you find the prisoner guilty or not guilty?'

The answer came without hesitation. 'Guilty.'

'And is that the verdict of you all?'

'It is.'

Darcy knew that he must have gasped. He felt Alveston's hand on his arm, steadying him. And now the court was full of voices – a mixture of groans, cries and protests which grew until, as if by some group compulsion, the noise died and all eyes were turned on Wickham. Darcy, caught up in the outcry, closed his eyes, then forced himself to open them and fixed them on the dock. Wickham's face had the stiffness and sickly pallor of a mask of death. He opened his mouth as if to speak, but no words came. He was clutching the edge of the dock and seemed for a moment to stagger, and Darcy felt his own muscles tightening as he watched while Wickham recovered himself and with obvious effort found the strength to stand stiffly upright. Staring at the judge he found a voice, at first cracked, but then loud and clear. 'I am innocent of this charge, my lord. I swear before God I am not guilty.' Wide-eyed, he gazed desperately round the courtroom as if seeking some friendly face, some voice which would affirm his innocence. Then he said again with more force, 'I am not guilty, my lord, not guilty.'

Darcy turned his eyes to where Mrs Younge had been sitting, soberly dressed and silent among the silks and muslins and the fluttering fans. She had gone. She must have moved as soon as the verdict was delivered. He knew that he had to find her, needed to know what part she had played in the tragedy of Denny's death, to find out why she had been there, her eyes locked on Wickham's as if some power, some courage were passing between them.

He broke free of Alveston and pushed his way to the door. It was being firmly held fast against a crowd outside who, from the increasing clamour, were apparently determined on admission. And now the bawling in the courtroom was rising again, becoming less pitiable and more angry. He thought he heard the judge threatening to call the police or army to expel the troublemakers, and someone close to him was saying, 'Where is the black cap? Why in God's name cannot they lay their hand on the damn thing and put it on his head?' There was a shout as if in triumph and, glancing round, he saw a black square being flourished above the crowd by a young man hoisted on his comrade's shoulders and knew with a shudder that this was the black cap.

He fought his way to keep his place at the door and, as the

crowd outside edged it open, managed to struggle through and elbowed his way to the road. Here too there was a commotion, the same cacophony of groans, cries and a chorus of shouting voices, more, he thought, in pity than in anger. A heavy coach had been drawn up, the crowd attempting to pull the driver down from his seat. He was shouting, 'It weren't my fault. You saw the lady. She flung herself right under the wheels!'

And there she lay, squashed under the heavy wheels as if she were a stray animal, her blood flowing in a red stream to pool under the horses' feet. Smelling it, they neighed and reared and the coachman had difficulty in controlling them. Darcy took one look and, turning away, vomited violently into the gutter. The sour stink seemed to poison the air. He heard a voice cry, 'Where's the death wagon? Why don't they take her away? It's not decent leaving her there.'

The passenger in the coach made to get out but, seeing the sight of the crowd, shrank back inside and pulled down the blind, obviously waiting for the constables to arrive and restore order. The crowd seemed to grow, among them children gazing incomprehensibly and women with babes in arms who, frightened by the noise, began wailing. There was nothing he could do. He needed now to return to the courtroom and find the colonel and Alveston in the hope that they might offer reassurance; in his heart he knew that there could be none.

And then he saw the hat trimmed with purple and green ribbons. It must have fallen from her head and bowled along the pavement and had now stopped at his feet. He gazed at it as if in a trance. Nearby a staggering woman, yelling baby under one arm, gin bottle in her hand, pushed forward, stooped and clasped it crookedly on her head. Grinning at Darcy, she said, 'No use to her any more, is it?' and was gone.

11

The competing attraction of a dead body had diverted some of the men by the door and he was able to fight his way to the front and was borne in with the last six to gain admission. Someone called in a stentorian voice, 'A confession! They have brought a confession!' and immediately the court was in an uproar. It seemed for a moment that Wickham would be dragged from the dock, but he was immediately surrounded by officers of the court and, after standing upright for a few dazed moments, sat down with his hands over his face. The noise increased. And it was then that he saw Dr McFee and the Reverend Percival Oliphant surrounded by police constables. Amazed by their presence, he watched while two heavy chairs were being dragged forward and they both slumped into them as if exhausted. He tried to push his way through to them but the dense crowd was a heaving impenetrable mass.

People had left their seats and were now approaching the judge. He raised his gavel and used it vigorously, and at last was able to make his voice heard and the clamour died. 'Officer, lock the doors. If there is any more disturbance I shall order the court to be cleared. The document which I have perused purports to be a signed confession witnessed by you two gentlemen, Dr Andrew McFee and the Reverend Percival Oliphant. Gentlemen, are these your signatures?'

Dr McFee and Mr Oliphant spoke together. 'They are, my lord.'

'And is this document you have handed in the handwriting of the person who has signed it above your signatures?'

Dr McFee answered. 'Part of it is, my lord. William Bidwell was at the end of his life and wrote his confession propped up in bed but I trust the writing, although shaky, is sufficiently clear to read. The last paragraph, as indicated by the change of hand-writing, was written by me to dictation by William Bidwell. He was then able to speak but not to write, except to sign his name.'

'Then I shall ask counsel for the defence to read it. Afterwards I shall consider how best to proceed. If anyone interrupts he will be made to leave.'

Jeremiah Mickledore took the document and, adjusting his spectacles, scanned it and then began to read in a loud and clear voice. The whole courtroom was silent.

I, William John Bidwell, make this confession of my free will as a true account of what occurred in Pemberley woodland on the night of 14th October last. I do so in the sure knowledge that I am close to death. I was in bed upstairs in the front room but the cottage was otherwise empty except for my nephew, George, in his crib. My father was working at Pemberley. There had been a loud squawking from the chicken pen and my mother and my sister, Louisa, fearing that a fox was about, went to investigate. My mother did not like me to get out of bed since I had so little strength, but I was desirous to look out of the window. I was able to support myself on the bed until I got to the window. The wind was blowing strongly and there was moonlight, and as I looked out I saw an officer in uniform come out of the woodland and stand looking at the cottage. I drew back behind the curtains so that I could observe without being seen.

My sister Louisa had told me that an officer of the militia, stationed at Lambton the previous year, had attempted an assault on her virtue, and I knew instinctively that this was the man and that he had returned to take her away. Why else would he be at the cottage on such a night? My father was not there to protect her and it had always grieved me that I was a hopeless invalid, unable to work while he worked so hard, and too weak to protect my family. I put on my slippers and managed to make my way downstairs. Taking the poker from the hearth, I went out of the door.

The officer began to come towards me and held out his hand as if he came in peace, but I knew otherwise. I staggered towards him and waited until he approached me, then with all my strength I swung the poker so that the knob hit his forehead. It was not a strong blow but it broke the skin and the wound began to bleed. He tried to wipe his eyes but I knew he could not see. He stumbled back into the trees and I felt a great surge of triumph which gave me strength. He was out of sight when I heard a great noise like the crash of a falling tree. I went into the woodland supporting myself by clutching at the trunks of the trees and saw by the moonlight that he had tripped on the curb of the dog's grave and fallen backwards, striking his head on the headstone. He was a heavy man and the sound of his falling had been great, but I did not know that the fall had been fatal. I felt nothing but pride that I had saved my darling sister, and as I watched he rolled from the stone on to his knees and began crawling away. I knew that he was trying to escape from me, although I had not the strength to *attempt to follow him. I rejoiced that he would not return.*

I have no memory of getting back to the cottage, only of wiping the knob of the poker on my handkerchief which I flung into the fire. My next memory is of my mother helping me up the stairs and into bed, and upbraiding me for my folly in leaving it. I said nothing of my encounter with the officer. I was told next morning that Colonel Fitzwilliam had called later at the cottage to tell her of the two missing gentlemen, but I knew nothing of that.

I kept silent about what had happened even after the announcement that Mr Wickham was committed for trial. I still held my peace for the months while he was in prison in London, but then I knew that I must make this confession so that, if he was found guilty, the truth would be known. I decided to confide in the Reverend Oliphant and he told me the trial of Mr Wickham was to take place in a few days' time and that I must write this confession at once to get it to the court before the trial began. Mr Oliphant sent at once for Dr McFee and I have tonight confessed all to them both and have asked Dr McFee how long he expects me to live. He said he could not be sure, but I am unlikely to survive for more than a week. He too has urged me to make this confession and sign it, and so I do. I have written nothing but the truth knowing that I shall soon be answering for all my sins before the throne of God, and in the hope of His mercy.

Dr McFee said, 'That document took him more than two hours to write sustained by a draught administered by me. The Reverend Oliphant and I had no doubt that he knew his death was imminent and that what he wrote was the truth before God.'

There was silence, and then the courtroom was again full of

clamour, people were on their feet yelling and stamping and a few men began again a chant which was taken up by the crowd and became a concerted shout of 'Let him go! Let him go! Free him!' There were now so many constables and court officials surrounding the dock that Wickham was hardly visible.

Again the stentorian voice called for silence. The judge addressed Dr McFee. 'Can you explain, sir, why you brought this important document to court at the last moment of the trial when sentence was about to be pronounced? Such an unnecessarily dramatic arrival is an insult to me and to this court and I demand an explanation.'

Dr McFee said. 'We apologise, my lord, most sincerely. The paper is dated three days ago when the Reverend Oliphant and I heard the confession. It was then late at night and we set out early the next morning for London in my carriage. We stopped only to take brief refreshment and to water the horses. As you will see, my lord, the Reverend Oliphant, who is now over sixty, is completely exhausted.'

The judge said pettishly, 'There are too many of these trials when vital evidence has been delayed. However, it appears that you are not at fault and I accept your apologies. I shall now confer with my advisers on the next step to be taken. The defendant will be taken back to the prison in which he has been confined while the question of a royal pardon, which is, of course, in the gift of the Crown, is considered by the Home Secretary, the Lord Chancellor, the Lord Chief Justice and other senior law officers. I myself, as trial judge, will have a voice. In the light of this document I shall not pronounce sentence but the verdict of the jury must stand. You may rest assured, gentlemen, that courts in

England do not sentence to death a man who has been proved to be innocent.'

There was some muttering but the courtroom began to clear. Wickham was standing, his fingers clasping the edge of the dock, his knuckles white. He was still and pale as if in a trance. One of the constables loosened his fingers one by one, as if he had been a child. A path opened between the dock and a side door and Wickham, without a backward glance, was helped in silence back to his cell.

Book Six

Gracechurch Street

1

It had been agreed that Alveston should be present with Mr Mickledore in case he was required at the formalities for the pardon, and he remained behind in the courtroom when Darcy, longing for Elizabeth, made his solitary way back to Gracechurch Street. It was four o'clock before Alveston returned alone to say that it was expected that all procedures for a royal pardon would be completed by late afternoon the day after next and that he would then be able to escort Wickham from the prison and bring him to Gracechurch Street. It was hoped that this could be done with a minimum of public notice. A privately hired chaise would be ready at the back door of Coldbath Prison and another one as decoy at the front. It was an advantage that they had managed to keep secret the fact that Darcy and Elizabeth were staying with the Gardiners and not, as was confidently expected, in a fashionable inn, and if the actual time of Wickham's discharge could be kept from public knowledge, there was every chance he would arrive at Gracechurch Street undetected. At present he had been returned to Coldbath Prison but the chaplain there, the Reverend Cornbinder, who had befriended him, had arranged for him to lodge with him and his wife on the evening of his release, and Wickham had expressed his wish to go straight there after he had told his story to Darcy and the colonel, refusing Mr and Mrs Gardiner's invitation that he should remain at Gracechurch Street. The Gardiners had felt it right that the invitation should be issued, but there was general relief that it had been declined.

Darcy said, 'It seems like a miracle that Wickham's life was saved, but surely the verdict was perverse and irrational and he should never have been found guilty.'

Alveston said, 'I cannot agree. What they saw as a confession was repeated twice and was believed, and there was too much left unexplained. Would Captain Denny have left the chaise and rushed into a dense and unfamiliar woodland on such a night merely to avoid the embarrassment of being present when Mrs Wickham arrived at Pemberley? She is, after all, Mrs Darcy's sister. How much more likely that Wickham had involved himself in some illegal enterprise in London and, since Denny was no longer a willing accomplice, had to silence him before they left Derbyshire?

'But there was something else which could have contributed to the verdict and which I only learnt in speaking to one of the jury while I was still in court. Apparently the jury foreman has a widowed niece of whom he is very fond, whose husband took part in the Irish rebellion and was killed. Ever since he has nourished an implacable hatred against the army. If this had been disclosed, undoubtedly Wickham could have challenged that particular member of the jury, but the names were not the same and the secret was unlikely to have been discovered. Wickham made it plain before the trial that he had no intention of challenging the selection of jurymen, as was his right, or of providing three witnesses to speak to his character. He seems, indeed, to have been optimistic but generally fatalistic from the start. He had been a distinguished officer, wounded when serving his country, and now was content to be judged by his country. If his sworn word was not enough, where could he look for justice?'

Darcy said, 'But I have one concern on which I would like your opinion. Do you really believe, Alveston, that a dying man could have inflicted that first blow?'

Alveston said, 'I do. I have known cases in the course of my profession in which seriously ill people have found astonishing strength when exertion is called for. The blow was light, and after that he did not totter far into the wood, but I cannot believe he regained his bed without help. I think it likely that he left the cottage door ajar and that his mother went out, found him and helped him home and to bed. It was probably she who wiped the knob of the poker and burnt the handkerchief. But I feel, as I am sure do you, that justice would not be served by making these suspicions public. There is no proof and never can be, and I think we must rejoice in the royal pardon which will be given, and that Wickham, who has shown remarkable courage throughout his ordeal, is free to begin what we hope will be a more successful life.'

An early dinner was eaten almost in silence. Darcy had expected that the relief of Wickham's escape from a public hanging would be so great a benison that other anxieties would shrink in proportion but, with the greatest anxiety relieved, smaller ones pressed in on his mind. What story would they hear when Wickham arrived? How were he and Elizabeth to avoid the horror of public curiosity while they remained with the Gardiners, and what part, if any, had the colonel played in the whole mysterious business? He was filled with a desperate need to be back at Pemberley and burdened by a premonition, which he accepted was unreasonable, that all might not be well there. He knew that, like him, Elizabeth had rarely slept soundly for months and that much of this weight of impending disaster, which she shared, was the result of an overwhelming weariness of mind and body. The rest of the party seemed infected by the same guilt that they should be unable suitably to celebrate a seemingly miraculous deliverance. Mr and Mrs Gardiner were solicitous, but the delicious dinner which Mrs Gardiner had ordered was left virtually untouched and her guests sought their beds soon after the last course had been served.

At breakfast it was apparent that the spirits of the party had lightened; the first night without dreadful imaginings had produced rest and sound sleep and they now seemed more ready to cope with whatever the day might bring. The colonel was still in London and now arrived at Gracechurch Street. After paying his compliments to Mr and Mrs Gardiner, he said, 'I have matters to tell you, Darcy, which relate to my part in this whole affair which I can now safely disclose and which you have a right to hear before Wickham arrives. I prefer to speak to you alone but you will, of course, wish to pass on what I tell you to Mrs Darcy.'

He explained to Mrs Gardiner his purpose in coming and she suggested that he and Darcy should make use of her sitting room, which she had thoughtfully made available as the most comfortable and restful room in which a meeting, which would invariably be difficult for all parties, could take place next day when Wickham arrived with Alveston.

They seated themselves and the colonel leaned forward in his chair. He said, 'I feel it important that I should speak first so that you can judge Wickham's story against my own. Neither of us has cause to be proud of ourselves but throughout I have acted for the best and have paid him the compliment of believing that he felt the same. I shall not attempt to excuse my conduct in this matter, only to explain it, and will try to do so briefly.

'It was in late November 1802 that I received a letter from Wickham delivered at my London house where I was then in residence. It said briefly that he was in trouble and would be grateful if I would consent to see him in the hope that I could offer advice and some help. I had no desire to be involved but I was under an obligation to him of a kind that I could not ignore. During the Irish rebellion he saved the life of a young captain under my command who was my godson and who was lying gravely wounded. Rupert did not long survive his injuries but the rescue gave his mother – and indeed me – the opportunity to say goodbye to him and to ensure that he died in comfort. It was not a service any honourable man could forget and when I read his letter I agreed to see him.

'The story was not uncommon and is simply told. As you know, his wife, but not he, was regularly received at Highmarten and on those occasions he would stay at a local inn or rooming house as cheaply as possible and occupy himself as best he could until Mrs Wickham chose to rejoin him. Their life at the time was peripatetic and unsuccessful. After leaving the army – in my view a most unwise decision – he moved from job to job, never staying in one place for long. His last employment had been with a baronet, Sir Walter Elliot. Wickham was not explicit in revealing the reason why he left, but he said enough to make it plain that the baronet was too susceptible to Mrs Wickham's charms for Miss Elliot's comfort and that Wickham himself was not above making advances to the lady. I tell you this to let you know the kind of life they were living. He was now looking for a new appointment; in the mean time, Mrs Wickham had sought a comfortable but temporary home with Mrs Bingley at Highmarten and Wickham was left to his own devices.

'You may remember that the summer of 1802 was particularly warm and beautiful and so, to save money, he spent some of the time sleeping outdoors; to a soldier this was no hardship. He had always been fond of the woodland of Pemberley and walked many miles from an inn near Lambton to spend the days and some of the nights there sleeping under the trees. It was there he met Louisa Bidwell. She too was bored and lonely. She had finished working at Pemberley in order to help her mother nurse her sick brother, and her fiancé, extremely busy with his duties, came to see her only rarely. She and Wickham met by chance in the woodland. Wickham could never resist a pretty woman and the result was perhaps almost inevitable given his character and her vulnerability. They began meeting often, and she told him as soon as she suspected that she was carrying a child. Wickham acted at first with more generosity and sympathy for her than those who know him might expect; he seems, indeed, to have been genuinely fond of her, perhaps even a little in love. Whatever his motives or emotions, together they concocted a plan. She would write to her married sister living in Birmingham, go there as soon as there was a risk of her condition becoming obvious, and there give birth to her baby which would be passed off as her sister's child. Wickham hoped that Mr and Mrs Simpkins would accept responsibility for bringing up the child as their own, but recognised that they would need money. It was for that reason that he came to me and, indeed, I do not know where else he could have looked for help.

'Although I was not deceived in his character, I have never felt as bitter towards him as have you, Darcy, and I was prepared to help. There was also a stronger motive, the desire to save Pemberley from any hint of scandal. Given Wickham's marriage to Miss Lydia Bennet, this child, although illegitimate, would have been nephew or niece both to you and Mrs Darcy and to the Bingleys. The arrangement was that I would lend him thirty pounds without interest to be paid back in instalments when convenient. I was not under any illusion that the money would be repaid, but it was a sum I could afford, and I would have paid more than thirty pounds to ensure that a bastard child of George Wickham was not living on the Pemberley estate and playing in the Pemberley woods.'

Darcy said, 'This was a generosity amounting to eccentricity, and knowing the man as you did, some would say stupidity. I must credit you with having a more personal interest than the wish for the woods of Pemberley not to be so polluted.'

'If I had, it was not to my discredit. I admit that at the time I harboured wishes, indeed expectations, which were not unreasonable but which I now accept will never be fulfilled, but I think, given the hope which I then entertained and knowing what I did, you too would have devised some plan for saving your house and yourself from embarrassment and ignominy.'

Without waiting for any response, he went on. 'The plan was

relatively straightforward. After the birth, Louisa would return with the child to Woodland Cottage on the pretence that her parents and brother would wish to see this new grandchild. It was, of course, important to Wickham that he could see that there was a living and healthy child. The money would then be handed over on the morning of Lady Anne's ball when Louisa and Wickham could be confident that everyone concerned with Pemberley would be busy. A chaise would be waiting on the woodland path. Louisa would then return the boy to her sister and Michael Simpkins. The only people in Woodland Cottage at the time would be Mrs Bidwell and Will, and they were the only people to be aware of this scheme. It was not a secret a girl could expect to keep from her mother or, indeed, from a brother to whom she was close and who was never out of the cottage; all three were adamant that Bidwell should never know. Louisa had told her mother and Will that the father was one of the officers of the militia, who had left Lambton the previous summer. She had at that time no idea that her lover was Wickham.'

At this point he paused and took a glass of wine, drinking it slowly. Neither spoke and they waited in silence. It was at least two minutes before he began again.

'So, as far as Wickham and I knew, all had been arranged satis-factorily. The child would be accepted and loved by his aunt and uncle and would never know his true parentage, Louisa would make the suitable marriage previously planned, and so the mat-ter rested.

'Wickham is not a man who likes to act alone when an ally or companion can be found, a lack of prudence which probably ac-counts for his folly in taking Miss Lydia Bennet with him when he escaped from his creditors and obligations in Brighton. Now he confided in his friend Denny, and more fully in Mrs Younge, who seems to have been a controlling presence in his life since his youth. I believe it is regular stipends from her which have largely supported him and Mrs Wickham while he has been un-employed. He asked Mrs Younge to visit the woodland in secret so that she could report on the child's progress, and this Mrs Younge did, passing herself off as a visitor to the district and meeting Louisa by arrangement as she was carrying the baby in the woodland. The result was, however, in one respect unfortu-nate; Mrs Younge took an immediate fancy to the boy and was determined that she and not the Simpkinses should adopt him. Then what seemed a disaster turned to her advantage: Michael Simpkins wrote that he was not prepared to bring up another man's child. Apparently relations had not been good between the sisters during Louisa's confinement and Mrs Simpkins already had three children and would no doubt have more. The Simp-kinses would look after the child for another three weeks to enable Louisa to find a home for him, but no longer. This news was confided by Louisa to Wickham, and by him to Mrs Younge. Louisa was, of course, desperate. She had to find a home for the child and soon Mrs Younge's offer was seen as a solution to all their problems.

'Wickham had informed Mrs Younge of my interest in this matter and of the thirty pounds I had promised and had, indeed, passed to Wickham. She knew that I was due to be at Pemberley for Lady Anne's ball since this was my invariable practice when on leave from the army, and Wickham had always made it his business to know what was happening at Pemberley, largely through the reports of his wife who was a frequent visitor to Highmarten. Mrs Younge wrote to me at my London address, saying that she was interested in adopting the child and would be at the King's Arms for two days, and that she wished to discuss the possibility with me since she understood that I was an interested party. An appointment was made for nine o'clock on the night before Lady Anne's ball when she assumed that everyone would be too busy to remark on my absence. I have no doubt, Darcy, that you thought it both strange and discourteous of me to leave the music room so peremptorily with the excuse that I wanted a ride. I had no option but to keep the appointment although I had little doubt what the lady had in mind. You will recall that she was both attractive and elegant at our first meeting, and I found her still a beautiful woman although, after seven years, I would not have recognised her with any certainty.

'She was very persuasive. You must remember, Darcy, that I only saw her once when you and I interviewed her as a prospective companion to Miss Georgiana, and you know how impressive and plausible she could be. She was obviously successful financially and had arrived at the inn with her own coach and coachman accompanied by her maid. She produced statements from her bank proving that she was well able to support the child, but said – almost with a smile – that she was a cautious woman and would expect the thirty pounds to be doubled but thereafter there would be no further payments. If the boy were adopted by her, he would be removed from Pemberley for ever.'

Darcy said, 'You were putting yourself in the power of a woman you knew to be corrupt and who was almost certainly a blackmailer. Apart from the money she received from her lodgers, how else did she live in such opulence? You knew from our previous dealings with her what sort of a woman she was.'

The colonel said, 'They were your previous dealings, Darcy, not mine. I admit that it was our joint decision that she should take over the care of Miss Darcy, but that was the only previous occasion on which we met. You may have had dealings with her later, but I am not privy to those and have no wish so to be. Listening to her and studying the evidence she brought with her, I was convinced that the solution being offered for Louisa's baby was both sensible and right. Mrs Younge was obviously fond of the child and willing to make herself responsible for his future maintenance and education; above all he would be totally re-moved from Pemberley or any association with Pemberley. That was the first consideration to me, and I believe that it would have been to you. I would not have acted against the mother's wishes for her child, nor have I done so.'

'Would Louisa really have been happy for her child to be given to a blackmailer and a kept woman? Did you really believe that Mrs Younge would not come back to you for more money time and time again?'

The Colonel smiled. 'Darcy, I am occasionally surprised at how naive you are, how little you know about the world outside your beloved Pemberley. Human nature is not as black and white as you suppose. Mrs Younge was undoubtedly a blackmailer, but she was a successful one and saw it as a reliable business provided it was run with discretion and sense. It is the unsuc-cessful blackmailers who end in prison or on the scaffold. She asked what her victims could afford but she never bankrupted them or made them desperate, and she kept to her word. I have no doubt you paid for her silence when you dismissed her from your service. Has she ever spoken of her time when she was in charge of Miss Darcy? And after Wickham and Lydia eloped, and you persuaded her to give you their address, you must have paid heavily for that information, but has she ever spoken of the matter? I am not defending her, I know what she was, but I found her easier to deal with than most of the righteous.'

Darcy said, 'I am not so naive, Fitzwilliam, as you suppose. I have long known how she operates. So what happened to Mrs Younge's letter to you? It would be interesting to see what promises she made to induce you not only to support her plan to adopt the child, but to pay over more money. You yourself can hardly be so naive as to suppose Wickham would return his thirty pounds.'

'I burnt the letter when we spent that night in the library. I waited until you were asleep and then put it in the fire. I could see no further use for it. Even had Mrs Younge's motives been suspect and she had later broken faith, how could I take legal action against her? It has always been my belief that any letter which contains information which should never be generally known ought to be destroyed; there is no other security. As to the money, I proposed, and with every confidence, to leave it to Mrs Younge to persuade Wickham to part with it. I could be sure that she would succeed; she had experience and inducements which I lacked.'

'And your early rising in the morning when you suggested that we sleep in the library, and your visit to check on Wickham – were they part of your plan?'

'If I had found him awake and sober and had the opportunity, I wanted to impress on him that the circumstances under which he received the thirty pounds must remain totally secret and that he should adhere to this in any court unless I myself revealed the truth when he would be free to confirm my statement. I would say, if questioned by the police or in court, that the reason I gave him the thirty pounds was to enable him to settle a debt of honour, which was indeed true, and that I had given my word that the circumstances of this debt would never be revealed.'

Darcy said, 'I doubt that any court would press Colonel the Lord Hartlep to break his word. They might wish to ascertain whether the money was intended for Denny.'

'Then I should be able to reply that it was not. It was important to the defence that this was established at the trial.'

'I have been wondering why, before we set off to find Denny and Wickham, you hurried to see Bidwell and dissuade him from joining us in the chaise and returning to Woodland Cottage. You acted before Mrs Darcy had a chance to issue her instructions to Stoughton or Mrs Reynolds. It struck me at the time that you were being unnecessarily, even presumptuously, helpful; but now I understand why Bidwell had to be kept away from Woodland Cottage that night, and why you went there to warn Louisa.'

'I was presumptuous, and I make a belated apology. It was, of course, vital that the two women were aware that the plan to collect the baby next morning might have to be abandoned. I was tired of the whole subterfuge and felt that it was time for the truth. I told them that Wickham and Captain Denny were lost in the woodland and that Wickham, the father of Louisa's child, was married to Mr Darcy's sister.'

Darcy said, 'Louisa and her mother must have been left in

269

a state of dreadful distress. It is difficult to imagine the shock to both of them at learning that the child they were nurturing was Wickham's bastard and that he and a friend were lost in the woodland. They had heard the pistol shots and must have feared the worst.'

'There was nothing I could do to reassure them. There wasn't time. Mrs Bidwell gasped out, "This will kill Bidwell. Wickham's son here in Woodland Cottage! The stain on Pemberley, the appalling shock for the master and Mrs Darcy, the disgrace for Louisa, for us all." It is interesting that she put them in that order. I was worried for Louisa. She almost fainted, then crept to a fireside chair and sat there violently shivering. I knew she was in shock but there was nothing I could do. I had already been absent for longer than you, Darcy, and Alveston could have expected.'

Darcy said, 'Bidwell, his father and grandfather before him had lived in that cottage and served the family. Their distress was a natural loyalty. And, indeed, had the child remained at Pemberley, or even visited Pemberley regularly, Wickham could have gained an entrance to my family and my house that I would have found deeply repugnant. Neither Bidwell nor his wife had ever met the adult Wickham, but the fact that he is my brother and still never welcomed must have told them how deep and eradicable was the severance between us.'

The colonel said, 'And then we found Denny's body, and by the morning Mrs Younge and everyone at the King's Arms, and indeed in the whole neighbourhood, would know of the murder in Pemberley woodland and that Wickham had been arrested. Could anyone believe that Pratt left the King's Arms that night without telling his story? I have no doubt Mrs Younge's reaction would be to return immediately to London, and without the child. That may not mean that she had permanently given up any hope of the adoption, and perhaps Wickham, when he arrives, will enlighten us on that point. Will Mr Cornbinder be with him?'

Darcy said, 'I imagine so. He has apparently been of great service to Wickham and I hope that his influence will last, although I am not sanguine. For Wickham he is probably too much associated with a prison cell, the vision of a noose, and with months of sermons to wish to spend any more time in his company than is necessary. When he does arrive we shall hear the rest of this lamentable story. I am sorry, Fitzwilliam, that you should have become involved in the affairs of Wickham and myself. It was an unfortunate day for you when you saw Wickham and handed over that thirty pounds. I accept that in supporting Mrs Younge's proposal to adopt the boy you were acting in his interests. I can only hope that the poor child, with so appalling a beginning, has settled happily and permanently with the Simpkinses.'

2

Shortly after luncheon a clerk in Alveston's office arrived to confirm that the royal pardon would be granted by mid-afternoon the next day, and to hand Darcy a letter to which he said no immediate response was expected. It came from the Reverend Samuel Cornbinder from Coldbath Prison, and Darcy and Elizabeth sat down and read it together.

Reverend Samuel Cornbinder
Coldbath Prison

Honoured Sir

You will be surprised to receive this communication at the present time from a man who is to you a stranger, although Mr Gardiner, whom I have met, may have spoken of me, and I must begin by apologising for intruding on your privacy when you and your family will be celebrating the deliverance of your brother from an unjust charge and an ignominious death. However, if you will have the goodness to peruse what I write, I am confident that you will agree that the matter I raise is both important and of some urgency and that it affects yourself and your family.

But I must first introduce myself. My name is Samuel Cornbinder and I am one of the chaplains appointed to the Coldbath prison where it has been my privilege for the last nine years to minister both to the accused awaiting their trial and to those who have been condemned. Among the former has been Mr George Wickham, who will shortly be with you to give you the explanation about the circumstances leading up to Captain Denny's death, to which, of course, you are entitled.

I shall place this letter in the hands of the Honourable Mr Henry Alveston, who will deliver it with a message from Mr Wickham. He has desired that you read it before he appears before you in order that you may be aware of the part I have played in his plans for the future. Mr Wickham bore his imprisonment with notable fortitude but, not unnaturally, he was occasionally overcome by the possibility of a guilty verdict, and it was then my duty to direct his thoughts to the One who alone can forgive us all that has passed and fortify us for what may lie ahead. Inevitably in our discussions I learned much about his childhood and subsequent life. I must make it plain that, as an evangelical member of the Church of England, I do not believe in auricular confession but I would like to assure you that all matters confided in me by prisoners remain inviolate. I encouraged Mr Wickham's hopes of a not-guilty verdict and in his moments of optimism – which I am glad to say have been many – he has addressed his mind to his future and that of his wife.

Mr Wickham has expressed the strongest desire not to remain in England, but to seek his fortune in the New World. Happily I am in a position to help him in this resolve. My twin brother, Jeremiah Cornbinder, emigrated five years ago to the former colony of Virginia where he established a business schooling and selling horses, at which, largely due to his knowledge and skill, he has prospered exceedingly. Owing to the expansion of the business he is now looking for an assistant, one who is experienced with horses, and just over a year ago wrote to engage my interest in the matter and to say that any candidate I recommend will be kindly received and established in the post for a trial period of six months. When Mr Wickham was received into Coldbath Prison and I began my visits to him, I early recognised that he had qualities and experience which would eminently make him a suitable candidate for employment by my brother if, as he hoped and expected, he was found not guilty of a grievous charge. Mr Wickham is a fine horseman and has shown that he is courageous. I discussed the matter with him and he is anxious to take advantage of this opportunity and, although I have not spoken to Mrs Wickham, he assures me that she is equally enthusiastic to leave England and to take advantage of the opportunities available in the New World.

There is, however, as you may well foresee, a problem about money. Mr Wickham hopes that you will be good enough to make him a loan of the sum required, which will comprise the cost of the passage and a sufficient income to last for four weeks before he receives his first pay. A house will be provided rent-free and the horse farm – for that is what my brother's business may be called – is within two miles of the city of Williamsburg. Mrs Wickham will not therefore be deprived of company and of those refinements which a gently born lady will require.

If these proposals meet with your approval and you are able to help, I will gladly wait upon you at any hour and place convenient to you and will provide you with details of the sum required, the accommodation to be offered, and letters of recommendation which will assure you of my brother's standing in Virginia and of his character which, I need hardly say, is exceptional. He is a just man and a fair employer, but not one who will tolerate dishonesty or laziness. If it is possible for Mr Wickham to take up an offer for which he shows enthusiasm, it will remove him from all temptations. His deliverance and his record as a brave soldier will make him into a national hero and, however briefly such fame may last, I fear this notoriety will hardly be conducive to the reform of his life which he assures me he is determined to make.

I can be reached at any time of the day or night at the above address, and can reassure you of my goodwill in this matter and my willingness to provide you with any information which you may require about the situation offered.

I remain, dear sir, yours very sincerely,
Samuel Cornbinder

Darcy and Elizabeth read the letter in silence, then without comment Darcy handed it to the colonel.

Darcy said, 'I think I must see this reverend gentleman, and it is as well that we know of this plan before we see Wickham. If the offer is as genuine and appropriate as it seems it will certainly solve Bingley's and my problem, if not Wickham's. I have yet to learn how much it will cost me, but if he and Lydia remain in England, we can hardly expect that they can live without regular help.'

Colonel Fitzwilliam said, 'I suspect that both Mrs Darcy and Mrs Bingley have been contributing to Wickham's expenses from their own resources. To put it bluntly, this affair will relieve both families of financial obligation. In respect of Wickham's future behaviour, I find it difficult to share the reverend gentleman's confidence in his reformation, but I suspect that Jeremiah Cornbinder will be more competent than Wickham's family in ensuring his future good conduct. I shall be happy to contribute to the sum needed, which I imagine will not be onerous.'

Darcy said, 'The responsibility is mine. I shall reply at once to Mr Cornbinder in the hope that we can meet early tomorrow before Wickham and Alveston are due.'

3

The Reverend Samuel Cornbinder arrived after church the following day in reply to a letter from Darcy delivered to him by hand. His appearance was unexpected since, from his letter, Darcy had envisaged a man in late middle age or older, and he was surprised to see that Mr Cornbinder was either considerably younger than his literary style suggested or had managed to endure the rigours and responsibilities of his job without losing the appearance and vigour of youth. Darcy expressed his gratitude for all that the reverend gentleman had done to help Wickham to endure his captivity, but without mentioning Wickham's apparent conversion to a better mode of life, about which he was incompetent to comment. He liked Mr Cornbinder, who was neither too solemn nor unctuous, and who came with a letter from his brother and with all the necessary financial information to enable Darcy to make an informed decision on the extent to which he should and could help in establishing Mr and Mrs Wickham in the new life which they seemed heartily to desire.

The letter from Virginia had been received some three weeks ago. In it Mr Jeremiah Cornbinder expressed confidence in his brother's judgement and, while not overstating what advantages the New World could offer, gave a reassuring picture of the life which a recommended candidate could expect.

The New World is not a refuge for the indolent, the criminal, the undesirable or the old, but a young man who has been clearly acquitted of a capital crime, has shown fortitude during his ordeal and has shown outstanding bravery in the field of battle appears to have the qualifications which will ensure his welcome. I am looking for a man who combines practical skills, preferably in the schooling of horses, with a good education and I am confident that he will be joining a society which, in intelligence and the breadth of its cultural interests, can equal that found in any civilised European city and which offers opportunities which are

almost limitless. I think I can confidently predict that the descend-
ants of those whom he now hopes to join will be citizens of a
country as powerful, if not more powerful, than the one they have
left, and one which will continue to set an example of freedom
and liberty to the whole world.

Reverend Cornbinder said, 'As my brother can rely on my judgement in recommending Mr Wickham, so do I rely on his goodwill in doing all he can to help the young couple feel at home and flourish in the New World. He is particularly anxious to attract immigrants from England who are married. When I wrote to recommend Mr Wickham it was two months before his trial, but I was optimistic both that he would be acquitted and that he was exactly the man for whom my brother was seeking. I make judgements about prisoners quickly and have not yet been wrong. While respecting Mr Wickham's confidence, I have in-timated that there are some aspects of his life which would cause a prudent man to hesitate, but I have been able to assure my brother that Mr Wickham has changed and is resolved to main-tain this change. Certainly his virtues outweigh his faults, and my brother is not so unreasonable as to expect perfection. We have all sinned, Mr Darcy, and we cannot look for mercy without showing it in our lives. If you are willing to supply the cost of the passage and the moderate sum necessary for Mr Wickham to support himself and his wife for the first few months of his employment, it will be possible for them to sail from Liverpool on the *Esmeralda* within two weeks. I know the captain and have every faith both in him and in the amenities of the vessel. I ex-pect you will need some hours to think this over, and no doubt to discuss it with Mr Wickham, but it would be helpful if I could have a decision by nine o'clock tomorrow night.'

Darcy said, 'We are expecting George Wickham to be conveyed here with his lawyer, Mr Alveston, this afternoon. In view of what you say I am confident that Mr Wickham will accept your brother's offer with gratitude. I understand that the present plan of Mr and Mrs Wickham is to go now to Longbourn and stay there until they have decided on their future. Mrs Wickham is very anxious to see her mother and her childhood friends; if she and her husband do emigrate, it is unlikely that she will see them again.'

Samuel Cornbinder was rising to go. He said, 'Extremely unlikely. The Atlantic voyage is not lightly ventured and few of my acquaintance in Virginia have either undertaken, or desired to undertake, a return voyage. I thank you, sir, for receiving me at such short notice and for your generosity in agreeing to the proposal I have put before you.'

Darcy said, 'Your gratitude is generous but undeserved. I am unlikely to regret my decision. Mr Wickham may.'

'I think not, sir.'

'You will not wait to see him when he arrives?'

'No sir. I have done him such service as I can. He will not want to see me before this evening.'

And with those words he wrung Darcy's hand with extraordinary force, put on his hat and was gone.

4

It was four o'clock in the afternoon when they heard the sound of footsteps and then voices, and they knew that the party from the Old Bailey had at last returned. Darcy, getting to his feet, was aware of acute discomfort. He knew how much the success of social life depended on the comfortable expectation of approved conventions and had been schooled since childhood in the actions expected of gentlemen. Admittedly his mother had from time to time voiced a gentler view, that good manners consisted essentially in a proper regard for the other person's feelings, particularly if in society with someone from a lower class, an admonition to which his aunt, Lady Catherine de Bourgh, was markedly inattentive. But now both convention and advice left him at a loss. There were no rules for receiving a man whom custom dictated he should call his brother and who, a few hours before, had been condemned to a public hanging. Of course he rejoiced at Wickham's escape from the hangman, but was that as much for his own peace of mind and reputation as it was for Wickham's preservation? The dictates of decency and compassion would surely compel him to shake hands warmly, but the gesture now seemed to him as inappropriate as it was dishonest.

Mr and Mrs Gardiner had hurried from the room as soon as they heard the first footsteps, and he could now hear their voices raised in welcome, but not the reply. And then the door was opened and the Gardiners came in, gently urging forward Wickham with Alveston at his side.

Darcy hoped that the moment of shock and surprise did not show in his face. It was difficult to believe that the man who had found the strength to stand upright in the dock and proclaim his innocence in a clear unwavering voice was the same Wickham who now stood before them. He seemed physically diminished and the clothes which he had worn for his trial now seemed too large, a shoddy, cheap, ill-fitting garb for a man who was not expected to wear it for long. His face still had the unhealthy pallor of his imprisonment but, as their eyes met and for a moment held, he saw in Wickham's a flash of his former self, a look of calculation and perhaps disdain. Above all he looked exhausted, as if the shock of the guilty verdict and the relief of his reprieve had been more than a human body could endure. But the old Wickham was still there and Darcy saw the effort and also the courage with which he attempted to stand upright and face whatever might come.

Mrs Gardiner said, 'My dear sir, you need sleep. Food perhaps, but sleep more than anything. I can show you a room where you can rest, and some nourishment can be brought up to you. Would it not be better to sleep, or at least rest for an hour before you talk?'

Without taking his eyes from the assembled company, Wickham said, 'Thank you, madam, for your kindness, but when I sleep it will be for hours and I am afraid that I am accustomed to hoping that I shall never wake. But I need to talk to the gentlemen and it cannot wait. I am well enough, madam, but if there can be some strong coffee and perhaps some refreshments . . .'

Mrs Gardiner glanced at Darcy, then said, 'Of course. Orders have already been given and I'll attend to it at once. Mr Gardiner and I will leave you here to tell your story. I understand that Reverend Cornbinder will call for you before dinner and has offered you hospitality for the night where you will be undisturbed and can sleep soundly. Mr Gardiner and I will let you know as soon as he arrives.' With that they slipped from the room and the door was quietly closed.

Darcy shook himself out of a moment of indecision, then came forward with his arm outstretched and said in a voice which even to his ears sounded coldly formal, 'I congratulate you, Wickham, on the fortitude you have shown during your imprisonment and on your safe deliverance from an unjust charge. Please make yourself comfortable, and when you have had something to eat and drink we can talk. There is much to be said but we can be patient.'

Wickham said, 'I prefer to tell it now.' He sank into the chair and the others seated themselves. There was an uncomfortable silence and it was a relief when, moments later, the door opened and a servant came in with a large tray containing a coffee pot and a plate of bread, cheese and cold meats. As soon as the servant had left the room Wickham poured his coffee and gulped it down. He said, 'Excuse my lack of manners. I have recently been in a poor school for the practice of civilised behaviour.'

After a few minutes in which he ate avidly he pushed the tray aside and said, 'Well, perhaps I had better begin. Colonel Fitzwilliam will be able to confirm much of what I say. You already have me written down as a villain, so I doubt whether anything I have to add to my list of delinquencies will surprise you.'

Darcy said, 'No excuses are necessary. You have faced one jury, we are not another.'

Wickham laughed, a high, short, raucous bark. He said, 'Then I must hope that you are less prejudiced. I expect Colonel Fitzwilliam has filled you in with the essentials.'

The colonel said, 'I have said only what I know, which is little enough, and I do not suppose any of us believes that the whole truth came out at your trial. We have awaited your return to hear the full account to which we are entitled.'

Wickham did not immediately speak. He sat looking down at his clasped hands, then raised himself as if with an effort and began talking in an almost expressionless voice as though he knew his story by heart.

'You will have been told that I am the father of Louisa Bidwell's child. We first met the summer before last when my wife was at Highmarten where she usually liked to spend some weeks in the summer, and since I was not accepted in that house, I made it my habit to stay at the cheapest local inn I could find where, by luck, I could occasionally arrange a meeting with Lydia. The grounds at Highmarten would be contaminated if on occasion I walked there, and I preferred to spend my time in the woodland at Pemberley. I spent some of the happiest hours of my childhood there and some of that youthful joy returned when I was with Louisa. I met her by chance wandering in the woodland. She too was lonely. She was largely confined to the cottage caring for a mortally sick brother and was rarely able to see her fiancé, whose duties and ambition kept him fully occupied at Pemberley. From what she said about him I conjured the picture of a dull older man, anxious only to continue his servitude and without the imagination to see that his fiancée was bored and restless. She is also intelligent, a quality he would not have valued even if he had the wit to recognise it. I admit I seduced her, but I assure you I did not force her. I have never found it necessary to violate any female and I have never known a young woman more eager for love.

'When she discovered she was with child it was a disaster for us both. She made it plain, and in great distress, that no one must

282

know, except of course her mother who could hardly be kept in ignorance. Louisa felt she could not burden her brother's last months, but when he guessed the truth she confessed. Her chief concern was not to distress her father. She knew, poor girl, that the prospect of bringing disgrace on Pemberley would be worse for him than anything that could happen to her. I could not see why a love child or two need be such a disgrace, it is a common enough predicament in large households, but that is what she felt. It was her idea that she should go to her married sister, with the connivance of her mother, before her condition became noticeable, and there stay until after the birth. The idea was that the child would be passed off as her sister's and I suggested that she should return with the baby as soon as she could travel to show it to the grandmother. I needed to ensure that there was a living and healthy child before deciding what best should be done. We agreed that I would somehow find the money to persuade the Simpkinses to take the child and raise him as their own. It was then that I sent a desperate plea for help to Colonel Fitzwilliam, and when the time came for Georgie to be returned to the Simpkinses he provided me with thirty pounds. This, I imagine, you already know. He acted, he said, out of compassion for a soldier who had served under him, but no doubt he had other reasons; gossip Louisa had heard from the servants suggested that the colonel might be looking to Pemberley for a wife. A proud and prudent man, especially if he is rich and an aristocrat, does not ally himself with scandal, particularly such a commonplace and sordid little affair. He was no more anxious than Darcy would have been to see my bastard playing in the woodlands of Pemberley.'

Alveston asked, 'I suppose you never told Louisa your true identity?'

'That would have been folly, and would only have added to her distress. I did what most men do in my situation. I congratulate myself that my story was convincing and likely to induce compassion in any susceptible young woman. I told her I was Frederick Delancey, I have always liked the idea of those initials, and that I had been a soldier wounded in the Irish campaign – that much was true – and had returned home to find my dearly beloved wife had died in childbirth, and my son with her. This unhappy saga greatly increased Louisa's love and devotion, and I was forced to embroider it by saying that I would later be going to London to find a job, and would then return to marry her, when our baby could leave the Simpkinses and join us as a family. Together, as Louisa insisted, we carved my initials on the trunks of trees as a pledge of my love and commitment. I confess that I was not without hope that they would cause mischief. I promised to send money to the Simpkinses as soon as I had found and paid for my London lodgings.'

The colonel said, 'It was an infamous deceit, sir, on a gullible and essentially innocent girl. I suppose after the child was born you would have disappeared for good and that, for you, would have been the end of it.'

'I admit the deceit, but the result seemed to me desirable. Louisa would soon forget me and marry her fiancé, and the child would be brought up by people who were his family. I have heard of far worse ways of dealing with a bastard. Unfortunately things went wrong. When Louisa returned home with her child and we met as usual by the dog's grave, she brought a message from Michael Simpkins. He was no longer willing to accept the baby permanently, even for a generous payment. He and his wife already had three girls and no doubt would have more children, and he could never be happy that Georgie would be the eldest boy in the family, having precedent over any future son of his. Apparently, too, there had been difficulties between Louisa and her sister while she was with them awaiting the birth. I suspect it seldom answers if there are two women in one kitchen. I had confided in Mrs Younge that Louisa was with child, and she insisted on seeing the child and said she would meet Louisa and the baby by arrangement in the woodlands. She fell in love with Georgie and was determined that he should be given to her for adoption. I knew that she had wanted children but had no idea until then that her need could be so overwhelming. He was a handsome child and, of course, he was mine.'

Darcy felt that he could no longer remain silent. There was much that he needed to know. He said, 'It was Mrs Younge, I suppose, who was the dark woman whom the two maids glimpsed in the wood. How could you bring yourself to involve her in any scheme relating to the future of your child, a woman whose conduct, as far as we know it, shows her to be among the most base and contemptible of her sex?'

And now Wickham almost sprang from the chair. His knuckles on the arms were white, his face suddenly flushed with fury. 'You may as well know the truth. Eleanor Younge is the only woman who has loved me, none of the others, including my wife, has given me the care, the kindness, the support, the sense of being important to her, as has my sister. Yes, that is who she is, my half-sister. I know this will surprise you. My father has the reputation of having been the most efficient, the most loyal, the most admirable of stewards of the late Mr Darcy, and indeed he was such. My mother was strict with him, as she was with me; there was no laughter in our house. He was a man like other men, and when Mr Darcy's business took him to London for a week or more, he lived a different life. I know nothing of the woman with whom he consorted, but on his deathbed he did confide to me that there was a daughter. To give him credit, I must say that he did what he could to support her, but I was told little of her early history, only that she was placed in a school in London which was no better than an orphanage. She ran away when she was twelve and he lost contact with her after that, and when increasing age and responsibilities at Pemberley were becoming too heavy for him, he was not able to undertake a search. But she was on his conscience at the last and he begged me to do what I could. The school had long since failed and the proprietor was unknown, but I was able to contact people in the neighbouring house who had befriended one of the girls and was still in touch with her. It was she who gave me the first hints of where I might find Eleanor. And in the end I did find her. She was very far from destitute. There had been a brief marriage to a much older man who had left her sufficient money to buy a house in Marylebone where she received boarders, all of whom were young men from respectable families who were leaving home to work in London. Their fond mamas were immensely grateful to this respectable and motherly lady who was adamant that no young women, either as boarder or visitor, would be received in her house.'

The colonel said, 'This I knew. But you make no mention of the way your sister had lived, no mention of the unfortunate men she blackmailed.'

Wickham had some difficulty in controlling his anger. He said, 'She did less damage in her life than many a respectable matron. She was left no jointure by her husband and was forced to live by her wits. We rapidly grew to love each other, perhaps because we had so much in common. She was clever. She said that my greatest, perhaps my only, asset was that women liked me and that I had the trick of making myself agreeable to them. My best hope of avoiding poverty was to marry a wealthy wife and she thought I had the qualities to achieve this. As you know, my most promising and earliest hope came to nothing when Darcy turned up at Ramsgate and played the indignant brother.'

The colonel had got to his feet before Darcy could move. He said, 'There is a name which cannot be on your lips, either in this room or elsewhere if you value your life, sir.'

Wickham gazed at him with a flash of his old confidence. He said, 'I am not so new to the world, sir, as not to know when a lady has a name which can never be smirched by scandal and a reputation which is indeed sacred, and I also know that there are women whose lives help to safeguard that purity. My sister was one. But let us return to the matter in hand. Happily my sister's wishes provided a solution to our problem. Now that Louisa's sister had refused to take the child, somehow a home had to be found. Eleanor dazzled Louisa with stories of the life he would have and Louisa agreed that on the morning of the Pemberley ball Eleanor would arrive at the cottage with me to collect the baby and take him with us to London where I would be look-ing for work, and she would care temporarily for the child until Louisa and I could marry. Of course we had no intention of providing my sister's address.

'And then the plan went wrong. I have to admit that it was largely Eleanor's fault, she was not used to dealing with women and had made it her policy not to do so. Men were straightforward to deal with and she knew how to persuade and cajole. Even after they had paid over their money, men were never at enmity with her. She had no patience with Louisa's sentimental vacillations. For her it was a matter of common sense: a home was urgently required for Georgie and she could provide one far superior to that of the Simpkinses. Louisa simply did not like Eleanor and began to distrust her; there was too much talk from Eleanor about the necessity of her having the thirty pounds promised to the Simpkinses. Louisa finally agreed that the child could be taken as planned, but there was always the risk that when it came to actually parting with her child she might prove obdurate. That is why I wanted Denny with us when we went to collect Georgie. I could be confident that Bidwell would be at Pemberley and every servant would be fully occupied, and I knew that there would be no problem with my sister's coach being admitted through the north-west gate. It is astonishing how a shilling or two can ease these small difficulties. Eleanor had previously arranged a meeting at the King's Arms at Lambton with the colonel for the night before in order to inform him of the change of plan.'

Colonel Fitzwilliam said, 'I had not, of course, seen Mrs Younge since the time when we interviewed her as a governess. She charmed me now as she had then. She gave details of her finances. I have told Darcy how I was convinced that what she proposed would be best for the child, and indeed I still believe it would have been best for Mrs Younge to adopt Georgie. After I made it my business to call at Woodland Cottage while we were en route to investigate the shooting, I then thought it right to tell Louisa that her lover was Wickham, that he was married and that he and a friend were missing in the woodland. After that there would never be any hope that Mrs Younge, Wickham's friend and confidante, would be allowed to have the child.'

Darcy said, 'But there was never any question of Louisa being able to make a choice.' He turned to Wickham. 'You had it in mind that if necessary you would take the child by force.'

Wickham said with apparent unconcern, 'I would have done anything, anything, to give Eleanor possession of Georgie. He was my son, it was his future which mattered to both of us. Since we came together I have never been able to give her anything in return for her support and her love. Now I had something I could give her, something she desperately wanted, and I was not going to let Louisa's indecision and stupidity stop that.'

Darcy said, 'And what life would that child have had, brought up by such a woman?'

Wickham did not reply. All their eyes were on him and Darcy saw, with a mixture of horror and compassion, that he was struggling to compose himself. The previous confidence, almost insouciance, with which he had told his tale, was gone. He reached out a trembling hand for the coffee, but his eyes were blinded with tears and he succeeded only in knocking it from the table. But no one spoke, no one moved until the colonel bent down and, picking up the coffee pot, replaced it on the table.

At last, controlling himself, Wickham said, 'The child would have been loved, more loved than I in my childhood, or you in yours, Darcy. My sister had never borne a child and now there was a chance that she could care for mine. I have no doubt she did ask for money, that was how she lived, but it would have been spent on the child. She had seen him. He is beautiful. My son is beautiful. And now I know I shall never see either of them again.'

Darcy's voice was hard. 'But you could not resist the temptation of confiding in Denny. You had only one old woman and Louisa to face but the last thing you wanted was for Louisa to become hysterical and refuse to hand over the child. It all had to be done quietly if you were not to alert the sick brother. You wanted another man, a friend on whom you could rely, but Denny, once he understood that you would take the child by force if necessary and that you had promised to marry her, would have no part in it, and that is why he left the chaise. It has always been a mystery to us why he was walking away from the path which would have taken him back to the inn, or why he didn't more reasonably remain in the chaise until it got to Lambton when he could have left without explanation. He died because he was on his way to warn Louisa Bidwell about your intentions. The words that you said over his dead body were true. You killed your friend. You killed him as surely as if you had run him through with a sword. And Will, dying his lonely death, thought he was protecting his sister from a seducer. Instead he killed the one man who had come to help.'

But Wickham's thoughts were on another death. He said, 'When Eleanor heard the word "guilty" her life was over. She knew that within hours I would be dead. She would have stood at the foot of the gallows and witnessed my last struggles if that could have given me comfort at the end, but there are some horrors which even love cannot endure. I have no doubt she planned her death in advance. She had lost both me and my child, but she could at least ensure that, like me, she would lie in an unsanctified grave.'

Darcy was about to say that surely that last indignity could be prevented, but Wickham silenced him with a look and said, 'You despised Eleanor in her life, do not patronise her now she is dead. The Reverend Cornbinder is doing what is necessary and requires no help from you. In certain areas of life he has an authority denied even to Mr Darcy of Pemberley.'

No one spoke. At last, Darcy said, 'What happened to the child? Where is he now?'

It was the colonel who answered. 'I made it my business to find out. The child is back with the Simpkinses and therefore, as everyone believes, with his mother. The murder of Denny caused considerable concern and distress at Pemberley, and Louisa had no difficulty in persuading the Simpkinses to take the child back and remove him from danger. I sent a generous payment to them anonymously and as far as I know there has been no suggestion that he should leave the Simpkinses, although sooner or later there may be problems. I have no wish to be further involved in this matter; it is likely that I shall soon be employed on more pressing concerns. Europe will never be free of Bonaparte until he is thoroughly beaten on land as well as sea, and I hope I shall be among those privileged to take part in that great battle.'

All were now exhausted and no one could find anything more that needed to be said. It was a relief when, sooner than expected, Mr Gardiner opened the door and announced that Mr Cornbinder had arrived.

5

With the news of Wickham's pardon a load of anxiety had been lifted from their shoulders but there was no outbreak of rejoicing. They had endured too much to do more than offer heartfelt thanks for his deliverance and prepare themselves for the joy of returning home. Elizabeth knew that Darcy shared her desperate need to begin the journey to Pemberley and she thought they could set out early the next morning. This, however, proved impossible. Darcy had business with his solicitors in connection with the transfer of money to the Reverend Cornbinder, and through him to Wickham, and a letter had been received the previous day from Lydia stating her intention of coming to London to see her beloved husband at the first opportunity and of obviously making with him a triumphant return to Longbourn. She would be travelling in the family coach accompanied by a manservant, and took it for granted that she would be staying at Gracechurch Street. A bed for John could easily be found at a local inn. Since there was no mention of the probable time of arrival the next day, Mrs Gardiner was immediately occupied in rearranging accommodation and somehow contriving space for a third carriage in the mews. Elizabeth was only aware of an overwhelming tiredness and it took an effort of will to prevent her breaking into sobs of relief. The need to see the children was now foremost in her mind, as she knew it was in Darcy's, and they planned to set out the day after tomorrow.

The next day began with sending an express to Pemberley notifying Stoughton when they could be expected home. With the completion of all necessary formalities and the packing, there seemed so much to arrange that Elizabeth saw little of Darcy. Both their hearts seemed too burdened for speech and Elizabeth knew rather than felt that she was happy, or would be as soon as she was home. There had been anxiety that once news of the pardon was mooted abroad a noisy crowd of well-wishers would find their way to Gracechurch Street, but happily no such disturbance occurred. The family with whom the Reverend Cornbinder had arranged accommodation for Wickham were utterly discreet and the location unknown, and such crowds as did gather were clustered round the prison.

The Bennet coach with Lydia arrived after luncheon the next day, but that too aroused no public interest. To the relief of both the Darcys and the Gardiners, Lydia behaved with more discretion and reason than could be expected. The anxiety of the last months and the knowledge that her husband was on trial for his life had subdued her usual boisterous manner, and she even managed to thank Mrs Gardiner for her hospitality with something approaching genuine gratitude and a realisation of what she owed to their goodness and generosity. With Elizabeth and Darcy she was less assured, and no thanks were forthcoming.

Before dinner the Reverend Cornbinder called to conduct her to Wickham's lodgings. She returned some three hours later under shadow of darkness and in excellent spirits. He was again her handsome, gallant, irresistible Wickham, and she spoke of their future with every confidence that this adventure was the beginning of prosperity and fame for them both. She had always been reckless and it was apparent that she was as anxious as was Wickham to shake off the soil of England for ever. She joined Wickham in his lodgings while her husband recovered his strength, but could only briefly tolerate her host's early prayer meetings and grace said before every meal, and three days later the Bennet carriage rumbled through the London streets to the welcome sight of the road going north to Hertfordshire and Longbourn.

6

The journey to Derbyshire was to take two days since Elizabeth felt very tired and disinclined for long hours on the road. By mid-morning on the Monday after the trial the coach was brought round to the front door and, after expressing thanks for which it was hard to find adequate words, they were on their way home. Both of them dozed for much of the journey but they were awake when the carriage crossed the county boundary into Derbyshire and it was with increasing delight that they passed through familiar villages and were driven down remembered lanes. Yesterday they had only known that they were happy; now they felt joy's irradiating power in each nerve of their being. The arrival at Pemberley could not have been more different from their departure. All the staff, their uniforms washed and pressed, were lined up to greet them, and Mrs Reynolds had tears in her eyes when she curtseyed and with emotion too deep for words silently welcomed Elizabeth home.

Their first visit was to the nursery where they were greeted by Fitzwilliam and Charles with squeals and jumps of delight and spent some time hearing Mrs Donovan's news. So much had happened during the week in London that it felt to Elizabeth that she had been absent for months. Then it was time for Mrs Reynolds to make her report. She said, 'Please be assured, madam, that I have nothing distressing to tell you, but there is a matter of some importance about which I must speak.'

Elizabeth suggested that they should go as usual to her private sitting room. Mrs Reynolds rang the bell and instructed that tea should be brought for them both, and they sat down in front of a fire which had been built more for comfort than for warmth, and Mrs Reynolds began her story.

'We have, of course, heard of Will's confession in connection with Captain Denny's death and there is much sympathy for Mrs Bidwell, although a number of people have been critical of Will for not speaking earlier and saving Mr Darcy and yourself, and Mr Wickham, from so much anguish and suffering. No doubt he was motivated by the need to have time to make his peace with God, but some feel that it was purchased at too high a price. He has been buried in the churchyard; Mr Oliphant spoke most feelingly and Mrs Bidwell was gratified by the large attendance, many people coming from Lambton. The flowers were particularly beautiful and Mr Stoughton and I arranged for a wreath to be at the church from Mr Darcy and yourself. We were confident that that is what you would like. But it is of Louisa that I must speak.

'The day after Captain Denny's death, Louisa came to me and asked if she could speak to me in the strictest confidence. I took her to my sitting room where she broke down in great distress. When, with much patience and difficulty, I was able to calm her she told me her story. She had no idea until the colonel visited the cottage on the night of the tragedy that the father of her child was Mr Wickham and I am afraid, madam, that she was gravely deceived by the story he had told her. She never wished to see him again and had also taken against the baby. Mr Simpkins and her sister no longer wanted him and Joseph Billings, who knew about the baby, was not prepared to marry Louisa if it meant taking responsibility for another man's child. She had confided in him about her lover but Mr Wickham's name has never been divulged or, in my view and that of Louisa, must it ever be in order to spare Bidwell's shame and distress. Louisa was desperate to find a good and loving home for Georgie, and that was why she had come to me, and I was glad to help. You may remember, madam, my speaking of my brother's widow, Mrs Goddard, who for some years has kept a successful school in Highbury. One of her parlour boarders, Miss Harriet Smith, married a local farmer, Robert Martin, and is very happily settled. They have three daughters and a son, but the doctor has told her it is unlikely that further children can be expected and she and her husband are anxious to have another son as playmate to their own. Mr and Mrs Knightley of Donwell Abbey are the most important couple in Highbury, and Mrs Knightley is a friend of Mrs Martin and has always taken a keen interest in her children. She was good enough to send a letter to me, in addition to those I received from Mrs Martin, assuring me of her help and continued interest in Georgie if he came to Highbury. It seemed to me that he could not be better placed, and accordingly it was arranged that he should return as soon as possible to Mrs Simpkins so that he could be collected from Birmingham rather than from Pemberley where the coach sent by Mrs Knightley would almost certainly be noticed. All went exactly as arranged; subsequent letters have confirmed the child has settled well, is a most happy and engaging boy and greatly loved by all the family. I have, of course, kept all the correspondence for you to see. Mrs Martin was distressed to learn that Georgie had not been baptised, but this has now been done in Highbury church, and he now has the name of John after Mrs Martin's father.

'I am sorry I could not tell you earlier, but I promised Louisa that all of this should be in absolute confidence although I made it plain that you, madam, must be told. The truth would have greatly upset Bidwell, and he believes, as does everyone at Pemberley, that baby Georgie is back with his mother, Mrs Simpkins. I hope I have done what is right, madam, but I know how desperate Louisa was that the child should never be found by his father, and that he should be well cared for and loved. She has no wish to see him again or to have regular reports on his progress, and indeed does not know with whom he has been placed. It is sufficient for her to know that her child will be loved and cared for.'

Elizabeth said, 'You could not have acted better and I shall of course respect your confidence. I would be grateful if I could make one exception; Mr Darcy must be told. I know that the secret will go no further. Has Louisa now resumed her engagement with Joseph Billings?'

'She has, madam, and Mr Stoughton has lightened his duties somewhat so that he can spend more time with her. I think Mr Wickham did unsettle her, but whatever she felt for him has turned to hatred and she now appears content to look forward to the life that she and Joseph will have together at Highmarten.'

Wickham, whatever his faults, was a clever, handsome and engaging man, and Elizabeth wondered whether, during their time together, Louisa, a girl whom the Reverend Oliphant considered highly intelligent, had been given a glimpse of a different and more exciting life, but undoubtedly the best had been done for her child and probably also for her. Her future would lie as a parlourmaid at Highmarten, wife of the butler, and in time Wickham would be no more than a fading memory. It seemed irrational to Elizabeth, and rather strange, that she should feel a twinge of regret.

Epilogue

On a morning in early June, Elizabeth and Darcy took their breakfast together on the terrace. The day was bright with the prospect of friendship and shared enjoyment. Henry Alveston had been able to take a short break from his London responsibilities and had arrived the previous evening, and the Bingleys were expected for luncheon and dinner.

Darcy said, 'I would be grateful, Elizabeth, if you would take a walk with me by the river. There are things I need to say, matters which have long been on my mind and which should have been spoken of earlier between us.'

Elizabeth acquiesced and, five minutes later, they walked together over the greensward to the riverside path. Both were silent, until they crossed the bridge where the stream narrowed leading to the bench put up when Lady Anne was expecting her first child to afford her a convenient resting place. It gave a view across the water to Pemberley House, an aspect which Darcy and Elizabeth both loved and to which their feet always instinctively turned. The day had begun with an early mist which the head gardener invariably prophesied presaged a hot day, and the trees, which had lost the first tender sprouts of the lime-green leaves of spring, were now in full luxurious leaf, while the banks of summer flowers and the sparkling river combined in a living celebration of beauty and fulfilment.

It was a relief that the longed-for letter from America had arrived at Longbourn and a copy sent by Kitty to Elizabeth had been delivered that morning. Wickham had written only a brief account, to which Lydia had added a few scribbled lines. Their response to the New World had been ecstatic. Wickham wrote chiefly about the magnificent horses and the plans of Mr Cornbinder and himself to breed chasers, while Lydia wrote that Williamsburg was in every way an improvement on boring Meryton, and that she had already made friends with some of the officers and their wives stationed in an army garrison near the city. It seemed probable that Wickham had at last found an occupation which he was likely to keep; whether he was able to keep his wife was a question from which the Darcys were grateful to be separated by three thousand miles of ocean.

Darcy said, 'I have been thinking of Wickham and of the journey he and our sister have faced, and for the first time, and with sincerity, I can wish him well. I trust that the great ordeal he has survived may indeed lead to the reformation of which the Reverend Cornbinder is so confident, and that the New World will continue to fulfil all his hopes, but the past is too much part of what I am and my only wish now is that I never see him again. His attempt to seduce Georgiana was so abominable that I can never think of him without repugnance. I have attempted to thrust the whole experience out of my mind as if it had never happened, an expedient which I thought would be the easier if it were never spoken of between Georgiana and myself.'

For a moment Elizabeth was silent. Wickham was not a shadow on their happiness, nor could he damage the perfect confidence, spoken or unspoken, that existed between them. If this was not a happy marriage the words were meaningless. Wick-ham's previous friendship with Elizabeth was never mentioned out of a delicacy which they both felt, but they were united in their opinion of his character and mode of life, and Elizabeth had shared her husband's determination that he could never be received at Pemberley. Respecting the same delicacy she had never spoken to Darcy about Georgiana's proposed elopement, which he saw as Wickham's plan to get his hands on Georgiana's fortune and avenge himself for past imagined slights. Her heart was so full of love for her husband and trust in his judgement that there could be no room for criticism; she could not believe that he had acted towards Georgiana without thought or care, but perhaps the time had come when the past, however painful, had to be confronted and spoken of between brother and sister.

She said gently, 'Is that silence between you and Georgiana not perhaps a mistake, my love? We have to remember that nothing disastrous happened. You came to Ramsgate in time and Georgiana confessed all, and was relieved to do so. We cannot even be sure that she would, in fact, have gone away with him. You should be able to see her without always recalling what is so painful to you both. I know that she longs to feel that she is forgiven.'

Darcy said, 'It is I who am in need of forgiveness. Denny's death has made me face my own responsibility, perhaps for the first time, and it is not only Georgiana who has been injured by my negligence. Wickham would never have eloped with Lydia, never have married her and been brought into your family if I had subdued my pride and told the truth about him when he first appeared in Meryton.'

Elizabeth said, 'You could hardly have done that without betraying Georgiana's secret.'

'A word of warning in the right quarters would have done it. But the evil goes back much further, to my decision to remove Georgiana from school and place her in the care of Mrs Younge. How could I have been so blind, so uncaring, so neglectful of the most elementary precautions, I who am her brother, who was her guardian, who was the one my mother and father trusted to care for her and keep her safe? She was only just fifteen at the time and had not been happy at school. It was a fashionable and expensive academy but there was no loving care, and it inculcated pride and the values of the fashionable world, not sound learning and good sense. It was right that Georgiana should leave but she was not ready to have an establishment set up for her. She, like me, was shy and unconfident in society; you saw that yourself when, with Mr and Mrs Gardiner, you first took refreshments at Pemberley.'

Elizabeth said, 'I saw, too, what I have always seen, the trust and the love which existed between you.'

He went on as if she had not spoken. 'And to set her up in an establishment, first in London, and then to sanction a move to Ramsgate! She needed to be at Pemberley; Pemberley was her home. And I could have brought her here, found a suitable lady as her companion, and perhaps a governess to further an education which in essentials had been neglected, and to be here with her to provide the love and support of a brother. Instead I placed her in the care of a woman whom, even now that she is dead and beyond any earthly reconciliation, I shall always think of as the personification of evil. You have never spoken about it, but you must have wondered why Georgiana had not remained with me at Pemberley, the only house which she knew as home.'

'I own that I did wonder from time to time, but after I met Georgiana and I saw you together I could not believe you had acted with any other motive than her happiness and well-being. As for Ramsgate, it could have been that medical men had recommended she should have the benefit of sea air. Perhaps Pemberley, where both her parents died, had become too imbued with sadness and your own care of the estate might have made it difficult for you to devote such time to Georgiana as you would wish. I saw that she was happy to be with you and could be confident that you had always acted as a loving brother.' She paused, then said, 'What of Colonel Fitzwilliam? He was joined with you as guardian. Presumably you interviewed Mrs Younge together?'

'Yes, indeed. I sent a coach to convey her to Pemberley for the interview and she was invited afterwards to stay for dinner. Looking back on it, I can see how easily two susceptible young men were manipulated by her. She presented herself as a perfect choice to have responsibility for a young girl. She looked the part, spoke the right words, professed to be a gentlewoman, well educated, sympathetic to the young, with impeccable manners and morally beyond reproach.'

'Did she not come with references?'

'Impressive references. They were, of course, forged. We accepted them mainly because we were both seduced by her appearance and apparent suitability for the task, and although we should have written to the so-called previous employers, we neglected to do so. Only one reference was taken up and the testimonial received later proved to have been from an associate of Mrs Younge and was as false as was her own original application. I believed that Fitzwilliam had written and he thought that the matter had been left to me and I accept that it was my responsibility; he had been recalled to his regiment and was much occupied with more immediate concerns. It is I who must bear the heavier weight of guilt. I cannot make excuses for either of us, but at the time I did.'

Elizabeth said, 'It was an onerous obligation for two young men, neither of you married, even if one were a brother. Was there no female relative or close friend of the family whom Lady Anne could have joined as guardian?'

'There lay the problem. The obvious choice was Lady Catherine de Bourgh, my mother's elder sister. To choose elsewhere would have provoked a lasting breach between them. But they were never close, their dispositions were so different. My mother was generally regarded as strict in her opinions and imbued with the pride of her class, but she was the kindest of women to those in trouble or need and her judgement never erred. You know what Lady Catherine is, or rather was. It is your great goodness to her after her bereavement that has begun to soften her heart.'

Elizabeth said, 'I can never think of Lady Catherine's defects without remembering that it was her visit to Longbourn, her determination to discover whether there was an engagement between us and, if so, to prevent it, that brought us together.'

Darcy said, 'When she reported how you had responded to her interference, I knew that there was hope. But you were an adult woman, one with too much pride to tolerate Lady Catherine's insolence. She would have been a disastrous guardian for a fifteen-year-old girl. Georgiana was always a little afraid of her. Invitations were frequently received at Pemberley that my sister should visit Rosings. Lady Catherine's proposal was that she should share a governess with her cousin and that they should be brought up as sisters.'

'Perhaps with the intention that they would become sisters. Lady Catherine made it plain to me that you were destined for her daughter.'

'Destined by herself, not by my mother; it was an additional reason why Lady Catherine was not chosen as one of Georgiana's guardians. But much as I deplore my aunt's interference with the lives of others, she would have proved more responsible than did I. Mrs Younge would not have imposed on her. I risked Georgiana's happiness, indeed possibly her life, when I placed her in the power of that woman. Mrs Younge knew from the start what she was about and Wickham was part of that plot from the first. He made it his business to keep himself informed about what was happening at Pemberley; he told her that I was seeking a companion for Georgiana and she lost no time in applying for the post. Mrs Younge knew that, with his strong ability to captivate women, his best chance of achieving the lifestyle to which he felt entitled was to marry money, and Georgiana was selected to be the victim.'

'So you think it was a scheme of infamy on both their parts from the moment you and she first met?'

'Undoubtedly. She and Wickham had planned the elopement from the first. He admitted as much when we saw him at Gracechurch Street.'

They sat for a time without speaking, gazing where the stream eddied and swirled over the flat stones of the river. Then Darcy roused himself.

'But there is more and it has to be said. How could I have been so unfeeling, so presumptuous as to seek to separate Bingley from Jane? If I had taken the trouble to converse with her, to get to know her goodness and gentleness, I should have realised that Bingley would be a fortunate man if he could win her love. I suppose I was afraid that, if Bingley and your sister married, I should find it more difficult to overcome my love for you, a passion which had become an overwhelming need, but one which I had convinced myself I must conquer. Because of the shadow which my great-grandfather's life had cast over the family I was taught from childhood that great possessions come with great responsibilities, and that one day the care of Pemberley, and of the many people whose livelihoods and happiness depended on it, would rest on my shoulders. Personal desires and private happiness must always come second to this almost sacred responsibility.

'It was this certainty that what I was doing was wrong that led to that first disgraceful proposal and the even worse letter which followed it and which sought to justify at least a part of my behaviour. I deliberately proposed in words which no woman who had any affection for, or loyalty to, her family, or any pride or respect, could possibly accept, and with your contemptuous refusal and my self-justifying letter I was convinced that all thoughts of you had been killed for ever. But it was not to be. After we parted you were still in my mind and heart, and it was when you and your aunt and uncle were visiting Derbyshire and we met unexpectedly at Pemberley that I knew with absolute certainty that I still loved you and would never cease loving you. It was then that I began, but without much hope, to show you that I had changed, to be the kind of man you might think worthy to take as a husband. I was like a little boy showing off my toys, desperate to win approval.'

After a pause he went on: 'The suddenness of the change from that disgraceful letter I put into your hands at Rosings, the insolence, the unjustified resentment, the arrogance and the insult to your family, all this to be followed so shortly by my welcome to you and Mr and Mrs Gardiner at Pemberley – my need to make amends and somehow to gain your respect, even to hope for something warmer, was so urgent that it overcame discretion. But how could you believe me altered? How could any rational creature? Even Mr and Mrs Gardiner must have known of my reputation for pride and arrogance and been amazed at the transformation. And my behaviour to Miss Bingley, you must have found that reprehensible. You saw it when you came to Netherfield to visit Jane when she was ill. As I had no intentions towards Caroline Bingley, why did I give her hope by seeing so much of the family? At times my rudeness to her must have been humiliating. And Bingley, honest fellow, must have had hopes of an alliance. For my part, it was not the behaviour of a friend or a gentleman to either of them. The truth is that I was so filled with self-disgust that I was no longer fit for human society.'

Elizabeth said, 'I don't think Caroline Bingley is easily humiliated when in pursuit of an objective, but if you are determined to believe that Bingley's disappointment at the loss of a closer alliance outweighs the inconvenience of being married to his sister, I shall certainly not attempt to disabuse you. You cannot be accused of deceiving either of them, there was never any doubt about your feelings. And as for the change in your manner towards me, you must remember that I was learning to know you and was falling in love. Perhaps I believed you had changed because I needed to believe with all my heart. And if I was guided by instinct rather than by rational thought, haven't I been proved right?'

'Oh my dear love, so very right.'

Elizabeth continued, 'I have as much to regret as have you, and your letter had one advantage, it made me think for the first time that I could have been wrong about George Wickham; how unlikely it was that the gentleman whom Mr Bingley chose as his best friend would have behaved in the way Mr Wickham described, would have been so false to his father's wishes and so activated by malice. The letter which you so deplore did at least some good.'

Darcy said, 'Those passages about Wickham were the only honest words in the whole letter. It is strange, is it not, that I should write so much deliberately designed to hurt and humiliate you and yet could not bear the thought that, parted as we would be, you would always see me as the man Wickham described to you.'

She moved closer to him and for a moment they sat in silence. She said, 'We are neither of us the people we were then. Let us look on the past only as it gives us pleasure, and to the future with confidence and hope.'

Darcy said, 'I have been pondering about the future. I know that it is difficult to prise me from Pemberley and there might be problems in travelling to Europe now, but would it not be a delight to return to Italy and revisit places where we spent our wedding journey? We could travel in November and avoid the English winter. We need not spend long abroad if you dislike leaving the boys.'

Elizabeth smiled. 'The boys would be safe in the care of Jane, you know how she loves looking after them. To return to Italy would be a joy but it is one which we must postpone. I was about to tell you my plan for November. Early that month, my love, I hope to be holding our daughter in my arms.'

He could not speak but the joy which brought a tear to his eyes suffused his face and the strong grip of his hand was enough. When he could find a voice he said, 'But are you well? Surely you should have a shawl. Would it be better to go back to the house and then you can rest. Ought you to be sitting here?'

Elizabeth laughed. 'I am perfectly well; am I not always? And this is the best of places in which to break the news. Remember, this is the bench where Lady Anne rested when she was expecting you. I cannot, of course, promise a daughter. I have a feeling that I am intended to be the mother of sons, but if it is a boy we shall make a place for him.'

'We shall, my love, in the nursery and in our hearts.'

It was in the silence that followed that they saw Georgiana and Alveston coming down the steps from Pemberley to the greensward beside the river. Darcy said with mock severity, 'What is this I see, Mrs Darcy? Our sister and Mr Alveston walking hand in hand and in full view of Pemberley windows? Is this not shocking? What can it mean?'

'I leave that to you to determine, Mr Darcy.'

'I can only conclude that Mr Alveston has something of importance to communicate, something he wants to ask of me, perhaps.'

'Not to ask, my love. We must remember that Georgiana is no longer subject to guardianship. All will have been settled between them and they come together not to ask but to tell. But there is one thing they need and hope for, your blessing.'

'They shall have it with all my heart. I can think of no other man whom I would be better pleased to call my brother. And I shall talk with Georgiana this evening. There shall be no more silence between us.'

Together they got up from the bench and stood watching while Georgiana and Alveston, their happy laughter rising above the constant music of the stream, their hands still linked, came running to them across the shining grass.